22:22:22

FREQUENCY SHIFT

ADAM ECCLES

❀ Created with Vellum

For Robin & Willow

ABOUT THE AUTHOR

Adam Eccles is a sarcastic, cynical, tech-nerd hermit, living in the west of Ireland for the last couple of decades, or so.

www.AdamEcclesBooks.com

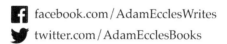

facebook.com / AdamEcclesWrites
twitter.com / AdamEcclesBooks

CHAPTER
ONE

I'M NOW ACCUSTOMED to the endless darkness. It's comforting, warm and embracing. Natural.

Rather than foreboding, I find it familiar and safe. Relaxing, even. You can lean back into the night, and it will engulf you in its velvet arms, smother and hide you from all. Gift the power of invisibility. You can pick out only the things you want to see in the darkness. Laser focus, flashlight beam, shrouding everything else and hiding it away. The night is my friend.

Conversely, the light is now my enemy. Harsh, accusing, pointing and rude. Squinting from over rooftops and leering into white skies. Casting revealing shadows, turning heads, flaring up like a stubbed toe. Overwhelming visibility, forcing everything into the foreground. You can't hide when you are bathed in ultraviolet radiation.

I welcome the night and rue the day.

I sleep when others do their business. They rest while I work. I'm nobody, hidden from view, keeping the world in motion in the quiet hours.

It wasn't always this way, but now this life has grown on me like five-day stubble, defining my profile, changing my outlook, and wrapping me in a comfortable blanket that I never want to leave behind.

I am the night. The darkness is within me.

I park my car at the far end of the empty carpark, away from sight and mind, then trudge across the dimly lit tarmac towards the office building, looming in the distance. A sodium glare casts an orange haze through the light mist. A constant buzz of electricity arcing in the moist air.

There's a shimmer of distant traffic from unseen motorways that never really subsides throughout the night, save the occasional random gap, that is quickly filled with the atonal drone of never-sleeping heavy-goods commerce. Aside from those baselines, which the brain learns to tune out almost entirely, there is silence this far away from the city. I take a moment to drink in the cool air and pause outside the building, letting the dark night swirl into my lungs and become a part of me. A tangible shadow that merges with my body and energises me, preparing me for the inevitable onslaught that is only a short walk away.

A frigid gust of wind carries the distinct smell of winter. It might yet snow. I turn and sweep a glare across the empty darkness, warning the world to stay away. The world ignores me. I'm okay with that.

Reluctantly, I scan my pass at the door and gain entry to the building, immediately shielding my eyes from the sudden barrage of fluorescent brightness.

There's no one at reception, no one in sight at all, which suits me just fine. I take headphones from my pocket and stream a playlist of heavy-metal music into my ears. More fuel to keep me powered up through the long shift.

The empty corridors stretch for exaggerated miles. I navigate by staring down at the worn carpet, and knowing when to turn or burst open a fire door by rote more than measure. I could close my eyes entirely, and every so often, I do. The melodic guitar riffs and intricate drumbeats keep me on time, in rhythm, and in step.

Outside my department entrance, I pause again and pluck out a headphone to check for any boisterous jostling, but there are no obvious sounds. I'm five minutes early, so I turn and head for the restroom instead.

Inside, I'm again glad of the late hour, as the cleaners have removed all traces and smell of the foul effluent of humans. Only the powerful and noxious scents of industrial cleaner and air freshener linger, mingling into something quite toxic. I turn my nose up, but there's no escape.

I splash my face with cold water, then take out a packet of ibuprofen and pop two capsules onto the counter, and dig in my backpack for a can of energy drink to wash them down. Not a great breakfast. Not likely that Kellogg's would push this as a healthy way to start your day, but needs must, and all that.

· · ·

I burst through the doorway into my realm. Steve is at his desk, ready to pounce. He sees me and looks up. I can't hear him, thankfully, because of my headphones and the music that brings me peace through its frantic guitars and drums, but I can read his lips, and because we go through the same pointless routine every night, it makes it easier to understand.

"Richmond is out of his room! He's supposed to be in his room. Why is he out of his room?" He sneers and cackles at his hilarious parody. An obscure reference to the colour of my clothing and the length of my hair.

I pretend I don't know what he said and do the usual sign language — a forefinger pointing at my headphones with raised eyebrows. A middle finger flip in his direction. Then a palm wave of exasperation at the same stupid charade every single day. I ignore his subsequent mimed tirade, that plays out to the sound-track of my symphonic metal, and watch as he grabs his phone and coat, then bolts out of the door without looking back.

Don't they ever tire of the never-ending battle?

Every day is a fight that I will lose. Every day is a reminder of the idiocracy in which we live, and the yearning desire to escape the self-inflicted social prison to which we are shackled.

I sigh, then turn and walk to my desk, flop down onto the worn seat and pluck out my headphones, returning them carefully to their case.

"Evening, Toby." I turn to see my boss, Vickie, beaming a smile in my direction. I nod hello. "Don't mind Steve, I'll have another word. Mention Human Resources and a reprimand."

I wave my hand. "Forget it, I just ignore him." The truth is that any well-meaning words from Vickie or Human Resources would have the opposite of the desired effect, and the bullying would only increase but in more devious and subtle ways. There's no point in trying to beat them. There are too many. Better to ignore and be unseen as much as possible. Invisible in the night.

Vickie smiles again, and then perches on the edge of my desk. She's a good-looking woman. In her fifties. She doesn't reek of 'bling' like so many career women do, and she eases on makeup and perfume. Subtle and discreet. I can admire that.

"I've sent you the list of tickets to complete. Quite a few we didn't get to today."

I nod. "No worries, Vickie." I know for a fact that half of the work I do every night is stuff that Steve, and the rest of the day crew, have somehow shirked off and dumped into my night-shift bucket.

She yawns and checks her watch. "Right, I better be off. You all set, then?"

I turn back to my screen and flick on the power. "Yup."

"Dunno how you do it, all night, on your own."

Vickie moves into my peripheral vision, and I turn back to face her with a shrug. "Don't mind. No distractions."

She grabs her coat from the rack and slips into it. "You don't get bored or lonely?"

"Nope." I shake my head. "I've got my music and plenty of work to do." I motion towards the computer screen.

Vickie laughs and rolls her eyes. "Well, if you say so. Have a good night. See you tomorrow."

"Yeah, night, Vickie."

She departs with a wave, leaving me alone in the building, save for the security chap who does his rounds every so often.

I reload the headphones and select a soundtrack of upbeat metal, increasing the volume enough to shake the remaining cobwebs out of my brain.

I log into my PC and glance through the long list of tasks awaiting.

I take lunch around one in the morning, but not before I've completed a chunk of my nightly tasks. I've done my rounds, nodded hello to Raymond, the security guard, fixed a couple of printers, rebooted a laggy server, and pruned some crud from a database. Nothing too difficult, and made easier by the lack of humans to slow me down. Why wouldn't I want to do the night shift? I get paid an extra fifteen per cent, and have total peace for my entire shift. Job satisfaction? Well, sort of.

I take my sandwich and flask of coffee to the table near the windows, and stare out at the world. Occasional lights in the distance, flickering, but otherwise a calmness to the night that spreads out, flows over me, and through some kind of spiritual osmosis, reaches my core. There was no such peace when I worked a day shift. The hubbub of life was always near. I would go home with a splitting headache from the constant stimulation.

After I gulp down the last morsel of dry bread, I get

up and take a wander around the room, avoiding Steve's area as if his desk itself emits his ugly violence and hatred, having soaked it up from his daily eight-hour stints sitting there and breathing out tainted air. I tap twice with alternating fingers on each of the familiar landmarks as I pass them. The printer, the water cooler, and the cubicle dividers that line the walkways. I usually turn the lights off when everyone else has gone. I can see enough from the light of screens, dozens of red and blue LEDs, and reflections from the carpark lamp posts.

"You don't smoke, do you?" A voice from the doorway suddenly startles me. I look around to see Raymond standing apologetically, making a lighter-flick thumb movement with his right hand. "Sorry, Toby, didn't mean to give you the willies."

"No worries. No, I don't." I flash a smile and motion for Raymond to come in. "Steve does, though. You might find a lighter on his desk." I point but feel more like I should make the sign of the cross towards it.

"Nice one." Raymond eagerly rushes towards the desk and peers down from his excessive six-foot-six stature, into the mess and relative darkness of Steve's desk. "Bingo." and he raises a hand triumphantly holding a leopard print lighter, flicking at the mechanism to test it. A small blue flame appears, momentarily lighting up Raymond's delighted face.

"Come out for a fag break?"

I ponder for a moment, but then nod and follow as Raymond leads the way, back into the brightly lit corridors, down the familiar path to the back door, and then out into the cold night, across the tarmac, towards where I park my car. I check all is well, and I'm relieved to see it is. I always wonder if Steve is going to slam into it with his car, or piss up against the door handles after he leaves the office. Would I know if he had? The misty drizzle has beaded over everything, so maybe it wouldn't be possible to tell.

We reach the 'smoking area', which is a bare concrete patch, covered over with a corrugated iron roof that, in daylight, is green with algae and red with rust. Now it just looks black and oppressive. A fat drip of rain lands on my face as I go under, and I wipe it away with a sleeve.

Raymond lights up, bristling a little in the cold, but then seems to warm as he sucks on the cigarette and puffs out a cloud of acrid smoke.

"I saw a documentary the other night on the telly … actually, no, it was on YouTube." He shakes his head slightly. "It was about the large hadron collider thing, you know, at CERN?"

I nod.

"They reckon it could cause a black hole to appear, just out of nowhere, and it would suck the entire planet into it, and we'd all be nothing but crumpled space dust." Raymond lingers after his revelation, staring at me wide-eyed, expecting me to react.

"Yeah." I pause. "Good."

He tilts his head.

"We're a virus, Raymond. A plague on the planet. Scourge of the galaxy. We deserve to be wiped out."

"Well, aren't you a cheerful prick, eh!" He laughs. "Aren't you worried?"

"Nah. Nothing I can do about it, is there?"

"Well, they could turn it off for a start."

"They are doing great work there. Let them have their fun."

Raymond shakes his head knowingly as he takes another drag. "There are places that science shouldn't go, Toby. When the entire planet could be destroyed just to get some answers to meaningless questions, that seems like it's too far to me."

I shrug. "Not bothered. If we go, we go."

"That's very bleak, mate."

I look up at him, gaunt, late fifties, sallow skin, hollow cheeks, wife left him years ago, kids all grown up and gone far away. He walks around an office building, pretending to secure the place every night, scanning sensors, checking cameras, and patrolling empty walkways.

And he thinks I'm bleak?

"You do know what we do here, at this company, don't you, Raymond?"

He shudders. "Yeah," then points towards me with his fag. "… and that's exactly what I'm talking about. Science gone too far."

"Pays our wages."

Raymond scoffs, then steps outside the fag-bunker, glances around, and flicks his glowing butt towards the business sign at the edge of the carpark. 'BioDigi Pharmaceutical' in a subtle and meaningless logo, muted colours lit from within, but fading and dirty with the same algae that colours the iron roof. "Fuck 'em."

I don't say it, but I have to agree with his sentiment.

"Any plans for the weekend?"

I double-take and raise an eyebrow. "It's only Tuesday."

"Oh, is it?" He takes a deep breath. "Hard to keep track of time."

"No plans, anyway. As usual."

Raymond nods. "Thought as much."

Back at my office, Raymond returns the lighter to Steve's desk, despite me telling him to keep it. Then he goes off on his rounds again. He'll probably read a book or paper, then nod off for a while between the hours of three and five. Can't blame him. I open a browser window, read up on the LHC, and try to figure out how I could help instigate a catastrophic, world-ending singularity in the middle of our office area.

Bored after a while, I carry on with my proper work. Making sure all the IT systems are functioning as they should; no downtime, no errors, and no disconnections. All seems well. There are no open tickets left, so all I have to do is wait in case something happens, or the morning light creeps up from the horizon, relieving me of duty. Whichever is sooner. I pull out my phone and play a crystal-matching game to pass the time.

CHAPTER
TWO

I'M WRAPPED in one of those emergency silver foil blankets when my senses stir me into consciousness. There's incomprehensible, lazy graffiti smeared onto pale orange brick, and a scrub of dirty grass in my line of sight, but everything is at ninety degrees to the plane I reckon it ought to be. Daylight. Broad daylight. I try to sit up, but a sharp pain triggers in my head. I cry out, and this, in turn, triggers an avalanche of activity.

"Sir, can you hear me?"

A kindly-faced ambulance paramedic appears in my field of vision, leaning down and staring at me. I look into her deep brown eyes with what I hope doesn't appear as love. I nod, but wish I hadn't moved my head. A pounding surge of pain overwhelms me, and I think I might retch. I cough and try to sit up. The paramedic turns to someone else and speaks, but I can't understand the words. I find myself being shuffled onto a stretcher, and then lifted into the back of an ambulance.

"Can you tell me your name?" The words seep in around blankets and an oxygen mask.

"Toby Steele." I say the words, but I'm not sure if they came out audibly.

"How are you feeling, Toby?"

"Ugh. Dunno." I pause for a moment to think about what is going on. No answer comes. "What happened?"

"A witness saw you being mugged by a man with a long metal pipe of some kind. You went down, the witness called 999, and we showed up."

"Pipe? … No. Wheel brace … He was changing a tyre."

"Changing a tyre?"

I shuffle up a little as my brain starts to function and pull the mask off. "I was going shopping. Thought I'd walk to get some air. Some bloke was pulled off the road, looked like he was trying to change a tyre." My head pulses with pain and I flinch a little.

"Take it easy, Toby."

"Yeah." I take a breath and wait for the pain to ease. Suddenly the memories of what happened flood back, and anger fills my veins along with whatever drugs the paramedics have injected me with. "I stopped to help as he looked like he didn't know what he was doing, then he turns to me with the wheel brace raised, a young lad, I think, hoodie, of course, couldn't see his face much. Demanded that I give him my phone. Told him to piss off." I laugh at the memory, and a fresh pain throbs in my skull. "Shit."

"Just try to get some rest. We'll be at the hospital in a minute."

"Okay." I look around me. "My shopping bag. Did you see it?"

"No, sorry."

"Bloody hell, that was my best bag for life."

———

"I told him there's absolutely no point in stealing a phone these days. It will be useless, locked, and wiped. He'll get nothing good out of it, and no one would buy it when it's locked and reported stolen."

I don't know how many hours have passed, but I'm feeling much better now, sitting up in a hospital bed, answering the questions that WPC Turner puts to me and then notes down my answers. I can't remember what type of car it was, or the registration number, but I think it was dark blue and small. A boy racer type thing. Now I think about it, the engine was running, and the wheel was perfectly pumped up when I stopped. I should have known it was a scam. But, as the jury will note, it was in fact broad daylight when the incident occurred. I rest my case.

"He made the executive decision to take it anyway, I guess, plus my wallet and empty shopping bag." I pat my pockets. "Oh, and my work phone, too." I still had that in my pocket after last night's shift. I only went out for milk and bread. The police officer makes a note of the work phone details and number.

"I had no cash, only cards, and they will all be useless, too. What he's nicked are two bricked phones and a cheap velcro wallet. Was it worth it?"

"Probably not, but unfortunately, criminals don't

tend to think rationally. We're going to check the CCTV cameras in the area and see if we can get a lock on the car." WPC Turner flashes a sympathetic smile, but I know there's nothing she, or anyone else, can realistically do.

"Nobody got a video?"

"We're still looking into that, but so far no one has come forward with anything. The witness who called 999 said he was too busy phoning for help to think of making a video."

"Right."

"It all happened very quickly, apparently."

"It did, yes." I wait for any more questions, but none come. "Am I okay to go, do you think? Only, I was on the night shift last night, and I'm exhausted."

"Might be best to wait for a doctor to see you before discharging." The sympathy smile again. "We'll be in touch if we come up with anything, Mr Steele."

I nod. "Thanks." I offer, half-heartedly.

I'm released back into the world after a lot more waiting and fussing, and I make a point to find a mirror to look at the damage. A black eye, a bump on my forehead, and some cuts and bruises, but no major damage. My ego, more than my body. Apparently, I was 'lucky' that the weight of the wheel brace didn't fracture my skull when impacting it. I'm sure everyone who gets walloped in the head with a heavy metal object is just perfectly lucky. Perhaps I should buy a lottery ticket today?

Last time I try to do someone a good deed, that's for

sure. I turn over the event in my mind once more, in case any details spring back, but it did happen very quickly. I knew I shouldn't have gone out during the day, but I had nothing in the fridge, and my stomach insisted I do something about that.

I get a taxi home, stopping along the way to get more painkillers, but then realise, as the driver pulls up outside the pharmacy, I don't have my wallet or phone to pay with. No spare bank cards at home, either. I can't even pay the driver. Shit.

"Err, sorry, mate. Change of plan. Can you take me to the bank?"

The driver looks at me in the mirror with implied scorn, but nods without a word, and pulls away.

"Hi, can I speak with Philippa Harrison, please?" The girl on the desk just inside the bank doors looks at me with a mixture of fear and contempt. I'm not looking my best, I admit, but I couldn't think of anywhere else to go for help. The taxi driver is waiting outside in a loading bay, so he'll not be too pleased if this doesn't pan out.

"Can I get your name?" She eyes me ever more suspiciously.

"Toby Steele."

"And do you have an account with us, Mr Steele?"

"I do, yes."

"What's it in relation to?"

"Err, can you just tell her I need a favour, quickly, please? She's a friend."

"Right."

She reluctantly picks up a desk phone and dials, but I can tell her heart isn't in it. I flick a smile and stand back from the desk. After a brief pause, she puts the phone down and then looks up at me with a smug grin. "Ms Harrison isn't at her desk right now. I imagine she's just gone for lunch."

"Ah… Do you know when she'll be back?"

"No. Maybe you can come back this afternoon?" There's an unspoken message in her tone; 'or, like, never?'

I feel myself deflate, mentally readying myself to start filling out lengthy forms to get new bank cards issued, and the old ones cancelled. Wondering if the hoodie'd menace has stripped my account with multiple tap-to-pay purchases already, or worse, weird transactions online. My primary worry now, though, is the taxi outside racking up a hefty fare.

I hate to use the term, but Philippa and I 'dated' for a while, a few years back. We were a couple, more or less, for about eighteen months. She's some high-up at the bank. I never figured out what she does exactly, but we had barely anything in common, aside from a mutual admiration for heavy metal music. A fact I think she hides from her fellow bankers. The establishment would frown on that sort of thing, I'm sure.

We met on a dating app. Doesn't everyone these days? And for a while, I thought it was going well. We went to a few gigs together, even some far-flung ones, in Milan, Prague, and Krakow. We had a good time, looking back, but anytime we got together without a gig to make things interesting, we sort of clashed and bounced off each other. She broke it off, citing a general incompatibility, and I didn't object. We're still friends, on and off, although I haven't seen her for a long time, probably partly due to my nocturnal lifestyle. Maybe it was for the best.

However, she was my only hope of borrowing some cash to pay the taxi driver. Shit.

I turn back to the reception girl, wondering how I get back into my bank accounts with no trace of identification on my person. No phone, no wallet. I feel naked.

"Toby?"

I turn around as I hear my name called. Philippa stares at me in shock. Do I look that bad?

"Oh, thank fu …" I stop myself just as I catch the eye of the reception girl again, who now beams a grin towards Philippa.

"What's going on? Are you okay?"

"I'll explain, but can I borrow a few quid? There's a taxi outside and I don't think he's very impressed." I pause and double-take at her. "Are you pregnant?"

It turns out that Philippa is pregnant, five months so, in fact.

Wow.

I guess we haven't caught up in a while. I didn't even know she was seeing someone. She paid for my taxi, then helped with cancelling my bank cards and getting new ones issued, and she checked the activity on my cards, finding that the little turd had indeed used my card to buy gambling credits on some dodgy site. She marked the transactions as fraudulent, and I'll get the money back once all the legal stuff is sorted. After all that, Philippa took me for lunch and offered sympathy for my poor throbbing head, and shock at the daylight robbery, literally. She even bought me painkillers and drove me home after, whereupon I flopped into bed, totally knackered.

———

When I wake up, about six hours have passed, and I instinctively reach for my phone, which, of course, doesn't exist. After a guzzle of coffee, I log into my PC and start checking the phone's location, which I probably should have done hours ago. Not surprisingly, the current location isn't available, but the last known signal was along the road, near where I was mugged. The thief must know what he's doing and instantly turned the phone off, or into airplane mode. I set it up to be locked and to notify me as soon as it's ever switched back on, and connects to the internet. I then order myself a new phone, the latest model, and remember the work phone, which will be more hassle. I'll have to report it to Vickie and get her to sort a new one. No doubt the company has insurance, whereas I don't.

My head rings with a dull ache, and I run my fingers over the bump on my forehead. Perhaps slightly less inflamed than it was, but sore, nonetheless. I ponder on calling in sick, but there's no point. Too late now to get someone to cover my shift, and it should be a quiet one, anyway, being Friday night. The Americans who log in to our databases and servers will be thinking more about the impending happy hour, than any actual work.

I prepare myself. Quick shower, more painkillers, and some kind of breakfast. Although, I didn't get my shopping done, so beans without toast, black tea and an apple.

I venture out into the darkness, but I feel just a little nervous. The day now proved to me how dishonest it is, but the night is still my friend. Isn't it?

I park in my usual spot in the office carpark, but then change my mind, and move the car closer to the door. I'm five minutes early, but I wait for a while, until I see Steve eject from the building and lope awkwardly towards his car, then speed away. I don't need his pathetic mocking today.

"Ah, there you are. I was beginning to get worried … Jesus, Toby! Are you okay?" Vickie stares at me in shock, eyes wide.

I offer a half-smile and flop down at my desk. I'm five minutes late now, but I couldn't send a message, due to the lack of phones.

"Got mugged."

"Oh, my God! What happened?"

I explain my wonderful day to my boss, who offers copious quantities of sympathy, then gets me a drink from the vending machine and tells me to go home. But I'm here now. I tell her I'll be fine, and that being in the building, guarded by cameras and Raymond with his hefty flashlight, is making me feel safer than I would at home.

Vickie logs back into her PC and orders a new work phone for me, then a pizza to be delivered to the building, because I mentioned I didn't have a sandwich, and she gives me a long, gentle hug, before asking me eight more times if I'm okay and need anything else. I smile, and bid her goodnight, then switch off the glaring lights and settle into my normal, boring routine.

CHAPTER
THREE

LIFE IS what happens when you aren't paying attention. It speeds by, like a train that isn't stopping at your station, and all you feel is the wind and noise, knowing you aren't getting anywhere fast.

Life is the cold night air that fills your lungs, then breathes back out, warm and visible in a cloud of mist, dissipating as you watch, helpless to catch it, taking away a tiny piece of your energy.

Life is the wealth of mistakes you make when you think you are acting in the best interest, then look back on later as worthless junk in a forgotten shed, tarnished and laden with webs.

Sometimes, it pays to pause a little, step back and away from the edge of the platform, look at the wider picture and the clouds above. Maybe you'll notice the signal lights change, an arrival on a different track, or a jewel lurking in the dimly lit realms.

Meeting Philippa, and noticing her blossoming belly, had an effect on me that I wasn't expecting. I'm forty-two years old, single, working a graveyard shift, let's be honest, and I wonder what I'm going to do with my life to make it worthwhile, to justify the oxygen I consume, the carbon footprint I leave in my path, the blood that circulates my veins. What legacy am I going to leave to the world if I depart this mortal state? Would anyone outside of work even notice? What if I had been killed with that stick of heavy metal impacting my head?

I should have just handed over the phone, the policewoman told me. Then he might not have walloped me. But, no. Why should I just repeatedly bend over and be shafted by the world? Why do I let Steve mock me every day? Why don't I fight back? Assert myself, dominate the office. Probably because I'm not made like that. I don't have a serial-killer childhood backstory that leaves me cold and angry. I just want to do my thing and be invisible, left alone. I have no desire to spread pain wherever I go.

The whole thing with Steve; I don't even remember how it started, but for several years now, he's been a total dick at every possible opportunity, and I think I've had enough of it. In fact, I know I have. Time for a change, I reckon.

The wonder of next-day delivery means a new phone is waiting for me on my doorstep when I get back from work. I pick up the parcel, wondering how it didn't get nicked as well, and fumble the key into the door.

On the doormat inside also waits an envelope with a new bank card. Very efficient.

I set everything up, taking much longer than I hoped, and reinstate my life into some semblance of normalcy, then order shopping to be delivered to me later today. Take charge of the situation.

I slump into my bed, but the soft edge of daylight filters through the thin curtains, taunting me. Soon the light will flood this corner of the world, and everyone else will start their day while I'm unconscious. I'll avoid the world and its treacherous light, once again.

Well, that was the plan, but despite my tiredness and the remnants of the headache, sleep does not come.

I send a text to Philippa, thanking her again for the help, and letting her know I'm back in the realm of the connected, and generally okay.

Over lunch, she told me she's with a guy called Jason, also working at the bank. They've been together about a year now, and obviously, since a baby is coming, things are pretty serious. Well, if they weren't before, they should be now. I asked if she was engaged to him, and she said no, with a hint of sadness, swept away with a laugh. Curious, I asked if she'd been to any gigs lately, and apparently not. Jason isn't into any kind of metal. He just 'likes whatever is playing on the radio.' I coughed out a laugh, causing pain in my head again. She smirked and nodded, but then shrugged. "It doesn't matter, in the grand scheme of things." So she said, but I think it matters.

She replies to my message with a thumbs-up and smiley face emoji. I put the phone down and close my eyes.

I feel like I should tell someone else about what happened, but I can't think of anyone who would care.

My parents sold up and retired to Aberystwyth, must be a good ten years ago. I visit occasionally on holidays, but they have their own lives and plenty of old-people activities to keep them busy. My elder brother, Duncan, buggered off to Australia with some woman when I was a teenager. We never got along, him being so much older than me. I was a pain in his backside when I was a kid, and I reckon he couldn't wait to get away from me. We haven't spoken in over five years, and I haven't seen him since, hmm, I can't remember. Donkeys. I'm sure he keeps in touch with Mum and Dad, but that's their business.

I don't have anyone else to tell my horrible news, and maybe it's for the best not to worry Mum with my tale of woe. I might go visit when I'm all healed up.

For now, I don't want the hassle of explaining everything over and over. I twist in the bed, away from the window and try to sleep, once more.

The memory of the mugging loops in my brain. I can't help but think about how I should have handled it differently, what I should have said and done. Maybe fought back, blocked the attack, ducked down even. Asserted dominance, not letting this kind of thing happen in the first place. Or, not stopped to help at all.

I should have crossed the street and avoided eye contact, called the police and reported a car parked on double yellow lines. What if someone older or more fragile had been in my place, they may not have survived. It boils venom in my veins to know I have to share the world with scumbags, who have no morals or empathy. Who believe the world owes them something when they have done nothing to deserve it. People who screw over others for their amusement. They need to be stopped.

As it is, I don't know what I might do about the situation, other than try to act differently if anything like this ever happens again. Will I, though? If I could rewind and do the last day over again, would I perform any better, or would exactly the same thing happen? I'm not a fighter, I don't even watch action movies or play violent video games. People think because I listen to heavy metal music, that I must be some hard-core scary bastard, but they couldn't be further from the truth. I could be a vegetarian, except that I like bacon too much.

I get out of bed, giving up on trying to sleep, and instead flip on some music and run a hot bath.

———

Cold, pruned, half-naked and half-asleep is how I receive my shopping. The delivery driver walloped on my front door, waking me from a bath slumber. I grabbed a dressing gown, and almost fell down the stairs in my haste. No matter, I'm sure they've seen it all before. The guy didn't flinch, and just dumped my groceries in the hallway before grunting a goodbye.

I put away the food and find my mind wandering again to the state of my life. Maybe I should try again on the dating app? Get out a bit and go to some more gigs. I have done nothing like that in ages. It all seems like so much effort, and what's the point in the end? Probably just more stress and hassle.

I sigh, then make a light meal, but I don't know what to call it. Lunch, dinner, or something in between? When your body clock is reversed, it's hard to gauge against societal norms.

I may need to think about my life and focus on some kind of direction. If not, I might end up dead in a ditch, or worse, stuck in a dead-end job until I'm seventy-five, working my days away because I don't know what else to do.

I'm reminded of school, and the career advice we were given, but of course, I paid no attention. I somehow drifted into IT, mainly because I'm a nerd, anyway. At work and home, I mess with computers a lot. It's easy for me. Perhaps I need a challenge? Something to take me out of my comfort zone, as they say.

Asking a sixteen-year-old what he wants to do for the rest of his life is a ridiculous concept if you ask me. How could he possibly know? With no life experience, no business experience, it all seems like a wild dream. Not reality or something tangible and achievable or even important. That stuff was for old people, not me.

I said I wanted to be a Private Investigator because of a series of books I was reading around that time. My classmates laughed, but I was serious. The teacher just looked at me, sympathetic, now I think about it, and said perhaps I could return to that later, but for now, to aim for something more traditional and solid, like getting points for college. What a knob-end.

You learn nothing at school except how to get out alive. If you are lucky.

I laugh at myself now. What do I know about any kind of investigation? Bugger all, if I'm honest. I should start with figuring out who the little bastard was who assaulted me, and then I should heed the words of the proverb; 'revenge is a dish best served cold'. Yeah, right.

On a whim, I decide to see if there are any local gigs on this weekend. Live music always raises the spirits in my experience. I'm not interested in the crowd atmosphere, but I enjoy witnessing an outstanding talent happening right there in front of me. I often marvel that instrumental music, with no singing at all, can trigger deep emotions, and can make you laugh or cry through tune alone.

I concede that outstanding talent and emotional melodies may be in sparse supply. You take what you can get.

I'm not looking my best, still with cuts and bruises all over my head, but at a metal gig, who cares? There's nearly always something on at *The Craufurd Arms*, and after a quick scan online, I find this weekend is no exception. There's a gig on tonight, so I decide based on the 'sod it' principle, and get dressed before I change my mind. I haven't heard of the bands before, but it doesn't matter as long as they don't suck too much.

I've walked the route before when I was younger and less paranoid, but today I take the simple path and order an app-based taxi. I'm dropped at the pub door without event or comment from the driver. Suits me fine.

The pub is nothing special, but not the worst. Red brick, decent size. I've been here a few times over the years, but usually with a particular band to see. I came here with Philippa. She would spend forever getting ready, but the result was worth it. Such a transformation from business banker lady to metal-goth chick. Don't know how she did it. I almost didn't recognise her.

The decor inside is your usual black paint that has seen better days, plenty of wood and dark corners, and a decent-sized stage. Stained glass windows depicting iconic musicians. They do 'intimate' gigs here, which I much prefer to stadium events. I can't enjoy a band if they are half a mile away and a pint of rain costs ten quid.

As I get into the pub, the first band is just starting. 'Stooge Monkeys'. I watch for a while as they flap around on the stage to a small audience that likely consists largely of their friends and family. They look like kids, and I guess you can't fault them for trying. They have decent equipment, and they make a lot of noise. I go to the bar and order a pint.

"You here for Placentophagy?"

I turn, startled. A guy has sidled up next to me, too close for my liking. Big grin on his mug, raised eyebrows, waiting for an answer. I don't think I caught what he said, over the music.

"Huh?"

"Placentophagy." He yells, with an unhealthy amount of spit, and nods towards a gig poster on the wall. I think he's half-cut, already.

I look up, and he's right. The headline band tonight

looks like some kind of grunge-metal. I've never heard of them and paid little attention when I came out. The guy seems overly enthusiastic about it, so I nod a 'yeah' and sip at my pint.

He seems pleased. "They're fucking brilliant, aren't they?" He points to his tee shirt, which is a band shirt for Placentophagy. A spiky blonde on the front almost eating a mic. "I mean, these guys are okay, but she's not a patch on Cherie." He motions towards the stage and the singer who's prancing around.

I'm at the disadvantage, having no idea who Cherie is, so I just nod and smile.

"I saw them in Northampton last night, and going to Luton tomorrow to see them again." He points to his chest. "Bit of a groupie, you could say." He laughs.

"Nice." I hope they are worth the build-up he's given them. I didn't want a gig pal tonight, just wanted to see some bands. A drunk super-fan is a liability I can do without. Drunk strangers that seem friendly can quickly turn nasty at the slightest thing. I'm looking around for an escape, but the bar is still fairly empty. Probably why this fellow pounced on me.

"She's bloody gorgeous, isn't she?" His eyes are far away now, gazing up at the gig poster. I assume he means the lead singer, the same spiky blonde that's on his tee-shirt.

I shrug. "Yeah, not bad."

"Eh?" His chest puffs up.

Here we go, the accidental spark that starts a blazing fire. I smile quickly, to defuse a potential situation.

"Bloody gorgeous, as you say, mate."

He deflates and backs down. Crises averted. "Yeah, amazing. I … I would marry her in a heartbeat."

This seems forward for a bloke I had only met seconds before. Thanks, alcohol, for bringing us together like this. I internally roll my eyes. He seems to want a reply, so I nod, enthusiastically and once again casually glance around for an escape. The dude is much younger than me, probably late twenties, and just a little desperate. He's well built, though, and likely dangerous if he wants to be. Maybe this was a bad idea, I'm feeling a pulse of headache rising, and I should probably be at home resting to heal, but I'm here now.

The groupie drifts away, to my relief, when Stooge Monkeys are finishing up. He seems to know them and helps them pack up their kit. I linger at the bar, nursing a pint and the headache that is ringing around my head like a ball bearing in a glass bowl. Maybe I should just go home. The first band was okay, nothing special, and maybe my craving is sated. I could nip out now, be home in twenty minutes and avoid bumping into the eager chap again later. I'm sure Placentophagy are spectacular and epic, as the groupie dude suggested, but I don't mind missing that show.

My mind made up, I swivel on my barstool to leave, just as a woman plops down on the stool next to me. I look up, and it's the blonde from the poster and tee shirt. Cherie, I guess, the lead singer. I pause. She smiles at me and then squints as she notices my bump and bruises.

"You been in a fight?" She's heavily made up, with

exaggerated black eyeliner and blushed cheeks. She's radiant in a sort of 80s way. Black and primary colours, ripped and netted. She turns as the barman slides a drink to her, without having to ask.

"Err, well, not really a fight." I flash a smile. "I was mugged."

"Shit! Here?" She knocks back the drink, probably vodka, and smacks her glass down on the bar.

"Well, nearby, yeah. In broad daylight."

"Really? Fuck."

"Indeed." Another drink is replaced in front of her and she takes a gulp.

"You seen us play before?" She nods towards the stage.

"No," I admit. "Never heard of you, sorry."

"That's good. A virgin." She grins and reaches over to me, lightly brushing her fingers over my damaged head. "Want me to kiss it better?" She leans in, and I can feel the heat from her body, smell her alcohol breath and perfume mixed into a potent cocktail.

"Err …" I feel my eyes widen.

She downs the rest of her drink and then grabs my hand. "Come on." She gets up, dragging me towards the back of the pub. What can I do, but follow?

Cherie needs to orgasm before a show, she tells me in the cramped dressing room behind the stage. She feeds on the energy, the endorphins. It boosts her confidence and makes the show all that much better. I am tonight's lucky contestant, she says with a sly grin. She wastes no time and helps me out of enough clothes to facilitate the process, before guiding my hand towards her groin and urging me into a rhythmic motion. She pushes into me, hard, and grabs my hand, increasing the speed. Then, when she's ready, she pushes me down on a chair and straddles me, riding me to an intense gallop. When we both explode in climax, Cherie yells out like an injured gazelle. I wonder if her act is similar.

Afterwards, she pauses and relaxes for a moment, before slowly getting off me and giggling.

"Thank you. Enjoy the show."

I get up, and zip myself back into jeans, feeling a tad shell-shocked, but in a good way. I'm warming to Placentophagy, as the evening progresses. "Yeah, no problem, err, I mean, thank **you**."

Cherie shoos me out into the main pub again, as she has to be on stage in a minute and needs to freshen up. Still in a daze, I wander back to the bar. Seems rude to go home now, without seeing the gig.

"You fucking prick!" Once more, I'm startled from my barstool. This time the groupie dude again, now with an aggressive stance, looming over me.

"Pardon?"

"I saw you going off with her. Don't think I don't know what happens backstage."

I realise the tone has flipped, not for the first time this evening. "Err, she was just …" I fade out, knowing there's no point. The guy is puffed up with jealousy and emotion, irrational, drunk and not listening. Killer instinct has taken over. "I think I'll just call it a night and head home." The guy is blocking me as I move to leave. I try to twist away, but he's there, darting around, staring intently at me. Jabbing at my chest and ranting something about how he knows very well what happens backstage, because it happened to him, once, and that I was a total bag of shit for going there with Cherie, and after he had confided in me his undying love for her. Bloody hell. How do I get into these situations?

I slip from the guys' attention and towards the door as the band comes out on stage, and a cheer erupts from the crowd. He gazes up at Cherie, spotlit and sparkling with glitter. I notice some of the same sparkles on my arm. She does have a certain presence, I'll admit that. Shame I'll miss the gig, but I best be off. I sneak outside and hurry away down the road, fumbling with my new phone to order a taxi as I walk.

CHAPTER
FOUR

Cypher: 22/02/42 00:01:
GZAN NEVL KIEQ ZRMR QCTS VGPO UIHL
HVPN MKQD
Interpretation:
KOHL SAUERKIRSCHE UNSINN
Translation:
CABBAGE SOUR CHERRY NONSENSE

"CABBAGE, Sour cherry, nonsense? What on earth does it mean? Are they playing with us?" I feel a pounding in my chest, my hand instinctively flies to cover my mouth. "My God, do you think they know we know?"

Alan shakes his head with a smile. "No, no. It's just a dummy. A test of the system. Notice the time we intercepted it? Just after midnight. That's when they broadcast a system test after they change the cypher. Still, well done breaking it, Evelyn. Top work."

Alan pats my shoulder and I feel my cheeks redden at my silly mistake. He's so understanding.

"Keep at it, I see great potential in you." Alan looks me in the eye, so intense I can feel my cheeks flush again.

"Really?"

"Absolutely, you will do amazing things, mark my words. Oh, and happy birthday. I'll buy you a drink, later."

"Why, thank you, Mr Turing, sir." He shakes my hand and then leaves my station.

My twentieth birthday and I'm sitting in this hut, reading through German gibberish, translating and interpreting. This was my first proper breakthrough, and I was so excited to show Alan, only for it to be a dummy. Oh well, never mind, more to come, I'm sure. Alan has been so welcoming, where the other chaps looked at me with scorn. I have made tons of friends in the girls' hut, though. Sandra was so jealous when they asked me to come to the boys' hut. Not as much fun as she thinks it might be, I'll wager, and we are sworn to secrecy on pain of death, literally, should we tell a soul what we do here. We work every hour God sends, but it's worth it, in the end. We will win this beastly war, by the power of our brains, not our brawn.

They gave me the job after completing a simple crossword puzzle in the paper, which was a clever recruitment technique to find capable codebreakers. I had the added bonus of being able to speak seven languages, at last count. Father is a diplomat, and we travelled frequently when I was a child. I was also top of my class in mathematics, which I think is why Alan was interested in my talents.

I was planning to attend college at Cambridge to study for a degree in mathematics, but I suppose that will have to wait until after the war, if we all survive.

Father tells me it is uncouth for a woman to brag, so I don't bring this sort of thing up often. It's hardly my fault my brain works in this way. I seem to instinctively understand a language quickly. German is simply a doddle.

I started at Bletchley only three weeks ago, and it was quite daunting at first, but I think I have settled in now. I'm already part of a knitting group in my lodgings with some of the other girls. They do like to gossip about the goings on, and the boys they fancy. I just listen, keeping to myself and quiet, especially about my work. Wouldn't do to be executed for treason when I'm so close to winning the war with intelligence.

Alan … Mr Turing, I should say, is such a lovely chap. Troubled in his own way. I do hope his work can be celebrated one day when this war is over. The world owes this man their livelihood, if not their lives, and to look at him you wouldn't think he could hurt a fly.

"We're going for lunch, would you like to join us, Evelyn? A birthday treat." I'm woken from my daydream by the chaps as they pass by my desk on their way out.

"Thank you, no. I want to work on cracking another message before I eat."

"Trying to impress him, eh?" Hugh laughs. "There's

no need, you are already the apple of his eye." I blush again, but smile, shake my head and look away.

"Well, suit yourself." The chaps leave me to it without fuss, for which I'm grateful.

It isn't Alan I want to impress. I'm sure he is the only man in England who believes in me. No, I'm trying to impress the rest of them. I want these men to know that I, a lowly woman, can crypto-analyse with the best of them. I know they pay us girls much less than the boys, and most of them still think we can't do anything more than file papers. But I'll show them. I'll be the best cryptanalyst in Europe. I'll be the best crypt-analyst in the whole bloody world! Pardon my French.

CHAPTER
FIVE

BACK TO MY usual parking space at the far end of
the car park. I reverse in so I'm facing the building,
leaving the lights on the 'guide you home' mode that
keeps them lit for a minute or so as I cross the tarmac.
My headlights carve out a projected cylinder of white
drizzle from the empty night that lends me, ever so
briefly, calmness in the chaos of my head. This is my
light, not the treacherous light of the world. No sounds,
save the distant drone of traffic, no other light, save the
sodium orange glare from sparse, flickering lamp posts.
No wind tonight, but a blanket of rain that's almost
graspable in handfuls. Antigravity water that doesn't so
much fall, as float from clouds, if it so pleases.

I would say this was like any other night, heading to
work while the rest of the world readies themselves for
bed, but already that isn't true. Instead of being
propelled by caffeine and non-steroidal anti-inflamma-
tories, tonight my belly is pre-filled with antipasto, aqua
minerale, pasta, and gelato, courtesy of the local Italian
restaurant. Feels strange.

I met Philippa for dinner, or breakfast, as I called it. She laughed, rolled her eyes, but compromised, and we decided on din-fast.

Nothing romantic, just a catch-up, as she called it. Not a date, so I suggested a 'date-up'? No, we didn't agree on that.

I think she wanted to know if I was okay after the attack last week.

I was.

I am.

The paranoia lingers, but the pain and swelling are gone, the cuts healing, the bruises fading. I'm as okay as can be expected. No lasting damage.

"Any word from the police?" She'd asked.

I scoffed, "You mean Sting, Stewart Copeland and them? Because I'm more likely to get a postcard from Gordon bloody Sumner than any news from the cops."

She nodded with a resigned acceptance that they probably have bigger fish to fry, murderers to catch — or worse; people splitting multipack cans of drink and selling them separately, or posting offensive memes on Facebook. My grievous bodily harm is merely a drop in the ocean of problems they have to care about. Never mind investigate.

I don't expect any kind of resolution, the criminal has got away with it, probably already sold the phone for scrap parts, made barely fifty quid, and gone on to rob many others since. A day job for him. Maybe he goes home to his loving family after work, talks about his day, laughs about who he's nearly killed with a long metal stick, and how he's ruined some people's lives who didn't bother using a password on their pocket supercomputers. They all laugh about it around the dinner table, then he watches TV, drinking cans of Bud, cursing at the sports news, wanking over the weather girl, and then they go to bed.

Philippa told me about the nursery she's painted with bright primary colours in her home, the vast amounts of equipment she's had to buy, the exercises she feels guilted into doing, and the embarrassing prodding and poking she's had to endure as her body has become almost public property, now that another human is residing in her belly. I listened with laughs and grimaces as appropriate. Over-all, I think she's happy about the baby, but I could tell she'd rather have a final clean and fed baby handed to her after a three-week holiday in Bruges or something. Skip the gore and pain, the inspections and the vampiric bloodletting, and just get to the bloody point.

It's a wonder the human race has continued, the amount of hassle and money it takes to make a new person.

I'm not so much happy for her, as glad she's happy. I'm sure there's a difference.

The dude, Jason, is not of much use. Well, aside from the initial sperm donation, he's not been called on to perform any further duties. He's assembled a cot, but it had to be reassembled by Philippa's dad after it fell down in the night. "What if the baby had been in it?" She shook her head in disbelief.

She asked if I'd been to any gigs, and I told her about some, but not all, of the events at the Placentophagy gig, and then we realised what that word meant. She won't be partaking in that practice.

We went our separate ways, Philippa back home, me to work, and with good cheer. Perhaps we'll do this again, but maybe not. Especially once the baby is out and needs constant attention. A nice way to end things, at least. Better than just gradually not talking anymore, and then forgetting each other exists.

I tread the lengthy corridor carpets, meandering in the worn path, occasionally stepping outside the beaten track where the plush comfort has not been stomped down. An extra bounce of softness to ease the last mile trudge to another night of tending to the needs of machines.

I'm early, by fifteen minutes, but I don't dawdle, because, in my head, I've rehearsed how I should handle any bullying or piss-taking that may come from Steve. With the contempt it is due, is how.

"Oh, look what the cat dragged in." I ignore him and go straight to my desk. "Hang on, he's early. Vickie, quick, call Sky News!"

"Hilarious, Steve. Evening, Toby." Vickie yells out but doesn't look up from her desk.

"Hey, Vickie." I make a point of not acknowledging Steve at all. Bullies want attention, that's what they feed on.

"Hey, Toby, have you seen my favourite **MUG** anywhere?" Steve stands up and makes a show of looking around the office. "Only, I haven't seen my

MUG for a week or more, and I thought you might know something about **MUGS**?"

I continue to ignore him and sit down, flicking my screen and desktop on, waiting for the progression of logos and then the login password.

"Maybe someone **STOLE** my **MUG**, do you reckon, Toby?"

"That's enough, Steve!" Vickie stands up and glares at Steve. He sniggers then grabs his coat and phone and buggers off through the door. Twat.

"I'm going to have a word with HR tomorrow. He's taking the piss now. Sorry, Toby."

"He's a dickhead, Vickie. Simple as that."

"True, but he gets the work done, so …" She rolls her eyes.

I pause, bite my lip, but then decide to just say it. "You know he dumps all his tasks into the night bucket, don't you?"

"Well, the stuff we don't get to over the day, yeah?" Vickie looks concerned.

"Yes, but did you know he doesn't reassign them to anyone? Keeps them all in his name, and when I finish them, they go back to his bucket, so all he has to do is press the complete button, and then he's got the credit for the work I did."

Vickie looks at me open-mouthed.

"I know he spreads them out, too, so it looks like he's hard at work all day. I check the time stamps."

"That sneaky prick!"

"Yeah."

"How long has this been going on?"

I shrug. "Dunno. Months, years, maybe."

"Jesus. Why didn't you say anything before?"

"Because he's a bully, Vickie, and I'll just get the shitty end of the stick, no matter what. I do my job, keep quiet, go home."

"Right. Fuck him, the little shit. He's out." She folds her arms.

I nod. I should feel relieved, chuffed, elated or something, but I feel nothing. "Don't say I told you, please?"

"God, no. Course not. I figured it out myself." She smiles. "Thanks, for telling me, Toby. I wish you had said it ages ago, but I understand."

"I'm sure he'll claim it isn't true, and that I've been fiddling the system somehow while everyone is asleep to set him up, but I assure you, that's not the case."

"I'll look at the log files tomorrow. I should be able to confirm who checked in what, and when things really happened?"

I nod. "Yup."

"Say no more, then. Tomorrow, Steve will pay a visit to the HR office." She puffs out a sigh. "For now, there's the big quarterly sync going on with Spokane tonight, so the yanks will be a bit delicate, if anything goes down, okay?"

"Yeah, right. I know."

"Good night, Toby. Take it easy, yeah?"

"Night, Vickie." I smile and she slides into a coat and leaves with a wave.

I'm choosing not to complete any of Steve's work, tonight. He can pick it up himself tomorrow … well, if he still has a job after half-nine, he can, otherwise, I suspect they will all somehow flow back into my bucket, anyway. It will be a shock for him to find all his tasks still need doing, but I'm beyond caring.

Will they give him the sack? I'm not convinced.

I quickly do my normal nightly tasks, then find I now have six hours of barely anything left to do, so I take out my phone and scroll around aimlessly, settling on a game, but swiftly getting bored.

My full belly makes it hard to stay awake. I switch the lights in the office back on after a short while, to stop me from nodding off at the desk. Extra heavy metal and a splash of cold water help a little, and I take a walk down to the smoking area to see if Raymond is around, but he isn't. I enjoy the cool air, though, and I linger for a while even though the rain persists.

My phone rings. The new replacement work phone that they have furnished me with. The support phone. Shit. It rarely rings. I normally just use it to delete email spam when sitting on the toilet. I answer, tentatively.

"Hello?"

"Jesus, finally. IT support? What the hell is going on over there?" An American voice blasts out of the speaker and I instinctively dash back to the office building, across the car park. What is going on, indeed? All was fine a few minutes ago when I headed out. Keep cool. Don't panic.

"Sorry?"

"Our goddam connection dropped in the middle of a transfer, we can't get back in. Are you having a power outage or something?"

Halfway across the carpark, I glance up at the office windows and see my lights still on. "No, I don't think so. Can you send me the details of what exactly happened?"

"What's your name, son?"

"Toby Steele."

"Well, Toby, I don't know if I mentioned it, BUT WE CAN'T GET BACK IN, we can't send you anything. Nothing is working. Get the damn systems back online ASAP!" He yells, and I have to move the phone away from my ear. I'm in the door now, and jogging along the corridors back to my desk to find out what he's on about.

"Okay, I'm just heading to the server room to see what's going on."

"See, this is why we need the mainframe here in Spokane. I've got techs sitting on their asses here waiting. Get it done, Toby!"

"Right."

He hangs up. Knob-end.

Mainframe? He must be 'old-school' as they say. We haven't run a mainframe for a long time.

I get to my desk and check the system dashboard. Everything is indeed 'dead' but I don't know why. Nothing is responding, not even email or server pings. We seem to be totally offline. Bugger.

The server room may as well be in a different time zone. I have to traverse the entire building and go up two floors to find it. I haven't visited the room for ages. Maybe years. We remote in, so there's no need unless something breaks, like this. I encounter Raymond on the way, and he asks why every bloody light on his security board is lit up like Christmas, and I imagine the root cause is the same issue as our whole system is having. He's in a panic, urgently checking in case there's a fire or something. He scuttles away and says he'll call me if the building is burning down. Great.

I scan my badge on the door, and thankfully that works. Lights come on as I step through. Inside is a cacophony of beeping and fan noise. No fire. There are several black metal racks of kit, which must be six feet high and the standard nineteen inches wide, like massive, ominous industrial fridges, but full of computers. Air-cooled with huge fans, the entire room is air-conditioned, sound and dust proofed. Every rack is jammed full of confused systems, beeping, blowing, flashing lights and neatly wrapped around with dozens of cables that connect us to the world. I check the main internet connection, but it looks okay, as much as I can tell from the lights on the box. None of this stuff has ever broken before, so I'm not an expert. Are we under some kind of DDOS attack?

I grab a mobile monitor and keyboard station and wheel it over, then plug it into … what? I don't even know where to start. I need a console that will show me some kind of error message. I grab two more screens, select machines at random that have video output ports, and plug everything in, hoping I'll find something useful.

The beeping changes tone to an oscillating whine on the system in the middle. The screen flickers to life and an empty terminal console appears. Something to work with. I hit a key and there's a pause.

A timestamp appears.

22/2/22 22:22:22:_

I check my watch. The clock is wrong, that was about fifteen minutes ago. It must be frozen at the point when things went bad. All the two's. Weird.

I type 'status' and hit return. Another pause … then the timestamp prompt appears again,

22/2/22 22:22:22:_

But nothing happens.

I try again on other machines, but they do the same. All the systems are stuck at that time. I go back to the first one and type 'help' then hit return.

Something happens.

Abruptly, the sounds cease. There's a moment of silence, where even the omnipresent fan noise fades out to nothing. I breathe. In. Out. In. Is everything rebooting? The beeps and fans come back, but with a different tone. Now with various screeching jitters, like an old modem dial-up handshake. Loud, pervasive, quite nauseating, even. I shake my head. The screens flicker back into life, but instead of the stream of text I'd expect to see after a reboot, there's a snow pattern like an old tube TV when it isn't tuned to a station. Background ambient radio interference causes nonsense to appear on TV screens. But this has more of a uniform pattern to it. A zigzag flash, then a sine wave blast in time with the beeps. Thousands of tiny white dots dance in an ever-changing motion around the monitors.

What the hell is going on? This must be some kind of virus or attack. What do I do? I've seen nothing like this before. Should I pull the plugs?

I look around the room, but can't see an obvious

point where I could shut off the power. The power distribution unit could be elsewhere and also go through a battery backup. Maybe I should call Vickie, but I don't think she would have any better ideas.

All the tiny lights on each computer are flashing in a pattern that seems synchronised with the snow on the screens, and the terrible beeping. How is that possible?

Some of the audio is high-pitch, loud and throbbing in the drums of my ears, causing pressure in my skull. Other systems blast low-frequency sounds that throb in my chest and stomach. They combine into an attack on my ears that is becoming worrying.

The middle screen flashes in colours now, a rainbow stream of the patterned snow, pulsating, warping, twisting around like an early 2000s screensaver. I stare at the symmetrical patterns, my eyes unfocused, blurred, and yet finding distant 3D shapes in the mess of static that morph and spiral around each other, fractal structures, then criss-cross shapes, wireframe explosions and bouncing fireworks. The screen flickers with a rhythmic cadence, shifting frequency and fluctuating in and out of detectable range.

I'm tired. I feel sick and I need to get out of here. But I can't move. My legs don't respond to commands, my arms are useless at my sides. All I can do is stare at the screen, and hear the buzzy, angry screeching. Feel the chaotic chorus of fans blowing air over me. I'm shocked when I hear a whimper, then more shocked when I realise it was me making the sound. I feel threatened by the servers, they shouldn't be doing this. What is happening?

I try to reach for my phone, but my hands stay slack.

I try to look away from the screen, and I somehow can't. It feels like a powerful magnet is pulling my eyes toward the display. The two screens on either side fill my periphery with the same chaotic mess. The audio is now blasting so loud it rivals some of the best metal gigs I've been to. I'm paralysed, completely frozen like the timestamp.

22/2/22 22:22:22:_

CHAPTER
SIX

I FIND myself waking with no recollection of going to sleep. I'm in a heap on the floor, face down on the cold tiles. I poll my various extremities and internal systems. A damage report is delivered promptly — I'm dehydrated, have a pounding headache, and I'm desperate for the bathroom. Otherwise, as well as can be expected. I'm still in the server room. A cool breeze of clinical clean air wafts around me and I shiver a little.

I stand up, slowly stretching out my cramped muscles and back, rubbing the life back into my face, and find the three screens still plugged into the servers. I check my watch. Now seven in the morning. I must have fallen asleep while standing at the screens last night. I have no memory of how long I stood there, watching the weird patterns evolve and spin around the screen, and listening to the screeching blasts before I must have collapsed in a heap. Nothing if not elegant.

The patterns and sounds have all gone, and now on each screen is a green status dashboard showing everything working as it should. No sign of trouble, completely operational and all circuits functioning perfectly. No beeping, no chaos. Fair enough.

I check my work phone. There's an email from the American chap who rang me last night. Ed Wagner. He offers a vague thanks for getting the systems up and running so quickly, but no apology for being an entitled, impatient prick. Did I fix the systems? If I did, I don't recall how.

There are a few other work spam emails that signify that everything is back to normal. Daily reports, automated notifications, and the usual chatter from the global offices. I put my phone in my pocket and tidy up the room. Unplug the monitors and roll them back to their stations, then I exit the server room, leaving it in a better state than I found it, and find the nearest toilet.

On the way back to my desk, I stop by and say hello to Raymond, who's just about to go home. He says his security system glitch cured itself after a few minutes, and it was probably just some weird anomaly. "Happens sometimes. Did you find anything strange in the server room?" he says, and I shrug with a vague "Nah." I probably should have told him about the weird sounds and patterns and all, but it seemed ridiculous, and embarrassing now I think about it. No harm seems to be done, so let's just forget about it. Just an anomaly, as he says. Jog on. Plus, I don't need word getting out that I fell asleep on the job. I'd never hear the end of it, or they'd fire me.

Which reminds me, Steve is destined to be ejected sometime today. I wish I could be a fly on the wall of that HR conversation. No doubt Vickie will fill me in with the details tonight, when I come back to work for more punishment.

I grab a bottle of water from a vending machine and chug it down in one go, dropping the empty bottle into the next recycling bin.

Having had a long nap all night, albeit, in a crumpled mess on a hard floor, I'm not feeling too bad now the headache is passing. Quite awake, for a change. Chipper, as our American friends would say.

I get back to my desk, write and send some status emails, and give a fairly scant review of the overnight status to Vickie.

> Quiet night, mostly. One minor glitch with the US sync, but I sorted it quickly. No other issues. See you later.

I shut down my PC, grab my coat and pop headphones into my ears, then saunter through the corridors and across the carpark. The morning grey light gently prods at the sky, nudging the night away to make room for the day. I head home, but I don't think I will flop straight into bed today.

I fancy a smoothie, so I stop at the supermarket on the way home and stock up on a load of fruit and vegetables. I grab some eggs and two litres of skimmed milk, a box of green tea, which I normally can't stand — but today it seems like a great idea, and also a big lump of steak. Not my usual trolley load, but I feel like a change.

I set about blending the fruit and veg when I get home, and surprise myself that kale doesn't have to taste like a tramp's sweaty underpants if you mix in avocado and pineapple. Breakfast sorted, I have the urge to go for a brisk walk, but then I remember my bike in the shed at the back of the yard, that I haven't used in years, and pull it out from the mess of tools and junk. A quick spray with a hose to remove any lurking arachnids, pump up the tyres, oil on the chain and I blast off for a spin. My legs aren't used to the exertion, but I push through the pain and carry on, buzzing through the town in no particular direction. The cool breeze is most welcome, but I'm glad that the rain has eased off.

After a while, I find myself outside Bletchley Park Mansion, the famous site where they cracked the Enigma code back in war times. A historic place. I remember visiting on a school trip, and being awed by the stories of Alan Turing and codebreaking. Maybe one of the things that compelled me toward computers as a hobby, and then, ultimately, a profession. I wonder what Alan would make of the computers we have now. Of the unfathomably powerful one that I have with me at all times in my pocket. So much progress in such a short time. Amazing.

I pedal on, taking a long route back home which takes me past the scene of the recent crime. Where the incomprehensible graffiti on the sickening orange wall is some kind of code itself, only decipherable to those who know how. A cypher to be broken. I guess that the words all mean something like 'knob' in this case, a phallic gesture depicting the anger of youth and over-running testosterone, juxtaposed against the modern dullness of supposedly civilised society. Or whatever.

I skid to a halt back home, rather enjoying my little jaunt on the bike. I should do it more often. Don't know why I haven't. I bought it years ago in one of those moments of madness where I thought I'd 'get fit', and I tried, in fairness, but then I transitioned to the night shift and it sort of went out of fashion. Maybe I just needed a break.

My legs throb, and I wobble to my bed, where I collapse into a jelly heap and succumb to slumber.

———

I should take a holiday. The last break I had was years ago; over to see a metal gig with Philippa. The gig was only one night, but we made a week out of it in Milan. That was probably the mistake. Pleasant city, nice food, but Philippa and I clashed a lot over stupid stuff. I think it was that trip that made up her mind for us to split up. The gig itself was brilliant, as I recall.

I'm tired of the monotony of this life, this job. It feels like I'm burning through the finite hours I have on the planet, and all for the good of some faceless corporation, that doesn't care a shit about my welfare and personal issues, even if the HR propaganda material says that they certainly do. If you have to make cartoon videos and slide decks showing how much you care about your staff, maybe you are working on the wrong things.

I'll mention it to Vickie, and see if I can book a couple of weeks off soon. No idea where I'll go. Maybe I won't go anywhere and just relax at home. Maybe I'll go see Mum and Dad. Just something different to the nightly churn would be good.

I trudge the endless corridors and slam open the fire doors with either foot or shoulder, alternating through the maze of passages until I land at my office door, where I pause, take a deep breath, and venture forth into the void.

Steve is at his desk. I don't flinch but quickly look away. Obviously, things have not gone to plan. I was sort of expecting him to be gone already. He doesn't look at me, doesn't say a word. I head to my desk and quietly sit down on my ancient, worn chair. It creaks, nonetheless. Vickie is in her cubicle. Headset on. Red lights on her covered ears indicate she's in a meeting, but muted. She waves at me, then rolls her eyes, pointing to her headset.

Steve quietly gets up, grabs his phone and coat, and calmly walks to the door and exits without a word.

Well, something has certainly changed. I switch on my PC and wait for the login screen, taking out my work phone and checking emails while my system boots up. Nothing unusual.

"Evening, Toby."

I turn around to see Vickie smiling. "Hey."

"Sorry, got caught in a meeting that went long." She waves back towards her desk.

I nod.

"You okay for a quick catch-up?" She flashes a nervous smile.

"Sure."

She pulls up her chair next to mine and sits, crossing her legs, but then uncrossing again. "So, I had a chat with HR this morning, regarding what we talked about yesterday, and Steve has been reprimanded and put on a performance improvement plan." She pauses for effect. "I shouldn't be telling you the details, but I think you deserve to know."

I remain poker-faced.

"They wouldn't fire him. Said it would be your word against his. Too risky for a social media backlash that our PR just doesn't need."

I open my mouth to protest, but even before the words form on my tongue, I know there's no point in speaking them. Vickie is on my side, the machine of industry is not. It's fine for one person to be victimised and bullied, as long as the company profile isn't tarnished. I get it.

"I know." She reaches out and lays a hand on my arm.

"What if I were to take to social media with my side of the story?"

Vickie retracts her hand. "Well, obviously that's your prerogative, but I can't see it going well … for anyone." She shuffles awkwardly. "Sorry, Toby."

"No, I understand. But I won't be taking on Steve's tasks anymore."

"Absolutely, and that's exactly what the deal is. Steve needs to show he's doing his work, and there will be an in-depth review in a month to see how things are going. If he hasn't pulled his socks up, he's out then."

"Fair enough."

"He's also been asked to leave you alone, and he may yet be moved to another department."

"Okay. Well, good."

"So we'll say no more about it, for now, okay?"

"Sure." I nod. Deal done, crises averted, so they reckon. I'm not so sure.

"On the plus side, I was just talking to Ed in Spokane. He sang your praises for last night."

"Really?"

"Yeah, he apologised for being brusque on the phone, but he was under pressure, he said you got everything back running quickly, and he was grateful and impressed. So, good job, Toby. Appreciate your dedication."

I shrug. "No big deal. Just had to reboot some stuff in the server room."

"Well, that's what you are here for. To keep things running smoothly." She beams a smile at me.

I get the feeling this conversation is ending. She gave me the classic open-faced shit sandwich. Bad news bread, but a spread of strawberry jam praise on top. I sigh internally and resign myself to the fact that work is just meant to be shit.

She smiles. "You all set, then?"

"Err, yeah. Sure. Thanks, Vickie."

She wheels her chair back into the realm of her cubicle, grabs her coat and heads away, turning back at the door and giving me a cheery wave.

"Night, Toby. You okay, yeah?"

"Yup, all good." I give her a thumbs-up sign and turn to my PC screen.

I blast quickly through my few tasks and then decide to go out for a non-smoking break with Raymond. Stopping on the way for a bio break, I notice the light is on as I go into the toilets. Odd. It normally goes off itself after a period of inactivity to save electricity. I pause and listen, but can't hear anyone. I shrug and relieve myself in my usual cubicle. As I pee, I notice a shadow that shouldn't be there, a slight change in the way the light reflects around the room, and a faint footfall under the sound of piss hitting the bowl. Someone is in the room with me.

I finish and zip up, but take my time. The only other person who should be here is Raymond, and if it were him, I'm sure he would either whistle or shout out a hello. I check both the phones in my pockets, but no messages. I set my personal phone to record audio, and slip it back into my pocket, then open the cubicle door, not sure what to expect.

"Evening, Toby." Steve. Should have guessed. He stands close to the cubicle that I came out of, facing me. Clearly, he was waiting for me. This doesn't bode well.

"What are you doing here?"

"Just fancied a little chat, you and me, no managers."

"Nothing to chat about." I shrug and try to push past him to wash my hands. He blocks my way.

"Oh, I think we do." He smiles a sickly grin. "I think we have lots to chat about."

I raise an eyebrow. There's a metal bin in this room, probably full of damp tissues, a hand dryer on the wall, water — hot and cold, and a fire extinguisher on the wall just outside the door. There's a fire exit about fifty yards along the corridor. I calculate all my options while he clenches his fists and then cracks his knuckles.

"For instance?"

"Well, for some strange reason, Vickie ran an audit on my work and then reported me to HR. You wouldn't know anything about that, would you?"

I shrug. "Can't say I do. Managerial tasks aren't my concern."

"Right. Strange, that." He steps closer to me. "What were you doing last night?"

"My work." I shake my head. "As normal."

"Well, funny that all the tasks I handed over didn't get done, isn't it?"

"Hilarious, yeah. Look, I don't have time for this. What do you want?"

"I just want to let you know, I'm going to be watching what you do, Toby, very closely. Very closely, indeed."

"Really? Maybe you should watch what you do, and none of this would be an issue."

"Are you fucking threatening me?"

I cough out a laugh. "I think it's the other way around."

"I've been put on half pay for the month because of your lies, you sneaky little shit. I have a family to feed, I can't afford you fucking my life up." He prods at me with a finger, staccato stabbing into my chest.

"Your inability to provide for your family isn't my

responsibility, Steve. What, do you need me to go home and fuck your wife, too?" Several things happen as I say this. First, I don't know where that came from, or why I said it. A shock to me as well as to Steve, who is suddenly white-faced and blank for a microsecond. Secondly, time seems to slow down to a slow-motion crawl as I see him ball his fist, then retract his arm and swing a punch towards my face. I watch with horror at first as he swings his arm, but as it all happens so slowly, I find myself laughing at the comedy of it. I wait for the punch to fly, and the velocity of kinetic motion to prevent any directional changes, and then I simply step aside just before his fist is near me. He slams hard into the wooden cubicle door behind me, and screams out in pain. I twist around and I'm behind him now, grabbing his other hand and pulling it up his back, twisting it hard, then slamming his body against the door. I jerk up on his twisted arm and he yelps again, muted as I press his face against the door.

I notice a dent in the cheap wood where his fist landed, and glance down at his hand, now red and already swelling. He may have broken a bone.

"You watch yourself, Steve. Because things are changing around here and I won't take your shit anymore, got it?"

He says nothing. I stamp down on the back of his knee. He falls, but I keep his arm twisted up. He yelps again.

"GOT IT?" I repeat.

"Yeah, yeah. Okay." He concedes, and I let go of him and step back.

"Now, get the fuck out of my night."

He picks himself up, nursing his hand and clutching his arm, he looks at me with anger and fear, then turns towards the door, and vanishes into the corridor.

I wash my hands in the sink, turn the audio recording off on my phone, and head out to the smoking area to have a chat with Raymond.

CHAPTER
SEVEN

ACCORDING to an app on my phone, I managed about five miles on the bike this morning, before my legs sent an official letter of objection to the high command, demanding all activity cease with immediate effect. I relented and made the slow, low-geared return home, then crashed on the bed with aching muscles in places I never knew I had muscles. I'm aiming to level up this activity gradually, building my body back into some kind of functioning vessel. I'm too old to ignore the facts now, I need to stay fit, or I risk turning into a slug-person, oozing from my bed to the couch, to the fridge and back again. A new diet, studded with leaves and protein, and as much exercise as I can manage is my vague plan. I should probably research a bit and get on some proper fitness regime, but for now, I'm content to ease into things at my slow pace. I can feel some change already. Sort of. My body reacts faster, I feel more awake, more vibrant, somehow. Still, my bed is most welcome, and I fade out of consciousness as the morning sun tries to burn through the thin curtains.

———

The audio is muffled through my jeans, but I amplify and clean it up without significant fidelity loss. I play back the recording of my encounter with Steve last night, on my home computer, analysing the frequencies and listening back to how it all played out. Weird thing; the time between me saying the words 'fuck your wife, too?' and then the slam of Steve's fist against the wood, is just over one second, verified with the waveforms, and the waveforms don't lie. The way I remember it, it felt more like thirty seconds. I had plenty of time to dodge the punch. I could almost have gone and made a cup of tea.

Aside from the occasional schoolyard scrap, I've never been in a fight before in my life. Yet somehow it seemed fluid and natural, the way I twisted behind him, and had his arm up his back before he even realised what was going on. Where did that come from?

As I recall it, I never lost my cool or panicked. The audio backs that up, too. No pauses or stutters, no tone changes. I could have been in a movie, scripted lines delivered perfectly. I don't know what to make of it. I save the file, uploading it to a cloud backup, in case I should need to reference it later.

I make a meal — don't know if it's breakfast or dinner anymore, so a random unnamed meal — of smoothie, followed by poached eggs on toast, and a mug of green tea instead of my usual coffee. Strange combination, but goes down well.

A notification sounds on my personal phone as I'm sipping my tea. I glance down at the screen, but then quickly pick it up and unlock it. After almost two weeks, my previous phone that was stolen has just connected to the internet, and is signalling to be rescued, reaching out across the void and pleading for help.

Interesting. I tap on the notification, and a map opens up, showing me the location of the phone. Not far away in the next town. I open a street view map of the location.

It seems to be in a house, deep inside a red-brick housing estate. I gulp down my tea and get in the car without a second thought. Time to teach the little twat some manners.

On the fifteen-minute drive, I have some second thoughts and reservations about my plan or, more accurately — lack of a plan. The person who just switched the phone on may have no idea it was stolen. They could have bought it from the robber, or a pawnshop, or eBay more likely, and assumed it was a legitimate sale. I can't go there, guns blazing, demanding justice. But I can inform the person, politely, that they are in possession of stolen goods. Perhaps they won't care, but more than likely they will, as without me unlocking the phone it won't be much use to them. They may help by telling me where they got it from, and that might give me a better lead to follow. Not much point in telling the cops; I highly doubt they would follow it up, even if I did hand them the answers and evidence on a silver plate.

I proceed with caution, glancing at my phone screen every so often to make sure the stolen phone hasn't moved. So far, it remains static. Probably charging. I arrive at the estate and then navigate the maze of roads until I'm outside the house where the phone is lurking.

The evening light is fading, but the streetlights are on, and I can see the house is a rundown box in various states of disrepair, with a front garden full of broken rubbish and knee-high weeds like Steptoe's yard. I drive on to a few houses down, as far away from any light source as possible, turn around and park facing the house in question, then turn the engine off. I glance at my phone again; the stolen one remains inside the house. I slide down low in my seat, monitoring the house and my phone screen. Thankfully, the area is quiet, and no one is around. I imagine all the good people of the world are eating dinner and watching Coronation Street, or whatever.

I linger for a while, trying to be invisible in my car. A couple passes by, walking a dog, but they don't acknowledge me or even look in my direction. I can't sit here all evening, though, as I'm due at work. I need some kind of plan.

A figure exits the house and crosses the road. I sit up but stay hidden in the shadows. I use my new phone to video the person, and zooming in, I can see it's a young woman. She gets into a car parked on the opposite side of the road. I zoom back out, and look at the car, grabbing the registration number. Something trips in my head. The car is dark blue and small, a boy-racer type thing. This is the car I stopped to help with the 'flat tyre' and then got attacked. This is them. They haven't sold the phone yet. I check my map, and the phone is still inside the house. The woman drives away in the car.

I think this is my sign.

I pocket my phone, get out of my car and casually walk up towards the den of crime. Just a bloke walking around an estate, nothing to see here. I glance at the house as I walk past. A light is on upstairs, but downstairs is dark. I walk on, then around the corner to see if there's an alley that goes behind the houses. There is, and I count back until I'm behind the right house. The backyard is behind a high fence, but the gate is half off its hinges, and not locked. I quietly let myself in and navigate through the mess, worse than the front yard. Old bikes, car parts, a broken toilet, three smashed flat-screen TVs, and an old fridge, are all being slowly absorbed by nature. I reach the back wall of the house and peer in through the biggest window. A living room, if you can call it that. Dark and nobody visible. I step back a few paces and look up at the second floor where the light is on. A figure crosses in front of the window for a moment. Too quickly to see if it was my assailant, but certainly, someone is in that room.

I check my phone, shielding the screen light with my hand and check again that the lost phone remains inside. It does, and is just a few feet away from my current position.

There's an option to connect to the phone, play a sound, and show a message on the screen. It's designed to be a 'lost phone' message, to show how a person can get in touch and say they have found the phone, but obviously, that won't be happening here. I can have some fun, instead.

I type a message and send it to the phone.

The Matrix has you …

I wait for the status to update and barely hear the chime as the message appears on the phone. It came from upstairs; the window is cracked slightly open.

A thought occurs to me. The little gobshite also stole my work phone. Maybe that is here, too? I reach into my jacket pocket. My new work phone is set to 'do not disturb' and silent mode, and it too has a notification on the screen. I chuckle to myself and send another message to that phone, which, coincidentally, is also in the room above me. I wonder how many other phones are there, all stolen.

> Follow the white rabbit.

A distant chime signifies the message is delivered. I edge back into the garden, looking up at the window. The figure crosses in front of the window again, maybe he's checking the phone beeps. I still can't see who it is.

I glance around the garden for inspiration, then grab a sizeable chunk of broken toilet cistern, and edge back out into the alley.

Checking up and down for signs of anybody first, I find a chink in the fence to observe through, and then I hurl the lump of ceramic over the fence into the garden. It has the desired effect, and satisfyingly smashes in a cacophony of noise on the concrete path at the back of the house. I watch the window upstairs, and sure enough, a figure appears with a 'what the fuck' expression on his face. I snap a photo with my phone, already focused and zoomed in on the glass, and then swiftly make my way back down the alley and around to the front of the house and my car. As far as I can tell, I manage this unobserved. No doubt the neighbours will wonder what the noise was, but maybe they are used to disturbances from this address.

In my car, I study the photo, and I can't be completely sure, as he was wearing a hoodie before that covered part of his face, but given that he is in possession of two of my phones, and the car is the same, I'm willing to bet on it. I've found my assailant.

A new plan gurgles into life in my head, and I drive away, down to the entrance of the estate where I noticed a dodgy-looking takeaway on my way in.

I grab the cheapest pizza — because there's no need to waste money — and drive back to the estate, but I leave my car a short distance up the road this time, facing the exit route, then I grab the pizza box, but I have another idea which brings a grin to my face. Resting the pizza box on the roof of my car, I check again to make sure the stolen phone is still in the house, then send another message to it.

> Knock, knock, motherfucker.

Then I stride casually up to the house, carrying the pizza flat on my left hand and bang twice on the door.

I wait, and nothing happens. I peer through the glass in the door, but it's frosted and I can't see anything. I bang again, louder.

A light comes on behind the door, and a blurry figure appears. It opens a crack, I stick my foot in quietly.

"Pizza delivery," I cheerily announce.

A face appears in the opening, confused. I recognise him now, it's definitely the wanker who cracked me on the head with a wheel brace.

"I didn't order no pizza." He scoffs in a high-pitched chav accent. I struggle to keep the bile down.

"Oh, that's strange. 38 Holland Way, yeah?"

"Yeah …" I estimate he's in his late twenties, wiry, angular features, decked in grimy, threadbare sweat-pants and another hoodie, but hood down this time.

I pretend to read off my phone screen. "Yeah, 38 Holland Way, medium pepperoni, paid for by card over the phone." I shrug.

"I didn't order no pizza." He repeats, and I notice in my periphery that he reaches for something with his left hand, and then passes it behind his back to his right. I assume a weapon of some kind.

"Well, someone did, and it's for this address. You want it or not? It's paid for."

He shuffles suspiciously, but who could turn down a free pizza? The nasty little shit opens the door a fraction more, and reaches for the pizza box with his left hand, his right hidden, no doubt clutching a wheel brace or something.

In my head, a chorus of intricate, elegant and orchestral heavy-metal music bursts from nowhere, and I move to the rhythm on autopilot. Many things happen in quick succession.

I slide my phone into my pocket with my right hand, and slam the pizza box up into the thief's face with excessive force with my left hand. A drum break punctuates the impact. I knock him back but he stays standing. He lifts his right arm, and I was correct, he clutches a metal baseball bat and makes to swing it towards me. The pizza falls slowly to the floor with moon gravity. I push into the house and slam the door closed while the pizza is still in motion. A guitar riff screeches in my head. He roars some abuse at me, and I watch with a grin forming as the baseball bat rises above him, and begins its descent towards my face. I read the words painted on the side, Optimum extreme, with a little logo of balls next to it. The bat continues to fly towards me, I reach up and pluck it from the air, twisting it out of his sweaty hand and kicking upwards at the same time, impacting him square in the stomach with my booted foot, knocking him back. He falls against the stairs with a thud, a cymbal crash coinciding in my mind.

He's winded for a moment, laying still, but then he reaches into a pocket and pulls out a knife, flicking it open. I laugh as a staccato melody plays out and I effortlessly bring the bat down in an arc, smashing the knife out of his hand. It falls down the stairs and I kick it away. He cries out, his broken hand flying to his mouth.

"What's the matter, you don't like pepperoni?"

"You fucking arsehole!" He whines, and I press the end of the bat into his chest. He lies prone, whimpering and white-faced. Terror rages through his veins and gears spin in his brain, trying to come up with a plan for escape and revenge. I laugh at his pathetic situation and slam down on the bat, a crack sounding in his ribcage. He roars out in pain, almost vomiting out his lungs.

"Where did the girl go?" I move close and stare into his weasely eyes.

"Wha?" He coughs out, confused.

"The girl who left in the car, where did she go?" I push down again on the bat for emphasis. He gurgles up some blood and spits it away.

"Fuck off! What do you want?"

I sigh and raise the bat, "Where," I bring down the bat with force on his right knee, he yelps and tries to shuffle away up the stairs. "did," I repeat the strike, this time on his left knee, "the girl," I lift the bat again, and now aim for his groin, he screams like a baby and squirms, but cannot move.

"Work, she went to work!"

"Go." I let loose the bludgeon and impact his scrawny body. He shudders, but then falls unconscious, sliding down the stairs until he slumps into a heap at the bottom.

"Twat."

I climb past him up the stairs and find the room at the back where I heard the phones chiming before. Inside is a rat's nest of chaos and a stink of sweat and farts. A table against one wall is loaded with dozens of phones. Maybe fifty. Some plugged in, some stacked up, some ripped apart, their guts spewing out with batteries and screens torn away from the chassis. No doubt all of them are stolen. There's a crappy laptop on the table, connected to two of the phones, running some kind of jailbreak software by the looks of it. He's trying to either crack the passwords, or wipe the phones entirely. This is a big operation, not just a casual tea leaf.

This changes things.

I go back to the stairs and look down. He's still slumped in a heap.

I think it's time to close down this redistribution facility.

I ping my stolen phone again, and find it in the mess plugged in and charging, but not connected to the laptop. I pocket it and do the same with the stolen work phone. It was further down in a pile, also charging. Waiting in the production line to be wiped and sold, probably.

He left his laptop unlocked, and I flip between the open apps. Predictably, he's got an eBay web page open, and I check the stats. He's already sold hundreds of phones online. A nice little business he's got here. Well, no more. I change his eBay password to 'IamANastyTw@!' and log him out, then do the same on his Gmail and Facebook which he also had open. That will be frustrating, for sure, but I don't think it's enough.

I glance around the room, looking for inspiration, and the answer is obvious, right there already laid out. A cascading resonance, an amplified frequency that rings through all these phones that sit with a lithium-ion incendiary within them, a catalyst to destruction.

I stack all the remaining functional phones on top of the laptop, and then place my right hand on the pile. I focus, concentrating energy into the block of silicon. Images race through my mind of patterns, waveforms, colours and light. A high-pitched whining sound comes from the stack of phones, a vibration in some of them, then a blinding flash and a fizz of fire spurting from midst the pile. It instantly melts the laptop screen, and heat floods up into my hand. I take it away quickly and step back as the rest of the phones repeat the process. They hiss and spurt, buckling and flipping onto the table, a noxious stink rises with thick smoke and I exit the room, slamming the door.

At the bottom of the stairs, I find the chav-boy's phone in his pocket, and dial 999.

"There's a fire at 38 Holland Way." I make sure they note the address, then disconnect and drop the phone on the floor, crushing it with my heel.

I pick up the pizza — as there's no need to waste it — open the door, and exit the house.

"Sorry, mate, must have got the wrong house." I laugh and close the door, then saunter back to my car and drive away towards work.

CHAPTER
EIGHT

THE PIZZA WASN'T BAD, as it happens. Four out of five stars, considering the low price and how it fell on the floor, and then got cold while I took care of business. I deposit a few left-over crusts in the pizza box, along with my two no-longer-stolen phones inside that I had unlocked, wiped, disassociated with my account, switched off and then snapped in half over a kerb stone with my boots, into a huge green bin beside Halfords on the other side of town. I had previously given the details of the phones to the police, and now they are evidence for more than one crime. Sad as it is to waste perfectly good technology, I can no longer be in possession of them. No matter, I have replacements. Justice has been served, no thanks to the system.

At work, I park in my usual spot, and trudge the endless route through darkness and light, over tarmac and carpet until I reach my office door.

I pause, then turn around and head back to the restroom, where I splash my face with cold water, and wash every trace of chav from my hands. I sniff my shirt, and there is a slight remnant of burning phones detectable. I reach into my backpack and dig out a can of body spray, wafting a mist over myself, covering the pungent chemical-electrical smell, and then go back to my office.

"Hello there, stranger." As I open the door, a friendly face smiles at me from the desk next to Steve's. Not him, obviously, but my daytime counterpart, Tracy Fisher.

"Well, hello. What a lovely surprise!" I drop my bag in my cubicle and then sidle over to Tracy. "What are you doing here at this time of night?" I perch on the edge of her desk and smile down at her. She's early thirties, with dark hair and ample cleavage, pretty enough, and I'm sure she once had a crush on me, years back. She's married, though, and I was never really interested. "Haven't seen you for ages."

We used to work together when I did the day shift. But since I switched to nights, I had completely forgotten she existed.

"Steve is out sick, so I'm covering." She giggles.

"Oh, no? That's a shame. What's up with him?" I feign sympathy.

"Fell over or something. Broke his hand on the ground trying to stop his fall."

"Ouch, that must have hurt!" I look at her, wide-eyed. "Still, it brought us back together, so silver linings, eh?" I wink.

"Yeah, he's in a cast, can't click a mouse button or

type for weeks, they reckon, so you're stuck with me for a while." She smiles.

"Could be worse." I raise my eyebrows. "I suppose you have to run off now, make hubby his dinner?"

"He's getting pizza, tonight. I wasn't expecting to be out all evening."

"Pizza? There's a coincidence. I grabbed one on the way here myself." I grin. "Stay and keep me company for a bit? Coffee and a catch-up."

"Oh, I'd love to, but I better be off. Maybe tomorrow?"

"Yeah, sure. There's always tomorrow. Take care, Tracy."

"See you." She picks up her handbag, and I quickly jump up and grab her coat from the stand, helping her into it, as a gentleman would, and then open the door for her with an elegant flourish.

"Lucky hubby." I note, as she walks away with a girlish giggle, and her short skirt shows off her elegant calves.

I sit down at my desk, switch on the PC and wait for the login screen to load.

"Evening, Toby." I turn and Vickie now beams a grin at me. "Sorry, was stuck on another meeting there. They are taking the piss now with these late ones."

"No worries, I was just catching up with Tracy."

"Ah, yes. Our dear friend Steve has had a bit of an accident, it seems."

"Indeed, did he say what happened, exactly?"

She shakes her head. "Apparently, he slipped and fell on the drive outside his house. When he reached out to break his fall, he broke his proximal phalange instead."

"His what?" I laugh.

"Middle finger bone." She holds up her hand and points to indicate. How ironic.

I nod. "Right. Unfortunate that should happen while he's on a performance improvement plan, isn't it?"

"I expect HR will make an allowance, considering."

I say nothing and turn back to my screen.

"Yeah, so Tracy will cover for the foreseeable. You two get on okay, don't you?"

"Oh, yeah, house on fire. No problems there." I stifle a chuckle at the words 'house on fire.'

"Right, good." She shuffles awkwardly. "Everything else going well?"

I shrug. "Yeah, fine."

"Great. Okay then. See you tomorrow. Usual stuff, I've sent the reports and dropped a handover note in your email."

"Cool. Thanks, Vickie. Have a good evening."

"Night, Toby."

I walk around the perimeter of my realm, glancing out into the ill-lit car park and catching myself in a shadowy reflection. The dark and peaceful night brings calmness to my soul, and I ponder on the events of the day.

I'm not normally violent in any kind of way, so the beating that I casually delivered earlier this evening now shocks me. The dark shadow of me in the window reflection shudders, but there's a smirk to his demeanour as well. I mean, the little twat had it coming, big time. Who knows how much violence he has dealt over the years? His stolen phone business seemed to be thriving, and no doubt many have suffered at his hand, even if they just handed over the phones without any need for a smack to the head. I gave him only what he deserved and probably not even enough.

I'm sure the fire brigade took care of the burning, and perhaps the police would be keen to investigate the cause of the fire, and why so many phones were in his back room, and then spontaneously combusted.

That point lingers in my mind and rolls around like a cat needing a scratch. How did all those phones catch fire? When I remember what happened, it doesn't make sense. I somehow instinctively knew how to start an exothermic reaction in the lithium-ion batteries, with a resonating frequency burst, delivered, it seems, by my touching the stack of phones. Once one started, they all quickly followed suit. A chain reaction triggered by my instigation? But, how, and what does that mean?

I walk over to my desk, but then decide against it and move to Steve's desk, and touch the tower case of his PC. I think about patterns and waves, fractal shapes and bursts of colour. I glance down at the computer; it remains off and inert. Maybe it has to be switched on? I'm not going to do that, though. If anyone is auditing Steve's systems, and it seems that he switched on the computer in the middle of the night, that would certainly put suspicion on me.

I step away and continue my meandering.

• • •

I find myself near the security office as I wander aimlessly around the building, so I grab Raymond for a non-smoke break. He obliges and we make the epic voyage out to the smoking area in the carpark. The air is moist, dark and chilled. An electric buzz from the lamp posts fills the night with a harmonic oscillation. I home in on the frequency. I can visualise the wavelength and all the irregular spikes and dips of power. The sound becomes null as I blank it out with a cancelling mirror in my head. The night is quiet again and we arrive at the fag bunker.

Raymond pulls out a packet of cigarettes and lights up, taking a deep inhalation of the acrid smoke into his lungs. He seems satisfied, but then coughs up a mythical creature, spitting it into a dark corner of the shed.

Chemicals and electricity, that's all we are. Atoms broken off from a distant star, formed together into the shape of a bipedal being, capable of so much, and yet doing so little, for the most part.

"You okay, mate?" I laugh and enquire with the smugness of a non-smoker evident.

"Absolutely top hole, old chap." Raymond fakes a posh accent and taps the ash from his fag with an effeminate gesture.

"If you found out you had some kind of super-power, would you use it for the general good, or for your own benefit?" I pose a question to Raymond the security guard, who has plenty of time in his life to ponder on such things. He doesn't flinch and takes another deep drag on his fag and squints at me.

"It all depends, Toby, on the type of world around me."

"Well, assume it is this very world in which we now exist." I hold out my hands and wave at the empty carpark before us. The night squelching its way into every nook and cranny, every gap in the walls, every leaf on every bush, that is ill-cared for and browning with disease around the edge of the lot.

"In that case, I'd certainly use it for my benefit, at least at first." He shrugs. "Do you think the world gives a shit about me now? Would humanity reach out and save me if I needed help?"

"I think it would, most of the time."

Raymond looks at me over his cigarette. "People are scared of difference. Petrified. You show them you have something they don't understand, and they will fear you, feel threatened by you."

"Hmm, yeah."

"And as soon as that happens, they'll be after you. Kill the freak. Doesn't matter if all you have ever done is benevolent, they'll want you dead. Buried, explained and put away. Nothing more than a story to tell. People can't handle anything weird." He looks me up and down. "Surely you know that already?"

"Oh, yeah, I sure do." I nod, thinking back to the bullying I've received over the years, and more recently from Steve. Well, no more. I'll be the one handing out beatings from now on. The world has had its last go at Toby Steele.

"Well, then. You take care of yourself and the people you love. Then, if there's time, you can help those who deserve help."

"Good answer."

"What is it, anyway?"

"What is what?"

"The superpower?"

"Oh, I dunno. Haven't worked it all out yet."

"You writing something?" Raymond stubs out the butt of his fag and flicks it into the hedge.

"Thinking about it, yeah." I lie. I don't think I know how to explain the truth, just yet.

"Good on you. Go for it, why not?"

We slowly amble back to our respective desks, far apart in the empty office. I check my status dashboard, and everything seems fine and normal. I check again that I've completed all my tasks for the night, and I have. Amazing how much more free time I have, now that I'm not doing another man's work every night.

Bored, I take to the corridors again, at least I can get my step count in while I'm stuck here. I find myself on the other side of the building, outside the server room where I was the other night. Curious, I tap open the door lock with my pass and go in. Everything is as I left it, clean and tidy, all functioning as it should. But I still can't explain the weirdness that happened. I pull over one of the wheelie monitor stations and plug it into the middle rack. The screen pops up with the green status display, as it should. I hit some keys to see what might happen. Esc, Enter, F2, F11. Nothing changes. Then I see an option to open a terminal — F12, so I try that. The green screen vanishes and is replaced with an empty black window with a single line of text and a cursor. The timestamp now is accurate, confirmed against my watch.

25/2/22 23:48:09:_

I type a command: 'help' — and hit enter. A page of text loads that lists all the available commands and what they do, but what doesn't happen is the weird screensaver patterns and buzzes that I experienced the last time. I look through the list of options, but none of them mentions a display of psychedelic images.

I try some commands, but they all seem to do what they are meant to do. I don't know enough about this system to dig too deep into it, and I know it is too important to the core business we do here to risk taking it offline, even for a minute. Angry Americans would call me immediately, especially now they know I can fix it when it goes down. That's the problem with doing a good job, you just get more work to do.

Instead, I unplug the screen and wheel it back home, then exit the server room, still confused, but perhaps resigned to never knowing what happened that night.

I wander back to my desk, intending to scroll through rubbish on Reddit until I can go home.

"Oh!" A pulse of adrenaline floods through me as I open the door to my office, expecting a dark empty room, but a figure lurks in the shadows. For a second, my fight or flight mechanism activated, and I was ready to see Steve, armed with something, ready to smash my head in, or a cop, having somehow sniffed me out after the fire at *Stolen Phones 'R' Us* on the other side of town. Instead, the silhouette is far more pleasing. Bézier curves and long hair. A high heel dangling from a leg that's resting on a desk.

"Hi, Toby."

"Well, hello again, Tracy. I wasn't expecting you here." I feel a grin splash against my face and I walk over to her. She remains sat on her desk, her hands holding onto the edge on either side of her. Her chest thrusts out at me.

"I wasn't expecting to be here, either, but … well, Ant is on earlies tomorrow and he went to sleep, so … I was thinking about you, all alone here in the dark and, you know, I thought I'd pop in to keep you company for a bit, as you said."

"That's kind of you, Tracy. Very thoughtful." A waft of perfume rises towards me from her hot body, and under it is a vague whiff of booze. She isn't drunk, but she's had a glass of courage. Fair enough.

"I brought a picnic." She grins and stands up from the desk, revealing behind her a half bottle of white wine, two plastic cups and what looks like homemade cookies. I remember she would often bring cookies to work when I was on the day shift, and they were always delicious. There's even a little tea-light candle. She's thought of everything.

"Amazing! I'm flattered that you'd do this for me, Tracy."

She smiles. "My pleasure. Shall I pour?"

I'm sure we aren't meant to drink alcohol whilst on duty, but one glass of wine won't hurt, and there's no one here to witness it, so … "Please do."

She picks up the little candle and flips a switch on the bottom. "I thought the smoke alarms might trigger if it was real, so I had these from Halloween." She shrugs, then opens the bottle of wine and pours some into each cup, then hands me one. "You like my cookies, don't you?"

"Absolutely, they are delicious as far as I remember." I take the cup of wine, not knowing where this might lead.

"Well, here's to a little company, now and then." She smiles and raises her cup to me, I tap mine on it and laugh.

"I'll drink to that."

Tracy's cookies are as yummy as I remember, and the little fake candle throws a flickering amber light around the otherwise dark office. We chat about the day shift crew I remember, and Tracy fills me in on all the mundane events that have happened since I switched to nights. New people joined, and some old people left. Susanna Fielding went to work for a rival company with much better pay. Paul Mandell was made redundant after eighteen years of service, and Gabe Sasso got promoted to another department. All information I could have lived my whole life without knowing, but Tracy was talking and I was listening. I know she didn't come here to talk about work, though, and I wonder what her real intentions are. She pauses for a moment and sips the last of her wine from the cup.

"Well, I should probably get going. Let you get on." She smiles, nervously and stands up.

I look up, "We both know you aren't leaving just yet, Tracy." I wink.

"Oh?"

"No, no. We haven't finished catching up yet." I stand up and move closer to her, then gently draw her into me and plant a kiss on her lips, soft, but passionate.

I can feel the flush in her cheeks but she hungrily responds and kisses back. Her hands move down my back. She steps backwards and perches on the edge of the desk again, then pulls me between her legs.

"I just need some passion, Toby. Things are fine with Ant, but … I don't know, it's become boring and perfunctory. I need something new and naughty to fire me up. This is just a one off, okay?"

I nod, "Okay, Tracy." I reach down and kiss her again for a long moist moment, then stroke my hand along her leg, noting that she's wearing hold-up stockings and an absence of knickers.

"Well, maybe a couple more times, after …?"

CHAPTER
NINE

EVERYTHING HAS ITS FREQUENCY, its rhythm and pulse. Even a static object like a table or chair, exists in a state of perpetual flux as much as it stands still. Solid and persistent, yet constantly spinning at the atomic level.

There's a baseline frequency to existence. A constant, buzzing, perpetual disturbance to be still and at rest, and then there's the resonant frequency that amplifies and shakes the core of being. The frequency that makes existence dance and jump, boil or burn. If you can find that precise value, then you control the world around you. Unlock the mysteries and play the game. Disrupt the status quo.

I'm in a pub.

There's no music playing, live or recorded, and no gig to watch later. Instead of my usual Saturday evening of farting around on the internet, and absorbing the spam that the world constantly creates, I felt like disrupting my status quo. I cycled here. Well, I was out cycling and this place caught my eye, so I stopped. Never been here before. Old-style pub. No TVs, no sport, no nothing apart from folks quietly enjoying a drink. There are some cheap B&B rooms upstairs, according to the pamphlets lying around. A slice of England's history, with no hint of corporate branding or franchise chain identity. A real pub.

I'm drinking fizzy water with ice and lemon. I don't want to dull my senses. Plus, I have the bike.

My glass resonates when I tap it with my nail. The ice clinks around in the glass, and the bubbles fizz with an apparently random pattern.

I absorb the relative peace, drink in the scene around me and sip at my water.

My mind frequently wanders back to the disturbance that happened at the phone thief's house. A looping ticker-tape reel of information spooling into my head, repeating endlessly with no answers, only more questions. Like, how I don't seem to be my usual self lately, and that I could cause a pile of phones to self-destruct. I don't understand it, yet I feel comforted and safe with it. I'm not worried, just curious.

I need answers, but I don't know where to look for them. Not like I can easily Google this question. I'm not sure I even know what the question is.

I finish my drink and stand up to leave. I'm not in a rush, but I suppose I should get back. Not that I have any other plans for the night. No work today, but no play either. I might read something or just go for a long walk in the middle of the night.

Someone comes into the pub. I don't see them, but I hear a door open and close, and then I feel a waft of wind, and a delicate scent of perfume on the breeze over the baseline beer aroma. I turn to look. A woman now sits three stools away from me. She waves to the barman and then orders a glass of wine. Her voice is soft and quiet, she's got an aura of happiness around her, but also a hint of sadness.

She turns to look at me. Maybe she felt me staring? She's bloody gorgeous. Natural, not caked in makeup and Instagram fake. Dark hair in long ringlets, blue jeans, simple blouse. Nothing ostentatious, but yet, so alluring.

We make eye contact and she flashes a brief smile, then turns back to the barman as he hands her the wine.

I don't hesitate and smooth my way over to her. Her perfume is like a rope, and I pull myself towards her with it.

"By any chance, is your name Anaesthesia? Because you are an absolute knockout."

She turns to me open-mouthed but then bursts into a laugh. A gentle laugh that makes me think of picnics and days at the lake.

"That was off the scale of cheesiness. Well done."

I raise my eyebrows and then motion to the stool next to her. "May I?"

"Free country." She shrugs and takes a sip of wine.

"What troubles you?"

She turns back to me, shocked. "Why do you think something troubles me?"

"I don't know," I say, honestly. "Just a feeling."

"Well, I'm fine, thank you." She politely remarks, then turns back to the wine.

"Vibrations, frequencies, waves. All around us, all the time. I think that has something to do with it."

She turns back to me. "Pardon?"

"Sorry. Let me start again?" I pause, but she doesn't react. "I'm Toby."

I stick out a hand, and after a moment, she shakes.

"Cassie."

"Beautiful name."

A thin smile briefly touches her lips. "Short for Cassiopeia."

"Oh?"

"Cassiopeia Andromeda, to be precise." She tilts her head with a smirk.

"Well, it was fifty-fifty, and I made the wrong choice. Damn."

"What was?"

"My opening line. The other choice was — Did you just fall from the stars, because you have a heavenly body."

She chuckles. "No, I think you made the right choice." She pauses. "Well, the slightly less cheesy choice, at least." She swigs at her wine.

"Can I buy you another drink?" I wave to the barman.

"I'm seeing someone, I'm not here for anything romantic, I'm tired and I've had a long day."

I pause for effect. "Is that a yes or a no?"

She guffaws. "… But I get the feeling you won't take

no for an answer, so yes, if you still want to, but my previous statement stands."

"Fair enough." I turn to the barman. "Same again please, mate." I change my mind. "Actually, I'll have a glass of wine, as well. Thanks."

"You don't look like a wine type. What were you drinking before?"

"Water."

"Really?"

"Yeah, fizzy water."

"Wild." Her eyes widen as she mocks me. I grin but say nothing.

We are furnished with wine. I take a sip, then turn back to Cassie, "So, what brings you to town?"

She's surprised for a moment but then glances down at the bar in front of her. Her phone is next to a purse, and on top of the purse is a room key with a big wooden block attached, and the name of the bar burned into it. Obviously, she's staying here in the rooms above. She doesn't flinch.

"Just visiting Gran."

"Oh, how is she?"

Cassie laughs again with that gentle giggle. "She's very well, thank you."

"Good to hear." I raise my glass. "To good health."

Cassie clinks my glass. "Good health, indeed." She smiles. "She just had her one-hundredth birthday."

"Wow, that's impressive."

"Still sharp as a knife, too." She shakes her head and then looks up. "I don't know why I'm telling you all this."

"Must be my affable demeanour." I grin.

"Must be!" She laughs.

"Staying long?"

"No, back home tomorrow."

I nod. "Do you live far away?"

"Far enough, yes." She pouts.

"That explains it, then."

"Explains what?"

"The undercurrent of emotional frequencies. The dark tints to your aura."

"What?" She stares at me.

"You want to see your gran more often, especially as she's a hundred years old, and you don't know if each trip might be the last time. You try to make time, but work and life make it hard to come all the way here."

She looks down at her wineglass. "Mm."

"I'm sure she appreciates when you can."

Cassie turns back to me, recovering her posture. "She does, but it really is none of your business."

"Sorry."

"You some kind of healer or hippie?"

My turn to burst out a laugh. "God, no. I'm in IT."

"But you read auras?"

I scratch my head. "Well, no, not really. I sort of feel frequencies."

"Frequencies?"

"Yeah … I'm not sure how to explain it."

"Okay …"

"Everything has a wavelength that it vibrates at, and somehow I can sense what that is."

"Really?"

"Yeah. Well, not as in a number value, but I just sort of, feel it."

"Interesting. I know something about frequencies, myself."

"Oh? What do you do?"

"I work in renewable energy. Analytics, data, statistics. That sort of thing."

"Nice."

"It is." She smiles.

"Lucky chap."

"Sorry?"

"The man you are seeing. He's very lucky."

She rolls her eyes at me. "Thank you, Mr Smooth."

I laugh. "Not serious, though?"

"What makes you say that?" She flinches back slightly.

I open my arms up. "He isn't here. You came to see your gran for her one-hundredth birthday, and he didn't come with you?"

She sniffs indignantly. "No. He didn't."

"Not serious." I nod.

She shakes her head with a laugh. "God, aren't you sure of yourself, Toby Smooth!"

"Steele. Toby Steele." I raise an eyebrow.

"Whatever. We aren't at that relationship stage, yet, if you must know." She flusters.

"Indeed." I flash a grin. "As I said."

"Look, I appreciate the effort and the compliments, but you aren't my type, Toby Steele. I feel I should be upfront and make that clear."

I tilt my head. "If you say so." I smile.

She laughs. "Men!"

"I just hope he appreciates you, that's all I'm saying."

She smirks and shakes her head again, but says nothing.

"Another glass?"

"Go on then."

We chat for a while about her work. She reluctantly tells me that Brian, her non-serious boyfriend, works with her at the same company, renewable energy solutions for large industries. That's how they met, only a couple of months ago. She politely asks me what I do, and even seems interested when I tell her.

As we talk, I get to ponder about my job and work — night shift IT support — it seems much less interesting than it used to.

Basically, I do very little, now I think about it. Fixing printers and making sure our network stays up. I'm not exactly taxing my abilities to their limits. I should do something about that, but I'm not sure what.

Cassie melts a little more as the wine glows inside her. She tells me how her grandmother was a significant figure in her childhood, and taught her almost everything she knows. An amazing woman. She worked most of her life for the government, but Cassie doesn't know, or won't say, exactly what she did.

Now, at one hundred years old, her grandmother resides in a care home. Very well looked after, but she's bored almost to tears, so looks forward to Cassie's visits.

Cassie tries to come at least once a month, but sometimes it is hard to find the time.

I nod in sympathy. It has been a long time since I saw any of my family. I should make more of an effort.

As well as being naturally beautiful, Cassie is smart and quick, raw and outspoken. Not shy about making herself clear. I know she said I'm not her type, but that only made me more interested. A challenge makes the prize all that more valuable. I don't count the non-serious Brian as a challenge. Her eyes never lit up when she mentioned him.

Cassie's phone buzzes on the bar and she taps at the screen, reading the message that has come in and then quickly turns the screen off. "Thank you for the drinks, Toby, but I should get some rest."

"My pleasure. Thank you for the conversation."

"Good night." She stands and sways a little, then smiles and heads for the door, turning to give me a wave.

I grab my bike and begin a slow, cautious ride home as the cold night air blows away all hints of alcohol warmth, chilling me to the core.

CHAPTER
TEN

MONDAY NIGHT, and the amount of willpower required to drag myself to work is wildly disproportionate to the amount of money I get in return. Effort outweighs bank balance by a factor of at least a thousand. I trudge, slowly, not caring if I'm late. Apathy has come to stay, brought a suitcase and bunked down.

There has to be something better to do than this with my life.

I have the urge to do something radical and wild. What if I just turned around now, walked back to the car, and drove away? No particular direction. Turn my phones off, and keep going until I run out of energy, money, or fuel. Whichever comes soonest. I have no real ties here. No family, no friends to speak of. No reason to stay in this town, and burn away the good years of my life, helping some faceless corporation get rich at the expense of my sanity. It doesn't seem worthwhile, or even vaguely right.

I don't think I want to do this anymore.

I don't know what I'll do instead, but right now it

doesn't matter. An opportunity will arise. A job will suggest itself. Something interesting, wild, ridiculous and dangerous even. Something worthy. Something that pumps the adrenaline around my body in a way that this graveyard shift never did.

My Dad always says — 'Do what you think is right until it doesn't seem right anymore, then do something else.' He's got a point.

When I ask myself the question; why am I doing this? I don't have a good answer.

— It's a job, so I do it.

That isn't enough.

— I'm lucky to have a job at all.

Bullshit.

It was never anything to do with good luck that I came to be here. If anything, it was probably bad luck that sent me along this dark path into the silent realms of night-shift IT work.

It was that conversation in the pub with a random woman, Cassie, that put my life into perspective. She's doing something useful and meaningful. Trying to help companies save energy, stop burning dinosaurs and polluting the world. She's making a difference in her small way. What am I doing?

I should be making a difference. Putting a dent in the universe, and generally, pushing the limits of everything I interact with.

Instead, I'm walking through empty hallways, and I don't even know what we as a company contribute to the world, aside from some expensive pharmaceuticals. Nothing to do with me. Chemicals aren't my strong point.

I reach the door to my office, but stop dead and stare through the thick dull wood into infinity. I've made up my mind. I'm getting out.

I turn and retreat to the restroom to formulate my plan.

"You're late." Vickie attacks me the moment I step through the door. She stands with arms folded by my desk. No one else here. Tracy must have already left. I'm relieved. I wouldn't want her to think my resignation was anything to do with her.

"Yeah." I shrug. Not even worth some empty excuse. I edge past her to my desk. "Vickie, I …"

"Toby, can we have a word?"

I turn. Her tone is dispassionate. Her vibrations are caustic. I put my plan on hold. "Okay."

"Come with me, please."

She exits the room, holding the door open for me, leading the way through the corridors, back the way I just came, down towards the entrance, but then turns left acutely, and along an unfamiliar path. A corridor that leads to a domain I tend to avoid.

'Here be dragons.'

The path opens into a clearing of intense beige. Sofas and tables, inspirational posters and acres of carpet, filthy with age, black spots of dirt trodden into the pile, with a greasy path worn into the fibres towards a section of open plan seating. Devoid of life, but lit with a voracious ferocity of fluorescent glare.

Vickie leads on to a glass-walled office at the back of

the area. She knocks on a door that is already open and steps into the room.

I know where I am, but I don't know why. Human Resources. A department full of synthetic platitudes and fake empathy. Lies, deceit and carefully constructed hatred for humanity. Even the name broadcasts the truth for anyone able to see it. They reduce people to a formulaic resource that can be tapped and discarded as needed.

A woman waits behind a desk. I'm sure she has never been here so late in her career before. Must be galling for her to have met me in my domain of night. She looks down at her laptop screen, no flicker of emotion on her face.

"Toby, this is Sharon O'Neil from HR."

I nod but stay silent.

"Good evening, please take a seat."

There's an awkward tension in the air. A drone of reluctance comes from both of them. Whatever this is about, they really don't want to be here. The feeling is mutual. Let's get this over with. I sit.

"What's this about?"

"I'll get straight to the point." Sharon flashes an insincere smile in my direction before looking to Vickie for inspiration. "We have evidence that you were drinking alcohol, and having sexual relations during your shift on Friday night."

I can't help it and blurt out a guffaw. "Do you, now?" I glance at Vickie, but she is stone-faced.

"We do, and obviously, that sort of behaviour is not tolerated."

I raise an eyebrow. Well, this is convenient. I was

planning to hand in my notice, but now it appears I'm about to be fired. No need to show my hand. I'll make this as difficult as possible. "And what kind of evidence do you have?"

Sharon shuffles in her chair. "An anonymous source sent us a video file."

"Really? Well, isn't that interesting."

"Yes. It is rather unusual, but nevertheless, the evidence is clear."

"There are no cameras in the office." I turn to Vickie. "So where did it come from?" She doesn't flinch.

"Are you acknowledging or denying the accusation, Mr Steele?"

"I'm doing nothing of the sort. I'd like to see this evidence, please."

With obvious distaste, Sharon taps on her laptop and then turns the screen to me and plays a video that was already cued up and ready. The scene is very dark, and the video quality is terrible. Night vision black and white, but grainy and low frame rate. The scene is empty, focused on what looks like Steve's desk. You don't have to be Einstein or Sherlock Holmes to figure out who recorded this. The sneaky little shit must have set up a camera in the office. I'm annoyed at myself for not noticing it, but the angle suggests it could be hidden up in the ceiling and poking down from a vent or something.

The scene changes, flickering to a frame of two people, barely identifiable, but one of them could be me, while a structural pillar obscures the other, Tracy. You can't see her face, only some hair.

On the screen, Tracy flicks on the little fake candle,

lighting my face up, and then she pours two cups of wine. We toast and then take a drink. The scene changes again to quite possibly the worst porn video ever made. Two blurry figures in a dark room, humping on a desk.

Sharon stops the video, then looks me in the eye and waits for my reaction.

"That's your 'evidence'?" I make air quotes with my fingers.

"Well, what have you got to say for yourself?"

"It's none of your business, to be honest, but during my mandatory one-hour unpaid lunch break, a friend from my amateur dramatics class popped over to rehearse a play we are both working on. The drink was sparkling water, and we acted out a passionate scene." I fold my arms with an air of smugness.

Sharon looks at Vickie for assistance. There's a slight shrug.

"I think the more pertinent question is; why was someone illegally videoing the office, and how did that video get onto your laptop? I would think the IT security department would be extremely interested in that, don't you?"

Vickie turns to me. "Look, Toby. Obviously, this is very awkward for all of us, but we can't have things like this going on in the office." She motions towards the screen, still showing a still image of a dark mess of bodies.

"What are you saying, Vickie?" I tilt my head.

"We think it would be best if you were to look for alternative employment."

"You're firing me?"

"No, no!" Sharon blurts out. "We didn't say that." She covers her arse with legal terms and conditions.

"No, Toby, we just think that with all the business with Steve, and now this, maybe you would prefer to work somewhere else. You are a talented technician, I'll give you a good reference. I'm sure you'll have no problem finding a suitable placement."

Well, she's got something right, at least. I don't want to be here anymore than they want me here.

"Six months' pay lump sum into my bank and I'm gone without a word."

Sharon's eyes widen. "That's out of the question, Mr Steele."

I pull out my phone and open Twitter. "Or I could just post a long Twitter thread about how I've been badly treated here. Bullied, now set up with an illegally gained video of a perfectly innocent event. Forced to leave for no good reason. I don't think that would look good for the company image."

Sharon and Vickie share another look.

"Two months pay, which is your accumulated vacation allowance, plus a generous severance amount in lieu of notice, and health insurance until the end of the quarter."

I scoff. "Six months pay. I don't think that's unreasonable, given the circumstances. You can keep your insurance."

I'm sure this isn't going how they planned. I was meant to break down in embarrassment at the video, plead forgiveness, and take whatever I can get to leave with my dignity. But that won't be happening. Now they are in a negotiation situation, and I reckon I have the upper hand.

I'm glad that Tracy isn't identifiable in the video. Hopefully, they will leave her alone.

"Four months." Sharon pouts, "and you need to leave immediately."

"Done." I flash a smile. "I'll wait while you make the arrangements." I motion towards her laptop.

She twists it around, then taps and scowls at the machine for a long few minutes. Vickie says nothing. I'm sure her primary concern is finding a replacement for me on the night shift. Perhaps she will have to do it herself tonight. I don't feel great about that, but they could have left this 'til the morning.

"There," Sharon announces. A sheet of paper spits out from a printer behind her. She hands it to me. Notice of severance, with a sum of money that looks about right, deposited to my account. I sign, and she countersigns below. We do the same on another copy that she keeps.

"Very well, Mr Steele. I trust you know the way out?"

"Can I just see that video once more, please?"

Sharon hesitates, then nods and turns the laptop back to me. I rest my finger on the touchpad, and scroll the video back to the start, the dark, empty room, and Steve's desk in full view. I tap the play button and smooth my fingers over the keyboard, feeling the heat from within the cheap plastic enclosure. I sense the operating frequency of the chips inside, pulsing and firing out billions of tiny blips of energy every minute. I focus on that energy and resonate with it, increasing the frequency and intensity, overwhelming the circuits with spurious noise. The heat intensifies, and the tiny fans inside ramp up and blow at full speed, but it's no use, they barely make any difference. The keyboard bulges in the middle, a creaking sound from within. The screen dims, then goes completely black. The fans stop, and the heat increases as the guts of the machine continue to expand. A key pops off. The F key, followed by G, H, and J. The bulge grows as the battery inside swells and melts.

"What's going on?" Sharon calls out in a panic.

The laptop case bursts open at the sides, a stench of burning plastic now pouring from it. Smoke rises from the blackening guts and the whole thing is now sparking and belching out acrid black smoke. I back away from the gurgling mess.

A shrill, excruciatingly loud alarm rings above us as the smoke detectors trigger the fire alarm.

"I think you need a new laptop." I look up at Sharon who is now white with terror. Vickie is already at the door and hurrying out of the office. I follow, making sure I have my severance letter, and Sharon is close behind, closing the door as she leaves. I turn back to look at the glass-walled office, now full of smoke with a dull glow coming from somewhere above the desk.

The two women exit through a fire door and I turn and run back down the corridor, then across the building.

My work here is not yet done.

· · ·

My badge still functions, and I enter the server room. I need to be quick, because, not for the first time in recent history, there seems to be an electrical fire in the building, caused by who knows what? Sharon and Vickie are both witnesses that the laptop seemed to explode, and catch on fire with no apparent cause. I barely touched it.

I grab a monitor and wheel it over to the main rack of servers, and plug it in, then wait for the green dashboard to appear. I pull up the list of commands and then enter the admin screen.

I find my user account on the company database and delete the entire thing. All my history, all my email, and all the files I have ever created will be gone in one sweep. I don't want to leave them anything to investigate, not that there's anything particularly incriminating on my work account, but it's the principle. The system asks me if I'm sure. I am, and a series of whirs and clicks, synchronised and connected all around the world get to work to remove all traces of Toby Steele.

I do the same for Sharon and her email, filled with lies and treachery, and the video file that obviously was made by Steve. I'm sure he still has a backup copy on his home computer, but I also wipe his corporate account. Why not?

I leave Vickie's account alone. No need to be nasty, then I log out, put the screen away and exit the room, going back to my desk where I have some bits and pieces I'd like to take home. The fire should be fairly well contained and nowhere near my office, anyway. The shrill of the alarm was dulled inside the server room, but now it rings loud around my head, painful and annoying. I blank it out, fixing on the stable frequency of the sound, and cancelling with an equally loud inverse version. The sound subsides and I can relax a little.

There's no sign of fire in this area, so I grab my bag that I had dropped on my chair when I came in, and scoop my belongings from the desk into it. Not much, in the end, mostly junk, memories I will probably chuck out in the cold harsh light of day, but again, it's the principle. There's also a mini yucca I bought in a moment of madness years ago. I grab the lot and find the nearest fire exit into the car park, take the long route around the building to where I parked my car, and note the distant sound of sirens approaching as I drive away.

Toby Steele has left the building.

CHAPTER
ELEVEN

I RECKON I owe Steve a favour, to the tune of about four months' pay. I was thinking I'd just leave and maybe get some of my accumulated holiday pay, if anything, but now, because of the evil intentions of Steve Twatly, I walked away with a chunk of cash. Not lottery or retirement funds, but something to keep me going for a while, or escape this dull world and move on to somewhere fresh and interesting.

Well, cheers, mate. I'll consider it payback for the years of anguish and hatred. No, I think Steve still owes me plenty.

What was he trying to achieve with the video camera? A paranoia that I was messing with his stuff? Did he sit up all night watching it for activity? It must have been the most boring TV channel ever, and Vickie must know it was him who planted the camera. I wouldn't be surprised if they fired him as well because of this. Was it worth it? Hardly.

I woke up with a Prodigy song in my head, so I put on headphones, blast some metal, and go out for a long cycle ride to clear the earworm and general funk in my brain. It works, more or less, and when I get home, I dive into an evening breakfast of porridge and fruit.

Cycling is fine, but I think I need to expand my exertions to more parts of my body. I'm reluctant because it's such a fad these days, but I should join a gym or something. Maybe even get a personal trainer, because I haven't got a clue what I'm doing. Getting fit, I suppose, but instead of farting around and guessing what best to do, I should probably use some of my well-earned severance pay to invest in my ongoing health and fitness.

I grab my phone and start some research.

A ring startles me away from scowling at gym propaganda online; I can already smell the stench of stale sweat and talcum powder just by looking at the photos. This sort of thing isn't me, but I feel compelled to do something about my general sagging middle age.

The phone in my hand isn't the source of the ring. It comes from upstairs. Shit. I forgot to leave my work phone at the office when I made my getaway. Whoops. I better post it back at some point.

The call is probably some American with a tech support issue. Well, sorry pal, you'll be out of luck this time. I'm no longer the lighthouse keeper of the night. No more fixing printers and resetting passwords for me. They can find some other mug to fill the role. I run upstairs and pluck the phone from my jacket pocket.

"Hello," I answer with the jolly tone of someone

who no longer has to give a shit. The caller ID shows a generic office line number.

"Toby!" The gasping voice of Tracy grates in my skull.

"Hey, Tracy. You okay?" A blurry picture of her from that terrible porno of us in the office flashes in my mind's eye. I wonder if she knows about the video.

"Oh, my God, Toby. I just heard!"

"What did you hear?"

"Vickie said they sacked you over some argument with Steve?"

"Interesting take on things. Well, not quite."

"What happened? She wouldn't say any more. It was all very suspicious … Oh, and there was a fire! The office was closed until after lunch while they checked it all out. It bloody stinks in here."

"Have you finished your shift?"

"Almost. Vickie is taking over from me and covering the night, but she wanted to pop out and get some food first."

No other mug was available I suppose. Well, shouldn't have fired me over nothing. I mean, who hasn't had a quickie on the office desk?

"Meet me in the Prince Albert when you finish?"

"Oh, Ant will expect his dinner."

"Seriously? He can't microwave some lasagna himself?"

"I don't want him to get suspicious, Toby, you know, after we …"

I cut her off in case there's now a microphone in the office somewhere recording her. "If you want to know what happened at work, meet me in the pub after."

She pauses, and I can hear cogs whirring in her brain. "Right, okay. See you in a bit."

———

The pub isn't crowded, but for a Tuesday night, there are a good few folks about. Close to the office, but not a particularly fashionable hostelry, so no annoying kids being loud and obnoxious. Just enough background noise to make our conversation invisible to anyone who passes by.

I sip a pint and wait for Tracy to appear. Keeping one eye on the door, and the other on my phone as I continue to search for a suitable gym. There's one nearby that's open twenty-four hours. Looks good enough from the promotional photos and videos. They offer personal trainers and the membership fee isn't too bad. I tap in my details, and receive a coupon for my first session free. Deal done.

"Hiya,"

I look up at Tracy's smiling face and get up for an embrace, then peck her on both cheeks. "Wine?"

She bites her lip. "I shouldn't, but just one. Thank you."

She sits down, and I go to the bar.

"Haven't been in here for years," she muses. "Work Christmas do, about three years ago, wasn't it?"

"Yeah, probably." I shrug. I never go to those things. Too forced and fake.

"So, what happened?" Tracy's face switches to sympathy and concern. "What are you going to do?"

"Vickie didn't explain anything more?"

"No, she was acting very strange. I thought maybe she was just in shock because of the fire and stuff. She only just got out in time, apparently."

"Really? Interesting. Do they know what started the fire?"

"Someone's laptop battery exploded, so they reckon. Must have been faulty or something and spontaneously caught fire. Scary, when you think about it."

"Indeed."

"We all had to wait outside this morning for hours before they'd let us in. I thought we'd get a day off, but no." She rolls her eyes.

"No such luck."

"Come on then, tell me what happened?"

I stroke my chin. Now I think about it, telling Tracy that our passionate affair in the office is what got me fired is going to be a delicate operation. If she doesn't already know about it, is there any point in stirring the shit? Then again, lying to her would be equally bad. I make a decision. "Steve, the sneaky little twat, had a camera in the office, for God knows what reason, pointing at his desk." I pause to allow her to put two and two together. Her face flushes and goes white at the same time.

"Oh, my God!" She covers her face with a hand.

"Yeah, but don't worry. The angle meant you weren't identifiable. It was pitch dark and there was a pillar in the way."

"For fuck's sake!"

"That was my thought as well, more or less."

"So they fired you for ... doing it in the office? Seems extreme. What did you say?" She's moved beyond shock to fear and panic. "Can't believe Steve grassed us up. That bastard!"

"Yeah, that's one way to describe him. I made up some bullshit about an amateur dramatics thing I'm in, and that I was rehearsing a passionate scene. Don't worry, they have no idea it was you. The video was terrible, and there was no audio."

"You do amateur dramatics?"

I laugh. "No."

"Toby, I'm so sorry. It was my fault you got fired!" She almost bursts into tears.

"No. Tracy, don't be. I was thinking about quitting, anyway. Forget it. You did me a favour. Anyway, it takes two to tango, as they say."

Her eyes widen. "You never said you were thinking about leaving?"

"It just sort of came to me recently." I shrug.

"Not because of … us?"

"Jesus, no. Tracy. Nothing to do with that. I think I just need a change. I've been doing this crap for years."

She seems placated. "I'll miss you." She flashes a sad smile.

"Same." I nod. "You'll be fine, though."

"What are you going to do now?"

"I genuinely do not know. Just see what happens, I suppose. Might up and move away."

"Oh?" She looks worried.

"Probably best. Don't want to get you into trouble, do we?"

"Yeah …" She seems wistful and takes a gulp of wine.

"So Vickie is doing the night shift?" I scoff.

"Yeah, well. Not all of it. She said she'll cover until midnight, and after that, it can wait. They're going to find someone else soon, she says."

"Be hard to replace me." I laugh.

Tracy grabs my hand on the table. "It definitely will, Toby."

"Well, nothing is forever. Move onwards and upwards, and all those clichés. I'm not sad about it. There's got to be something better for me to do with my life."

"I hope you find something you love, Toby."

I nod. "Yeah, cheers, Tracy. Same for you."

I head to my new gym after the pub, stopping briefly at home to change into sweatpants and a t-shirt. No point in dawdling, I need to kick this off before I convince myself it's a bad idea. Not really knowing what to expect, I find it fairly busy with various people entwined with all manner of equipment, grunting and sweating with a background track of upbeat pop music. It seems daunting, and I feel my confidence dwindle, but a nagging feeling in my guts tells me to carry on. I've never done anything like this before, but I have the urge to wake up all my atrophied muscles, from years of sitting on my arse at a desk.

I linger in the reception area, waiting for a staff member to notice me.

A young girl approaches in a garish bright yellow leotard with the company logo sprawled across her chest.

"Hi, can I help you?" She's got a generic Eastern European accent.

"Yes, I just joined today on your website and I got a coupon for a free training session."

"Okay, that's awesome. I'll take your details and we can get you started straight away."

"Right, thank you."

"My name is Eva, and I'll be your trainer today if that's good with you?"

"Sure, fine." I smile and nod.

"So, I'll just ask you some basic questions about your fitness level and goals first, then we can get started on some warm-up."

She taps at an iPad on the counter and reels off a scripted dialogue, rabbiting on about privacy and legal bullshit that no one ever pays attention to, then asks about my height, weight, age, and activity level. My mind is elsewhere. Something about what she said struck a chord in my brain, a resonant frequency, amplified and violent, vibrating out all other input. I see her mouth moving, and feel myself nodding and robotically answering her inquisition, but I'm not present in my head. Eva. I know that name. Eva … Eve. Not someone I know, but the name ... There's something about it.

Synapses trigger, neurones fire, memory vaults unlock and spew their contents into my consciousness. Eve … Where do I know that name from? I flick through a mental contact database trying to match the name to a face. People from work, people I've known through my life, school, other jobs I've had, pubs I've been in, gigs I've seen, but none of those seem right. Eve … Evelyn? Yes! A puzzle piece fits into place.

Evelyn. But who is she? The name is important. A powerful déjà vu feeling overwhelms me, and I need to pin this down or it will drive me insane. Eva still taps at the iPad, her hair is tightly pulled into a braid and there's not an ounce of fat on her. Muscles delicately ripple on her arms and she finally has all the information she needs from me. I'm led into the main gym where she begins a brief tour of the equipment, and suggests which complicated machinery she thinks will work best for me. I try to pay attention, but the nagging of the name is all I can hear.

Evelyn, Evelyn, Evelyn.

More important than the gym, more important than anything. This name takes over my entire brain like a repetitive dream that loops into infinity. I feel my throat tighten, sweat breaks out on my forehead, and confusion flusters me.

"Are you okay, Toby?" I hear Eva ask with some concern in her tone.

"Yeah, sorry, I'm just … excited to get going."

She smiles and carries on with her legal, health and safety-influenced spiel.

I nod in what I hope are the right places.

Evelyn Greenwood.

The name suddenly appears in my brain like a Boeing 747 emergency landing in a hurricane. It snaps so hard that my head is knocked backwards and a nauseous wave bursts over me. Breathe. Pause. Breathe. Just a name, nothing more. No emergency, no panic. Just a name.

Evelyn Greenwood. Who the bloody hell is Evelyn Greenwood?

CHAPTER TWELVE

09:22, MONDAY, 14TH JUNE, 1965.
MEDICAL RESEARCH COUNCIL
HOSPITAL, MILL HILL, LONDON.

"EVELYN GREENWOOD?"

I look up and an awkward, weaselly man steps into my field of vision. "Yes?"

"My name is Spencer Jenkins of GCHQ. May I have a word?"

Oh, bloody hell. I thought all that ridiculous poppy-cock was long since behind me. What do they want, now? I smile, pleasantly. "Certainly."

"Come with me, please." He waits at the door to the office, and I reluctantly follow, silently grieving the loss of my freshly brewed cup of coffee that will no doubt be cold by the time I get back. I know from previous experience that there's no point in trying to avoid these people. They are as relentless as they are obnoxious.

I'm led to a bare room two floors up that I've never been to before, and I'm ushered in by Mr Jenkins and asked to sit at a table. He sits opposite me and puts a briefcase down, taking out some papers and laying them neatly in front of him. He then takes out a silver cigarette case and offers me one.

"No, thank you. I don't."

"Mind if I do?"

"Suit yourself." I shake my head.

He lights his cigarette and takes a long draw.

"I'll get straight to the point. Miss Greenwood, you worked at Bletchley Park with Turing during the war, correct?"

I tilt my head. "I'm going to need to see some identification, Mr Jenkins."

"Of course." He produces a badge that seems to corroborate his claim, although I'm not an expert in these things.

"Yes, I worked at Bletchley."

"What exactly did you do at Bletchley?"

"What's this about, Mr Jenkins? The war was a long time ago."

"Can you answer the question, please?"

"No, absolutely not. I'm not at liberty to discuss my work during the war."

"Very good." He smiles. "Just a test, Miss Greenwood. I am already fully aware of the nature of your work."

I raise an eyebrow. The fool will have to get up very early in the morning to trick me. Although, if he knows, then he must be pretty high up the chain. Everything was highly classified, if not destroyed.

"And since then, you have worked here at the MRC?"

"More or less, but I'm sure you already know that, too, Mr Jenkins, so please do cut the crap and get to your point."

"Very well. A woman with spirit. I like that." He

grins. "You have been working on brainwave pattern analysis on human subjects during various medical procedures. Your work has been at the forefront of medical science, and in the last five years you have published several papers on such wide-ranging subjects as," he bends down to read from one paper on the table, "Let's see — measuring delta waves during sleep cycles, easing patient pain with alpha waves, the effects of disruption to circadian rhythm, and recording brainwave pattern fluctuations after traumatic events."

"Indeed. Your point, Mr Jenkins?" I raise my eyebrows.

"Her Majesty's Government requires you to start work on a new project immediately. We will refer to it only as Project Flash Gordon henceforth. You will be given every resource you need in a private office and laboratory equipped with the very latest in technology, and a generous salary accordant to your seniority and experience. This project is of extremely high importance and absolutely top-secret. You will not speak of this to anyone outside of this room, is that understood?"

"I … What? But, my work?"

"We will find a replacement to fill your current position."

"Well, I need to think about …"

"Miss Greenwood, this is not an offer, this is a requirement." He taps a finger on the table for emphasis. "Failure to comply would be considered treason."

"I see. And may I ask, what exactly is Project Flash Gordon?"

He smiles a sickly, greasy smile, but then pulls out

another sheaf of papers from his briefcase and puts them down in front of me.

"You'll find all the details contained within these pages. We must destroy this brief at the end of the meeting."

I raise an eyebrow.

"In a nutshell, Project Flash Gordon is an investigation into possibility. You will research and develop a method to reprogram a man's mind using brainwave patterns, light, sound, and vibrations. Whatever technique is required to do the job."

He pauses and stares at me intently. "Take any simple man of basic military training and rapidly make him exceptional. Strong, intelligent, quick and effective. Remove all his fears and cowardice, and replace them with bravery and confidence. Furnish him with distilled knowledge in many subjects, and a loyalty to his masters that is unbreakable. In short, create a superman from any stock. We believe the brain is capable of this transition by means of applied technology."

Ideas and thoughts race around my head. What he's asking sounds incredible and the stuff of science fiction, but what if there's something in it? There must already be something in it if he's pushing this task on me. They must have some intelligence that strongly indicates brainwashing and reprogramming a man's mind, is something that we can simply switch on with the push of a button. I'm intrigued, but I keep my poker face. I'm also not a huge fan of the codename. Flash Gordon? A bit obvious, don't they think?

"And what if it isn't possible?" I enquire.

"It will be your job to find out and make it possible."

He states, matter-of-factly. "This is a necessary step for the ongoing safety and protection of Her Majesty's realm."

"I take it this would be a military application?"

"Government intelligence, but certainly, there will be military interest."

I nod.

"The Americans have been looking into the effects of strobing lights at certain frequencies causing seizures and epilepsy, they are also working on a device that could be presented to youth for future … manipulation … this research, amongst many other classified documents will be made available to you for reference."

I raise an eyebrow. "This is all very fascinating, Mr Jenkins, but why me?"

"Your expertise, Miss Greenwood. We believe that in the United Kingdom, you alone possess the skills in the new field of computer programming, along with your neuroscience history, psychology, language, mathematics, cryptology and not to mention, you have already signed the Official Secrets Act and proven to be loyal."

"I see."

"Indeed. Please, take your time to read and digest the brief in full, and then we'll head to your new offices."

"Straight away?"

"No time like the present."

"I need to gather things from my desk, my research and personal belongings."

"Already being taken care of as we speak, Miss Greenwood."

I puff out a sigh. "Make sure they don't forget my yucca."

He takes a note and then motions to the pages on the table. I start reading.

True to his word, after I read through the papers and ask some more questions, he burns the documents in a metal bin, opening the window to let the smoke out, and then smashes the ashes into dust with a pencil.

We leave the room. I'm led through the maze of corridors and downstairs, through a guarded doorway to a large open office. Mostly empty, but for a desk and some expensive-looking equipment stacked up along one edge.

"Welcome to your new home, Miss Greenwood."

I walk around the perimeter of the room and note the DEC PDP-8 that stands monolithic against the back wall.

"More equipment will follow over the next month. We will provide a list. If you need anything else, simply requisition it. There is ample budget for this project."

"How about some support staff?"

"Ah, and there's where we draw the line. Because of the sensitive nature of this project, you will conduct the work alone, I'm afraid."

"What? That's ridiculous. I can't manage everything!"

"I'm sorry, but we cannot risk anyone else knowing the full nature of the project. Staff will maintain the heavy equipment, but they will do so under your watchful eye, and must not understand the work you are doing. We will choose suitable candidates and frequently rotate them in and out of service."

"What about test subjects? Trials, experiments?"

"You will use animal tests until you are ready to trial on some volunteer military staff."

"Animals?"

"Monkeys, rats, whatever you need."

"Good lord. It's going to stink in here."

"We'll install a ventilation system."

"You've thought of everything, haven't you?"

"No, Miss Greenwood, that's why we need you. To think of how to implement this project."

"Indeed. And how long have I got?"

"As long as you need. We'll review the status every three months, and we'll be in touch regularly." He beams a smile. "We're going to become best friends, Miss Greenwood. May I call you Evelyn?"

I glower at him. "No, you may not."

"Very well. Now, if you have no more questions today, I'll leave you to get acquainted. Remember, you answer to me, and I answer to the Prime Minister. You will speak with no one else on these matters."

"I understand."

"Excellent. I'll be in touch." He exits the room, leaving me alone in a chaos of thoughts and ideas, questions and objections.

He wasn't joking about the generous salary. My income has doubled since I arrived at work this morning, according to a document on the desk. I'm officially conducting unspecified government research, not part of the hospital staff anymore, but still located in the building.

I feel like I'm back at Bletchley, lost and immature, trying to fit in with a group of men who mostly despise my presence. Only Alan cared enough to tutor me, to make me feel at home and guide us all to victory, and look what happened to him. Poor Alan. I always knew he was a troubled soul.

Father always said my brain would get me into trouble, and just when I thought I was finished with this sort of nonsense, here we are back in the thick of it.

I suppose it could be worse. Plenty of money, a lab full of equipment, and an incredible project to put my brain to use. What more could a girl ask for?

CHAPTER
THIRTEEN

FREEDOM. A lovely concept. Free to do whatever I want all night and day.

I could read, take up more hobbies, watch TV, play games, sleep, or stay awake. The night is my own again, and yet I don't feel free.

I'm not at work, slogging through the darkness for the benefit of industry, which is something, but I'm not using my time wisely. Life seems empty and dull, and I crave some kind of adventure.

I need to give myself time to acclimatise. I should ease into my new life gently. But I'm impatient. Life is now, not tomorrow. Seize the day, and all that.

Yet, I'm still a slave of the system. Consume, purchase, excrete, sleep and repeat. The game is different now, but there's a game nonetheless. At some point in the not-too-distant future, the money will run out, and to stay living in this house, this town, country or even world, I'll need to have value. Signing on the dole and stamping out a prescribed life has little appeal. I need a plan.

I'm Player One in a cutesy puzzle platform adventure, where the rules change from level to level with no clues. I'm confused, but safe for now until I choose to walk into danger. The outside world looms heavy and bright, and I stay inside. Security by obscurity. I hide within my domain.

I woke early. Well, early for my usual routine. Restless and disconnected.

After the gym session last night, I came home and collapsed into bed. Spent adrenaline still burning through my veins. My dreams were vivid and odd. That name, Evelyn Greenwood, still knocking from one side of my brain to the other like a tennis ball, each impact firing memories I can't explain. The smell of hospitals, flickering lights, nausea, ecstasy. Knives, but weapons — not kitchen. Computer code in languages I don't know. Places I've never been to, sounds I've never heard.

I don't know why the name is important, but it certainly is. The reason is swimming deep in a frozen lake in my brain and I'm at the top, fishing through a hole in the ice, trying to catch the elusive beast with no bait.

I shower, wash away the stale sweat and fog in my brain, and then flick on the coffee machine and my desktop computer.

Evelyn Greenwood.

I try a basic Google search first; unsurprisingly, millions of results come back. I'm overwhelmed with spurious irrelevant information.

I add quotation marks to narrow the search for the exact phrase, but there are still tens of thousands of hits. I start scrolling, but I don't know what I'm looking for. I switch to image search, in case a photo of her triggers more memories. A long gallery appears. I scroll and scan for far too long. My bell remains un-rung.

I flip back to the text results and trawl through the first page of Google, then the second, and into the third before I get up for more coffee. I can't read every single one of these pages, but as I'm mining blind, I don't think I have any choice. Will I know it when I see it? Who knows.

Time passes, and so does my patience. I need a distraction, and to get double exercise, I brave the world and cycle to the gym for another session, hoping that stepping away from the problem will allow thoughts and ideas to brew and percolate, perhaps coagulating into something tangible and useful. Memory is a strange thing. A trigger at the gym brought that name to the surface, but now I need to dive deeper and find the hidden treasure.

Eva isn't here today, but a guy called Mike puts me through my paces. I'm forced into machines that stress my muscles and bend me into painful shapes. I'm assured that pain and suffering are all part of the process, and I'm coerced into going the extra distance, pushing outside of my comfort zone, where exhilarating energy awaits my tired, aching body. So he reckons, anyway.

I now regret cycling, and tentatively make my way

home, stretching my muscles that had already issued formal complaints to head office. There will be a rebellion soon.

Part of me thinks I should start looking for a new job. A small part, admittedly, but I shake away the thoughts. I don't even know if I want to stay here, in this town. What's stopping me from going somewhere totally wild and off the grid like my brother, Duncan? I could pack my stuff and be out of here in a few days. Trouble is, I don't know where I'm going, or what I want to do. I just know it isn't here, or this. Australia fits the purpose, and maybe I could try to build up a relationship with my brother, and find work and perhaps, even love. What a crazy notion.

But if I stay here, and get another dead-end job, I'll be stuck again in the rat race. Consume, purchase, excrete, sleep and repeat. No, I will not do that.

I have an opportunity and it would be stupid not to take it.

I still need a plan.

My phone buzzes in my pocket. A rare event in itself lately. I pull it out.

Toby, I need your help, urgent!

The message is from Philippa.

I call her immediately, but the call is cut off. I try again and the same thing happens. What the hell?

Another text message pops in.

Can't talk.

I reply.

What's going on? Where are you?

Jason's house. He's gone a bit mental.
I've locked myself in the bathroom.

What? What's the address? Are you
okay?

Adrenaline pumps through my body, electrifying
me. I tense up.

4 Ouzel Close. Yes, I'm okay, but I've
never seen him act like this. He's taken
some drugs, I don't know what, and
he's shit-faced drunk. Slamming stuff
all over the place. I don't know if he'll
hit me, even if it isn't intentional. Can't
risk the baby.

What the fuck? Do you want me to call
the cops?

What a piece of shit. He's gone psycho with his
pregnant girlfriend?

No, God. That will just make it all
worse. Can you just come over? Try to
talk some sense into him.

Right, yeah.

I check the address on maps, and I'm about an eight-
minute drive away.

I'll be there asap.

Thanks, Toby. I'm so sorry to drag you into this. I just didn't know who else to ask.

I jump into the car and start the engine.

No worries. I owe you one anyway. Driving now. Keep texting so I know you are okay.

I slam the car into gear and floor it out of my street, following the directions on my phone screen. A flurry of messages pops up and I keep one eye on the screen and one on the road.

I probably shouldn't have picked this moment to break up with him, but oh well, lessons learned.

How was I meant to know he had speed or something? I've never suspected anything like that before.

We were having dinner and a glass of wine. I was trying to be civilised about it.

I know the last time we spoke things all seemed great. Baby and all, but he's been acting suspiciously, and so I did some snooping and found he's been shagging around with some woman called Lorraine Holland. Found his messages and photos with her. Really dirty stuff.

So I confronted him this evening, and, yeah … obviously it didn't go so well.

He started ranting on about how he didn't want the baby and didn't want to be tied down in his life yet. Career and promiscuity are apparently more important.

He's just been promoted and gone to a bigger branch of the bank to become manager, too.

I stupidly thought that was a good thing for us. I was planning a celebration until I saw that name pop up on his screen, and he tried to say it was just someone from his new bank.

Oh, God. Toby, he's walloping on the door now, I don't know if it will burst open.

He was in the Army reserve. I probably should have mentioned that. God, I'm sorry, please be careful.

Jesus Christ, he's punching a hole through the door! Toby, hurry!

I screech to a halt outside the house, squinting in the half-light to check the house number is correct, then run to the door, take a deep breath, and then pause. I was going to bash it down, or at least thump on it repeatedly until it caught the raging psycho's attention, but a new plan floats like a feather and lands down into my brain. I ring the doorbell once, briefly, and step back.

I send a message to Philippa while I wait.

I'm here. Hang on. Say nothing.

I wait and listen, but I can't hear anything. I ring again, this time with two short bursts.

There's a faint sound of someone thudding down the stairs. Then the door cracks open. Dark behind, I can't make out his face.

"What?" An angry voice barks out.

"Yeah, taxi for Philippa Harrison." I chirp the words in a jovial tone with a cheery smile.

He scoffs. "She won't be going anywhere, mate. You better fuck off." The condescending tone of a bank manager oozes through his inebriation. I shudder inside, repulsed.

I lower my voice, both in tone and volume. "No, I don't think so. I'm here to take Philippa Harrison away from you."

He opens the door wider now and steps out onto the doorstep, puffing up his chest. Streetlight orange lights him up. "I don't think you heard me." He snarls. "I said you better FUCK OFF." He steps forward again to within a few inches of me. He's tall, but the stink of booze from him puts me at an advantage, regardless.

The drugs, though, well I'm not sure. I've heard stories of people gaining inhuman strength when taking drugs. Too late to worry about that. God knows what Philippa ever saw in this lanky, radio-listening, banker-twat.

I shrug. "Meter's running, better hurry."

"I'm not telling you again, get lost." He moves back into his hallway pulling the door shut. A flash of light-ning fires in my mind, a pulse of condensed adrenaline, slowing time, speeding my body, and tensing my muscles.

I spring forward, getting a foot into the doorway before he can slam it closed. Surprised, he lunges at me with a fist, and I watch his face contort into an ugly scowl with it. The door bursts wide open as I twist myself around and crouch down in one motion. He punches the air in front of him and staggers forward into me. I jam my elbows backwards into his gut, knocking him back into the hallway further. I feel myself becoming unstable, falling backwards, so I spring up, and punch straight up with my right fist, catching him squarely under the jaw. There's a sickening crack as his neck whiplashes back, and he chokes out a roar of pain. He goes down, slamming onto the tiles of the hallway, another crash as his head impacts the cold floor, and he's out. Slack and unresponsive.

"Well, I hope you've learned your lesson, Jason. Don't piss off a pregnant woman." I consider booting him in the nuts, but for a moment I wonder if he's already dead. I bend down to inspect the carcass, and his chest is moving. I back off and bolt up the stairs, three at a time, finding the bathroom where Philippa is waiting, face streaked with makeup tears, hand clasped to her mouth.

"Hey, it's okay now. Grab your stuff and let's go."

"What happened?"

"Ah, he didn't want to pay the taxi fare. Come on."

Philippa, stunned, pokes a head out of the bathroom, then rushes into another room, coming out shortly with a bag. A thought occurs to me.

"Do you know if he's got more drugs, and where they are?"

"Yeah, bread bin." She nods. "Little bag of something."

"Good. Okay, you got everything?"

"Yeah, I think so."

"Come on then."

I lead Philippa carefully down the stairs, straight out into the night air. "Don't look at the twat."

"Jesus, what did you do?"

"He's fine. Come on."

I install Philippa in my car, then dash back to the house and straight through to the kitchen. On the counter, there's a bread bin, and inside, under a Hovis best-of-both loaf, there's a small plastic ziplock bag of some off-white powder. I don't know what it is, could be flour for all I know, but the chances are that it is speed. I grab it, using my t-shirt to avoid finger-printing it, then go back to the inert body of Jason still lying in the hallway, and sprinkle the powder over his face and down his shirt, then drop the bag on the ground next to him. I prod at his pockets and find a phone-shaped outline in his jeans, and squeeze it out carefully, then make an emergency call to 999 and lay the phone on the ground next to the bag of drugs.

Leaving the door cracked open, I exit the house, casually and calmly, walking back to the car and nodding hello to a passing dog-walker as I jog down the pavement.

The trip back to my house is in silence as Philippa ponders on the evening, and I concentrate on driving safely. Another dickhead incapacitated in his hallway. That's two for two.

————

"What will you do now?" I fish in the back of my cupboards for the sachets of hot chocolate that Philippa left here ages back, hoping they are still in date. I can't stand the stuff, but she isn't drinking tea, coffee, or booze, so hot chocolate it is.

"No idea." She has cleaned up and changed into a red silky pyjama top that accentuates her bump, and my fluffy white dressing gown, loosely tied and much too big for her. There was no need for discussion. She is staying here with me tonight.

She sits at my kitchen table. "Is he dead?"

"No," I laugh. "He'll be fine. Well, headache for a week or so, and after he gets out of prison in a few years, he'll be fine." I shrug. "Probably."

"Prison?"

"Yeah, I assume the cops will want to prosecute when they find the drugs all over him."

"How did you knock him down so quick? He's a hard arse."

"Just got lucky." I shrug. "Here you go." I hand her a mug of chocolate with a reassuring smile. "Plus, he was wasted."

"Thank you, Toby. I don't know what I would have done without you."

"No worries. All part of the service." I sit down opposite her and sip my coffee.

Philippa shakes her head slowly. "I thought everything was great. He was sweet, kind, and generous. Then he just flipped into a nutcase with no warning."

"People change."

She looks up at me. "Yeah. You've changed, too, Toby. For the better." There's a sadness in her eyes.

"Thanks."

She puts down her mug and fixes me with a look I recognise. "Let's go to bed."

A smile creeps onto my face. "You don't have to ask me twice."

————

"We're not back together or anything," Philippa screws up her face as I drop a plate of toast and scrambled eggs in front of her. "You know? I was just, emotionally unstable last night. Needed comfort."

I chuckle. "I know, Pip, it's fine. Don't worry."

We made love slowly and gently last night, warm and close, passionate and emotional. It was wonderful, and I slept with my arms around her and my hand on her baby bump, protecting and reassuring.

"Baby and all, it would just be too complicated."

"Yeah, to be honest, I'm not even sure I'm staying around here." I sit down. "I got fired from work."

"What? Oh, my God, what happened?"

"A misunderstanding, shall we say." I raise my eyebrows. "Doesn't matter, I was going to resign, anyway. I've had enough of it. Need a change."

"Wow. Well, what are you going to do now?"

I shrug. "No idea."

"Aren't we a great pair!" She laughs.

"Yep." I nod and smile. "We could have been, but that time passed and now we're just friends. I know."

"Thanks, Toby."

"Welcome. Eat up. Baby needs her breakfast."

Philippa smiles but then bursts into tears. I stand up, not sure what to do, but she waves me away. "Sorry, bloody hormones. I'm fine."

My schedule is disturbed now and I'm wide awake during the day like some kind of normal person. We spend some time rehearsing a story in case the police contact Philippa for a statement of where she was last night. She was at Jason's house, but after he became drunk and violent, she called a friend — me, and I took her home. No need to mention drugs and the beating that he took, keep it simple. Let them piece together the jigsaw I left for them. He fell over after getting fucked up on speed, or perhaps a dealer got annoyed with him. Serves him right.

A thought occurs to me. "Hey, Pip, does the name Evelyn Greenwood mean anything to you?" Perhaps she was one of Philippa's friends or relatives that I'd half forgotten. That name still flips around in my mind, desperate for a landing place.

"Evelyn Greenwood," She repeats. "No, can't say it does. Who is she?"

"I don't know, but I can't get that name out of my head."

"Oh? A fancy woman?" She grins.

"No. Nothing like that. Just someone who seems

really important, but I can't remember why. Been bugging me for a couple of days."

"Actually, hang on, it does ring a bell. Wasn't she one of the code breakers during the war?"

"Code breakers?"

"Yeah, here at Bletchley Park. I remember seeing a documentary about it recently. Maybe that's where you heard the name?"

"Hmm, no I don't think so. Haven't watched anything properly for ages." I ponder. "Interesting."

I tap the words into my phone, 'Evelyn Greenwood, Code breaker, Bletchley' and a page full of search results immediately fills my screen. At the top is a photo of her — black and white, young, smiling, standing in front of a complicated machine in one of the code-breaking huts, next to Alan Turing. A stab of electricity bolts through my body.

Holy shit.

It's her.

CHAPTER
FOURTEEN

12:42, MONDAY, 20TH JULY, 1970.
MEDICAL RESEARCH COUNCIL
HOSPITAL, MILL HILL, LONDON.

"I DO WISH you would give me some notice, Spencer, instead of just showing up as if I'm your mother." I glance around my laboratory and the piles of mess everywhere. Paperwork, animal feed, circuit boards, valves and wires, screens, tape reels, cages, lights and speakers are all over the place. I may as well live inside the rat cages where at least there is some order. "I would have tidied up a bit." No, I wouldn't, but still, it would be nice to know when I'm to expect company. Mine is a solitary existence, here, only crawling out of my hole for meals and sleep, unable to discuss my work with a living soul, apart from this one chap, whom I suspect has no soul. Perhaps I will end up the same way, a husk of a woman, bereft of substance.

"I prefer to find you in the thick of it, Evelyn. No need to stand on ceremony for me."

"Nevertheless, it would be polite to at least mention a vague date."

"Duly noted. Now, shall we go somewhere for lunch, it stinks to high heaven in here."

I scowl at the weasel of a man, but once again swallow my pride and calm myself. "Where is my ventilation system, Spencer? I do seem to recall you promised me facilities?"

"Ah, yes. All in good time. We may have some news around that, but first, let's eat."

"Fine."

We leave the confines of my laboratory, and glide along the streets in the opulent comfort of Spencer's Bentley T1, to the same restaurant we always visit when he bursts in on me like this; Swinton's Townhouse in Soho. I daren't ask how much this lunch costs the taxpayer, but it is nice to be pampered every so often. He says he chooses this place because they are duly discreet and staff know never to hover around when secrets are being discussed. I'm sure a park bench and a sandwich would do equally well. Still …

We travel in silence, and I watch the cars, buildings and people pass, wondering how I'm going to present my lack of progress to the man. Five years have flown by since I started this thankless task, and I've worked every hour God has sent me, to seemingly no avail. I've been close to walking out many times, but I know that would do me no good. There's nowhere on earth I can hide where they wouldn't find me.

After much fuss and fawning by the restaurant staff; 'So nice to see you again Mr Jenkins,' we are seated at the back of the restaurant, far from any other patrons. Spencer orders wine, and I wonder how I'll get any work done for the rest of the day.

"Now we are settled, shall we begin?"

I pout and scowl, but Spencer ignores me and takes out a small notebook and pen.

"What do you want to know?"

"Progress, Evelyn. Have you made any?"

I sigh. Of course, what else would he care about? "Yes, and no."

"Perhaps start with the yes."

"No, why don't we start with all the problems, hmm, how about that?"

He leans back. "Very well."

"Because of your obstacles and bureaucracy, I wasted three weeks last month fixing a bloody broken amplifier." I feel the heat of anger building up in me and pause to take a breath. "I had to fix the damn thing myself in the end. Absolutely ridiculous. You can't send me a single sodding valve without requisition forms in triplicate, justification, competitive quotations and only from sources in Europe. Spencer, I simply can't work like this!"

"Processes are in place, Evelyn, we can't just bypass them."

"Then don't expect quick results." I fire out the retort that I've practised so many times.

He says nothing, but I can tell he is condescending me with a berating in his head.

"Not to mention the animals. I can't take care of everything. I demand you do something about the smell."

"Are you finished?"

I shake my head. "No, but there's no point in talking

to you. Empty promises and unreasonable expectations. That's all you care about."

He pretends he hasn't heard my objections. "So, to get back on track. You were saying. The yes?"

I sigh. "The yes … I was able to communicate a memory to Jenkins." I feel myself grinning. "A rat. That's his name. I tried Flash Gordon, but it didn't seem to fit."

He raises an eyebrow. "What was the nature of the memory?"

"Simple colour-coded direction markers to get through a maze."

Spencer tilts his head.

I take a deep breath. "A maze, made of wood, where the walls are painted in various colours, the correct path, indicated by the good colours, leads to a treat. Other paths lead to death. I implanted the correct colour sequence in his memory via three sessions of the shifting, strobing light frequencies. He followed it precisely, eight times in a row, having been nowhere near the maze before. I'm calling it 'FSMI' — frequency shifting memory implantation."

"Excellent work. Mr Heath will be delighted to hear it."

"Thank you. But this was Jenkins the thirteenth. The others perished, unfortunately."

"Progress, nonetheless."

"Indeed. I would publish a paper on this technique, but obviously, I can't do that."

"Certainly not … and the no?"

"I'm afraid that poor old Jenkins the thirteenth died soon after."

"Ah. In the maze?"

"No, in his cage a few days later. Perfectly healthy otherwise. I don't know why. Heart stopped beating, simple as that."

"Not ideal."

"No."

Spencer jots down some notes on his pad, then looks up and calls over the waiter.

"Usual, please Alfonse, if you will."

"Certainly, sir."

Spencer asks me about my home life, outside of work. I know his patterns now, this is to lull me into a false sense of security that my best interests are being considered. I know this to be a lie. All he cares about are results and getting this bloody project finished. I'm five years into it and frustration is building. As much time as you need, I remember him saying, well that may as well be the rest of my life. I don't know if this will ever be possible, and I've told him as much many times. Persevere, he says, believe in yourself. I always sneer at these remarks.

"I've barely seen my son or husband in months, I'm exhausted, burned out, sick of the whole thing, Spencer."

He takes another note. "Perhaps a holiday would do you good. Why don't you go somewhere for a break? Two, three weeks even."

"Ha!" I scoff. "Chance would be a fine thing."

"Make that an order, Evelyn. I am ordering you to take a three-week holiday. I'll make the arrangements. You can choose where."

"Really?"

"Absolutely. You'll come back refreshed and ready to jump in again."

"Well, I don't know what to say. Thank you."

"No need. Take a break, enjoy life."

I nod, my mind already drifting to exotic climes and places we could go.

"… and it will give us some time to move you over."

I promptly snap back to reality. "Move me over to where?"

"Porton Down." He says, with a casual tone, as if it is no big deal.

"What?" My eyes widen. "I can't just up and move to Wiltshire!"

"Lovely area, beautiful countryside."

"Spencer, I don't give a damn about that. I have a life outside of work, you know?"

"Do you?" He chuckles. "You just told me you didn't."

"You know perfectly well what I mean!"

"You've been complaining about the facilities at Mill Hill for years now, so we've built you a brand new laboratory at Porton Down, kitted out with everything you've been asking for."

"But … what?"

"It simply wasn't possible at the hospital, now you'll be in the right environment for your line of work."

"I … " I start to complain, but I know there's no point. Clearly, this deal has already been done and I'm the last to know about it, as usual.

He's built me a lab? Another new lab. "Where will I live?"

"A lovely house has been found for you and your family. Excellent school for Anthony."

"I do wish you would tell me about these plans, Spencer. Not just drop bombshells on me without consultation."

"I have spoken with Gerald already, he helped me choose the house and school."

"You what?" My mouth drops open. "You went to my family behind my back and schemed to uproot us, and no one, not even my husband, thought to tell me anything at all?" I stand up to leave. "This is outrageous, oh just you wait until I see that man!"

"Please, Evelyn, sit. It's all for your benefit. We didn't want to bother you when you were so close to a breakthrough."

"How did you know I was close to a breakthrough?"

He raises his eyebrows and then nods to the chair. I sit but only under duress. "Evelyn, in my line of work, I have the privilege and curse of knowing far more than I care to discuss. Now, never mind that, I rather think you are going to like your new facilities."

As our lunch is served and consumed, Spencer goes on to detail the technical capabilities of my new laboratory at Porton Down, buried amid the science and technology buildings and connected to something called ARPANet, which I'm told is a brand new and highly classified communications network for computers in America. All very expensive sounding, but I will have direct access to databases around the world, eventually. Another new thing for me to learn. There will be proper animal facilities — hallelujah, and a capable staff of technicians to assist with the mechanical and biological needs. I must still work in the utmost secrecy, but I will no longer be buzzing around like a bee, fixing every minor issue and tending to the rats.

All in all, quite an eventful lunch — and the food is pretty good, too.

CHAPTER FIFTEEN

THESE PLACES GIVE me the creeps. People, devoid of autonomy, are reduced to become stalagmites, stationary in front of a television, absorbing drips of food, and regular pacifying drugs from nurses who pretend to care. Gently decaying, ever so slowly. You know going in that you aren't getting out alive.

Cherryoaks Lodge Care Home.

It could be worse. This seems to be a better example of your typical old folks' home — probably costs a fortune, even so, there's no denying the underlying reason for it. People age and wither. You lose structural integrity and cohesion, then become fragile and brittle, tired and despondent. Apathetic, waiting to expire.

Not that I've been to many of them, but I have memories of when my grandfather was briefly interred in such a place, albeit much less salubrious, before he kicked the bucket when I was a young lad. I think it's the odour that has stayed with me the most. Cheap cleaning product, barely masking the breakdown of human life.

I shudder as I enter the reception area, and sidle up to the nurse on duty with a hopefully disarming smile.

"Yeah, hi. Here to see Evelyn Greenwood, please."

She looks up with a total lack of interest. "Name?"

"Toby Steele."

"Friend or family?"

"Ah, more of an old acquaintance."

"Is she expecting you?"

Good question. I suppose that depends on why her name is so potent a drug in my veins. Maybe she is, maybe she isn't.

"No, I was just passing and thought it might be nice to pop in and say hello, you know?"

"Is it about the documentary?"

"What? Do you mean the Enigma stuff? No, no. Not at all." I lie. Of course, that's how I found her. Well, via Philippa. I dug up the documentary on YouTube and watched it, where it outlined Evelyn's previously secret involvement with Turing, and cracking the Enigma code back during the war. Fascinating stuff, but that isn't why I'm drawn to come and visit a stranger in an old people's home today. At least, I don't think so.

It wasn't quite that easy, anyway. The documentary didn't name this place, but mentioned a care home in the Bletchley area, and had several shots of the outside grounds. A quick fart around on Google Street View and I had narrowed down the location within a few minutes. I've even passed it on my bike half a dozen times when out on rides. Hidden in plain sight.

The interview was done with Evelyn about two years ago, and she seemed unnaturally lucid for someone in her time of life. It was brief, but she spoke about Turing and Enigma like they were both old friends. There was something about her that cemented the thoughts that had been circling in my mind. I knew her, and yet I had never even heard of her before a few days ago. Her voice, soothing and familiar, stirred something deep in my subconsciousness. I knew I had to come and visit immediately.

I didn't stop to put together a back story as to why a chap should come to visit an old lady in a care home. I suppose I imagined I'd just walk in and say hello. Perhaps somehow she would know me? Maybe we do know each other from some huge event, of which I have since repressed all tangible memories. Maybe she was a friend of my parents from my early childhood. I can't narrow it down, but I also can't leave it alone. Like a scab that I can't stop picking at, it bleeds and cries out for attention.

I take it from the apathy and nonplussed look on the nurse's face, that I'm not the first to have tracked down the infamous Evelyn; code breaker and unsung war hero.

"Wait here and I'll ask if she'll see you."

"Great. Thanks."

"What was your name, again?"

"Toby Steele."

"Right."

It takes all her effort, but Nurse Rosey Macredie, according to her name tag, gets up from her chair and ambles towards a hallway, then disappears from view.

What am I going to say to Evelyn? I have to admit, it does sound a bit odd that a stranger would just show up, and tell her he can't get her out of his head. She could assume I'm some kind of pervert and call for security, or she could be flattered. Who knows. Maybe she won't want to see me at all and I'll have no choice but to walk away. I'm not going to make a scene here.

Maybe I should have called, or even written to her first. A brief outline of who I am and my background, and then mention that her name has become some kind of obsession for me of late.

There's no doubt about it, whichever way I look at it, this is weird as hell. Well, I'm here now, may as well try to get to the bottom of this.

Rosey appears in the hallway and trudges back to her desk. She sits down, and then pulls out a book and pen from under the counter, sliding them toward me.

"Sign your name in. Evelyn will see you, briefly."

"Oh, great. Thank you." I smile, but my efforts seem to be lost on disinterested Rosey.

I glance down the list of names, in various shades of ballpoint ink, some scrawled, some carefully penned. I add my name to the bottom and push the book back.

"Through there?" I point to the hallway.

"Yes, straight through. Evelyn is by the back window."

"Thank you so much for your help."

Beige, so much beige. Wide corridors with padded corners at wheelchair height, serene paintings of landscapes and animals, and doors leading off left and right with an offset regularity. Some open showing glimpses of private rooms. Most shut, hiding the private worlds of previously vibrant, now dulled people beyond. The worn path in the carpet leads me to a large open dayroom, where a dozen or so folk are seated on comfy chairs. It is visiting time, so there are some families gathered around grandmas and grandpas, others sitting alone, some smiling into a void of their memories, and some half asleep.

I scan around the room, but quickly spot the lady I'm looking for. A thud of adrenaline pulses through me as I notice her, fragile as a bird, but sharp and alert as a fox. She stares out at the neatly trimmed garden, away from the room. I slowly walk over and pause, somewhat awkwardly.

"We've never met, and you say it isn't about Turing, so what is it?"

She doesn't turn, but I assume she's talking to me. Silver hair, long and neatly braided, she sits upright, not slumped like most of the other folk.

"Evelyn Greenwood?" I suddenly feel nervous as the words come out.

"Yes, young man, obviously." She turns towards me finally and pierces me with a stare.

"My name is Toby Steele, and you are right, we have never met, and it isn't about Bletchley Park, or Enigma, or Turing."

"I believe I had already established that." She tilts her head slightly. "You young people do make a habit of repeating yourselves."

"Sorry, yes."

"So, what is it?"

"Err, well, this is going to sound odd, but …" I pause, feeling my face redden. "A few days ago, your name just sort of popped into my head, and hasn't left since. I don't know why."

She raises her eyebrows. "Really?" She bursts out a

laugh, then quickly composes herself. "No doubt the TV thing, you must have seen it."

"I have watched it, but only afterwards. A friend told me about it. Before that, I had never heard of you. Sorry."

"Curious." She squints and looks me up and down.

"Indeed. And, not just the name, but a sort of deep compulsion that drew me to find you. I know this sounds strange, but, I don't know the cause."

"You had better sit down, young man." She nods towards a chair opposite her.

"Thank you." I take the seat and try not to be eaten by its soft cushions.

"Perhaps you read an article in a paper or magazine? Bletchley has become very fashionable of late. I think there was a film about poor old Alan or something like that."

"Ah, that's true. There was a film about cracking Enigma, but I don't think I saw it. Of course, I knew about the history. I've been to the museum, but I don't think that's it."

"What exactly happened, then?" Evelyn leans forward closer to me, and indicates that I should shuffle forward. "My ears aren't what they were, you understand. But don't shout, I'm not deaf."

I do as she suggests. "Well, I was in a gym, just signed up to get some exercise, and the trainer girl, her name was Eva, and as she told me, the memory sort of sprang forward. It took a moment, but from Eva, I gradually remembered Evelyn, then Greenwood, and then all kinds of other distant things bounced around in my mind. Memories I can't explain, sounds, smells, experiences. But most of all, this gnawing drive to come and meet you."

"Memories, you say?" She meshes her fingers together, bringing them up to her lips and peers at me over them, as if in some kind of prayer.

"Yes, but nothing solid. Hard to describe. I'm quite disturbed by it. I don't know if you can explain this, but I had to try something, and your name was my only lead."

"What is it you do, Toby Steele?"

"I'm in IT. Computers and tech support. Well, I was. I recently lost my job. Long story …"

"Technology … I see." She pauses. "And aside from the memories, and my name, have you had any other odd experiences?"

An image of those burning phones in the robber's backroom springs into my mind's eye, and then the bulging, creaking laptop on the HR woman's desk that seemed to spontaneously combust in front of me. Then my uncanny ability to win fights, where previously I'd never even dreamt of such a thing. "Well, now you come to mention it. Yes." I'm reluctant to explain, but there's something about this woman that makes me implicitly trust her. I know that she's on my side, even though we've only just met. "I seem to be able to cause things to catch fire."

Evelyn's eyes widen, and she jolts forward. "How?"

"Err, I'm not sure. By starting a resonating pulse or something, I think it makes the batteries in phones and laptops short out, or just overload. They contain lithium, and I seem to know how to make them vibrate at the right frequency. I have no idea how." I flash a nervous smile. "Sorry, I know this sounds utterly ridiculous. I'm sure you are regretting letting me in now."

"Fascinating, Toby. No, no. I'm intrigued. Always like a good yarn."

I flinch. Does she think I'm making this up? "No, this is real. I can also fight. I have speed and power I never knew I was capable of."

Evelyn's face drains of colour, and she seems to tense up. "Dear boy, will you please fetch me a glass of water? I suddenly feel parched."

"Oh, yes. Of course." I stand up to go, there was a vending machine in the reception area.

"And a notepad and pen, if you will."

"Right."

She smiles at me thinly but then goes back to staring out of the window.

I return with a bottle of water, plus a paper cup and a notepad and pen, which I had to beg nurse Rosey for at reception.

"Thank you." Evelyn takes a long sip of the water, and then reaches for the notepad, scrawling something down on it. She motions for me to sit again, so I do.

"Now then. I'm going to show you this text. You tell me exactly what you see written here. Understand?"

She hands me the pad and I duly nod.

*GZAN NEVL KIEQ ZRMR QCTS VGPO UIHL
HVPN MKQD*

I look at the mess of letters that Evelyn has written.

Then up at her, wondering if this is a joke, but she stares at me intently and nods down at the pad.

"Read it."

I do as she suggests. The letters are obviously a cypher. A code hash. I look again, and after a moment, like a cherry blossom rain of petals on a breezy spring day, words somehow gently fall into my mind as I look at the gobbledegook text.

"Cabbage. Sour cherry. Nonsense."

Evelyn covers her mouth and coughs. "Say that again?"

"Cabbage. Sour cherry. Nonsense." I shake my head with a shrug. What a strange thing for me to say.

Evelyn gasps. "It can't be?"

"Sorry? Was that wrong? I don't know why I said that. I mean, it must be a code. But I don't know how I understood it."

"My God. It's true."

"What is? How did I know that? It's just a mess of letters."

"It's Enigma. My first break." Evelyn stares down at her hands now wrung together on her lap. "Help me up, young man. We must go into the garden. I need some air."

I grab a wheelchair as Evelyn is a little unsteady on her legs. Then she points me in the right direction to push her, out into the covered area of the garden, just outside the back doors. There's a cool breeze, and Evelyn wraps a crochet blanket around her shoulders. I park her next to a bench and then sit next to her. She turns to me with piercing eyes.

"Where did you work … Government?"

I shake my head. "No, not for the government. A pharmaceutical research company. BioDigi Pharmaceutical. A huge global thing, head office here in Milton Keynes. We, sorry, they have a big place in Spokane, Washington state, as well as branches all over Europe and even Japan."

"Hmm."

"What was that code you showed me?"

"A checksum."

"Sorry, a checksum? You mean like for validating data integrity."

"Precisely."

"Okay, I'm not sure I understand."

"Have you heard of Flash Gordon?"

"The TV shows? I mean, yeah, but I don't think I've watched it since I was a kid."

"No, no. Project Flash Gordon."

I shake my head again, confused. "No, I don't think so."

"Then how on earth did this happen?"

"What is Project Flash Gordon?"

"All in good time, young man. I need to be certain."

I shrug. So far, I'm feeling much more confused than when I got here. This isn't going quite how I expected.

"Do you speak any languages?"

"Err, no, not really. Outside of basic school French that I've completely forgotten."

"Je pense que vous pourriez être surpris." She speaks with a strong and fluent accent, obviously in

French, but, somehow I can completely understand her.

"Qu'est-ce qui vient de se passer?" The words spill from my mouth without friction. What the … ?

"You can speak French, very well."

"What? How?"

"Sie können viele Sprachen sprechen, auch Deutsch." She pauses, then counts on her fingers, "Española, Nederlands, Polski, Norsk, and Русский."

"I … what?"

"Try it."

"Err. Okay." I think for a moment. "Umiem mówić po Polsku."

"Bardzo dobry. Very good. Accent a little rusty, but that will be down to muscles."

"But, this is insane. How can this be possible? I never learned these languages."

"How indeed. That is what we need to get to the bottom of."

"Do you know what is going on here, Evelyn? Because, I have to admit, I am feeling rather freaked out at the moment."

She shivers a little in the chilly breeze but looks at me with those piercing eyes. "Yes, and no."

"Can we start with the yes?"

Evelyn sighs. "This is going to take some time, and it is getting chilly out here. Wheel me to my room, and I will try to explain."

Evelyn's room is a spacious ground-floor apartment that connects to the main hallway through one of the locked doors. She unlocks the door with a keycard and we roll in. The temperature here sizzling in the mid-twenty degrees.

She transfers herself to a comfy armchair, opposite a television, and I am told to bring over a small wooden chair from by the bed, and to sit and listen.

Evelyn takes another drink of water and then seems to wrestle with some thoughts internally, before finally shrugging and shaking her head. "Well, it's done now, so I suppose it doesn't matter anymore."

"What doesn't?"

"What I'm going to tell you now, Toby, has never been spoken to another living human. Not my son, my late husband, my closest friends, nor even my grand-daughter. I have never broken the promise I made over fifty-seven years ago."

"Okay." I feel like there should be more ceremony in my reply, but no words come. This sounds very heavy.

"And you must make the same promise, Toby. You cannot tell a soul about this. Do you understand?"

"Right, yes. Got it."

"For your own good."

"Understood."

"Very well." She takes a deep breath, and I wonder if she's getting tired. She is old and frail, but her mind is sharp as a pin. The body doesn't stay so agile as we grow older, unfortunately. "In 1965 I was assigned to work on something called Project Flash Gordon."

I raise an eyebrow but stay quiet.

"It was a government intelligence project. Cold War, spies, James Bond, all that sort of thing was going on, you must understand the political climate of the time.

They had an idea to create a superhuman spy from any average chap who underwent the procedure."

"Procedure?"

"My work was to find a way to make it possible. To flash a man's mind and give him all these special abilities, overnight."

"Wow."

"Wow, indeed."

"Special abilities? Like … being able to suddenly speak a load of languages?"

"Yes, and the knowledge of hand-to-hand combat, speed, increased intelligence, and a few extras that I threw into the pot along the way."

An unsettling feeling weighs heavy in my chest. What has happened to me? Was I part of some experiment that I have no memory of? "How was this done?"

"I spent many, many years developing and perfecting the technique. I called it frequency-shifting memory implantation. FSMI." She pauses. "The details would take too long to explain, but the nub of it was strobing lights, sounds, and patterns that interfered with one's brainwaves and altered the stored state."

"Sorry, did you say, strobing lights, patterns and sounds?" A deep knot in my guts makes me tense up. A throb of adrenaline pulses through me. "Oh, my God."

"Yes. Are you all right, young man?"

I stand up, but my knees don't support me. I sit back down. "Yes, I just … I think I know what happened."

"Do elaborate."

"It was at work, recently. I worked the night shift on tech support, and there was a complete server freeze-up. A guy from America rang me to complain that the systems were all down. So I went to the server room and tried to see what was going on, and then something strange happened." I look up at Evelyn who is staring at me. "Lights, flashes, patterns and sounds. As you said. I plugged in some screens to the servers and this stuff just started happening. I don't remember how long I was there, but I couldn't look away from it, like I was mesmerised. The next thing I knew, I woke up on the floor in the morning and all the servers were functioning as normal again."

"Heavens. Did you tell anyone what happened?"

"No, I didn't want to get into trouble for sleeping in the server room all night."

"Well, that's something, at least." Evelyn holds her head in her hands.

"What happened to me?"

She looks up at me. "You ran my code, Toby. You ran Project Flash Gordon."

"DOCTOR GREENWOOD?"

I look up, startled, as two strange people enter my domain. A woman, sharp and prim, and a man, tall and furtive. Both seem very young, early twenties perhaps, but they are dressed as if much older. They linger by the door as if scared to come further in case toxic fumes come from one of the experiments. A wise assumption, this place is riddled with things that can kill you, or worse.

"No. I'm not a PhD. Who are you and how did you get in here?" I demand, because this is my lab, and nobody gets in here besides Spencer, me, and my support staff. This is alarming.

"Calm down, Evelyn." Spencer, breaking the suspense in a sing-song voice, appears behind them and ushers the visitors further in towards me. "These good people are unrestricted, as it were."

I raise an eyebrow at him. I'll have words, later. "Very well, but my first question stands."

The woman thrusts a hand forward. "My name is Cynthia Payne, and this is Doctor Ian Davidson."

I shake her hand, then follow with the chap, who seems distracted, gawking around my lab. He doesn't speak but shakes with a powerful grip.

"Of?"

"Ah, now then, Evelyn, don't be rude. They are on our side and work for the Department." Spencer toadies around them, very much unlike his usual self.

"Sorry, which department?"

"No, just the Department." Cynthia corrects me.

"What?"

"Never mind that, now, Evelyn. We have guests who are keen to see your progress on Project Flash Gordon."

"Spencer, would you mind telling me what on earth is going on?" I stare at the weaselly man, who now resembles his spirit animal even more than usual.

"Well, I very much thought that I already had. These fine people have agency and authority to inspect the project progress, and wish to see the current status, and a briefing on the history, next steps, and projected completion timelines."

I scowl at Spencer.

"It would be in all of ours, but especially your best interest to cooperate, Ms Greenwood." The woman interjects before Spencer does himself a mischief with all the obnoxious, sycophantic bootlicking.

I relocate my glare to her.

"What's this?" The man picks up a strobe light bulb and holds it close to his nose, peering at it.

"Don't touch that! They are very delicate. One tiny fingerprint can blow the bulb from the excess heat."

"Ian, please." The woman flashes a smile at me as if her child has just farted in church. He puts it down.

I turn back to Spencer. "This is highly unusual."

"Agreed, and we can talk about it later. For now, please, relax and we can give Ms Payne and Doctor Davidson a demo of your amazing work."

Spencer gives me a sideways glance that suggests he is as offended by this intrusion as I am, but he cannot prevent it. When you have worked with someone for this long, you get to know their mannerisms.

I don't know what is going on here, but it seems as if we are being investigated by some unknown government agency, and these children outrank even Spencer. I suppose I should have expected something like this after all this time with no questions. The political environment changes all the time, new leaders want answers, and details on things that were left alone for many years. Well, I certainly won't be giving away all my years of research work to any young pretender. It occurs to me that these whippersnappers have already played me, and the first greeting that Ms Payne uttered — 'Doctor Greenwood' was a dig at me. She must know perfectly well I have never finished a PhD. Never had the time.

I bite my tongue and plan my campaign of misdirection. I grab the sheaf of paperwork from my desk that I was working on when I was rudely interrupted, and slide it into a drawer. The papers are nothing special, mostly log files regarding the guinea pigs' temperature readings, food intake and faecal output over the last month. I make sure to catch Cynthia's eye and then quickly look away after I close the drawer. I assume that given their age and free rein inside a highly classified government facility, these people must be the crème de la crème, but we'll see if that's true. With any luck, she'll assume the documents are far more valuable than they really are, shifting the focus away from the real good stuff — unless this Department places high value on rodent shit. They wouldn't be the first government agency to do so …

I'm not used to doing presentations, especially to strangers. Of course, Spencer pays his regular visits and I update him on progress, occasionally with a live demonstration, but mostly I email an encrypted message to him once a week and that's the end of it.

We use a simple Vigenère cypher with a key that changes daily, according to a monthly set of words that we decide upon, and then memorise and never write down. Mostly mundane things like 'breadboard', 'fryingpan', or 'crocus', but if you don't know the word of the day, the text of the message is indecipherable. We take turns choosing the words, and it has even become a silly game between us. Spencer chose the keyword for today, and coincidentally it is 'gatecrash', but now I think about it, perhaps that wasn't a coincidence, and I should have seen its hidden meaning. I may have slipped up, there. Codes within codes, messages inside messages. So much misdirection in this game. Certainly keeps you on your toes.

I wrote a program that encrypts and decrypts the messages as a learning project in FORTRAN, mostly as a distraction, and yet it turns out it's the most useful thing I've produced in years.

My typical messages to Spencer are scant in detail and heavy on problems, and I consequently only have to put up with his visits every few months. This unexpected party is something quite new.

I give the 'visitors' a tour, starting with the Cray-1 because it cost an eye-watering amount of money, and because it looks impressive with the C-shaped towers and bright red bench seats around the sides. Doctor Davidson claims to have seen one before, and now I really am curious about their mission and origin. There aren't many of these in existence, let alone easily available. I log on and show them some of my FORTRAN code, but can't tell if they understand any of it or not. I'm developing a syntax and codebase that allows me to effectively write a 'memory' for one of the test subjects, without having to start from scratch every time. I'm lucky to have the facility of the Cray and this lab, it certainly has made the task much easier, over the years. Still painstaking and unfathomably complex, but I feel I'm making progress now, having sunk a good chunk of my life into this thankless task.

I then give them an edited and brief lecture on the basics of the FSMI process, the aim of Project Flash Gordon, and a quick overview of my progress to date, over the last fifteen long, tedious years of research, development, trial and error, mostly error, up to the point of where I am today. I glanced at Spencer throughout the diatribe and he nodded and interjected when he saw fit. It certainly feels strange to be telling anyone about the project after so much silence. Cathartic, in a way.

We move on to the animal cages, and I introduce the guinea pigs to Ms Payne and Doctor Davidson. The pigs don't seem to be impressed. Can't say I blame them.

Finally, we get to the main act, the moment they have been waiting for. Presumably, they already knew the gist of what Project Flash Gordon was all about, otherwise, they wouldn't be here in the first place, so I've taken my time getting to the good stuff.

I ask the guests to choose one of the guinea pigs randomly and pick the poor chap up out of his cage, setting him into the preparation chamber. This is GP-PFG-072. I gave up giving them names long ago, as it was becoming unmanageable. 072 sniffs around in the box and I close the lid. The box has a mesh at the front so they can see he is alone, and no magic or subversion is taking place.

Now we move to a computer console and I ask Doctor Davidson to choose a six-digit code at random.

"8-0-0-8-1-3." He grins like a schoolboy.

I raise an eyebrow but say nothing. I enter the code into the computer. After a few seconds of churning and whirring, the screen updates with the text: **READY**.

"I will now teach that code to the chap in the box, using the FSMI process of strobing lights and ultrasonic sounds. The process will only take a minute or so."

"Intriguing." Ms Payne leans over my shoulder and peers at the screen, then walks over to the preparation chamber. Spencer beams and beckons Doctor Davidson to follow him over.

"Won't we be brainwashed as well?" Doctor Davidson bends down and looks into the cage.

"It isn't brainwashing, Doctor, just memory implantation. Quite different."

"Yes, yes, of course. But won't that memory be implanted in us, as well, if we witness the strobing, or have I misunderstood your explanation?" He looks between Spencer and me.

"There's a blackout curtain, and you should put on ear protectors. Otherwise, yes, there is a chance that this memory could be implanted into your brain, too."

"Gosh, how exciting!"

"May I ask, Doctor, what field are you in?"

"Statistics." He beams.

"I see."

"Yes, fascinating subject. Stochastic prediction, data analytics, social modelling."

"Intriguing." I use the phrase that Ms Payne uttered. She glances at me with barely hidden disdain. "Forgive me, but you seem awfully young to be a PhD."

"Ha, yes. I was rather precocious." He snorts a laugh, hiding a slight blush by looking away.

"And what have you predicted?"

"Ah, well it's an ongoing process. Early stages, but we hope to be able to predict all kinds of things …"

"Ian." Ms Payne flashes a smile. "We don't want to bore Ms Greenwood, do we?"

"Sorry. No, of course."

"Not at all." My fishing line has been cut.

I busy myself finding four sets of ear protectors and handing them out.

"Now, I will run the FSMI process."

I make sure the little chap is still safe in his box, then pull the curtain across the cage, and back at the computer console, I type in the command to start it off, and hit enter. So simple, now, but this kicks off a process I have been developing for so long, that I can barely remember doing anything else with my life. This project has become my life. Project Flash Gordon … Who would have thought it?

Even through the ear protectors, the whining sound is audible, but muffled enough that the high frequencies aren't active. The blackout curtain obscures most of the strobing light, but a glimmer spills around the edges, flashing in the patterns needed to burn a memory into the brain of the guinea pig. The process is quite harmless now, after many, many iterations and tweaks to remove errors and spurious noise that could creep into the signal, corrupting the data, spoiling the memory, and sometimes introducing fatal brain damage. 072 will be right as rain after his fairground ride through the FSMI box.

A minute passes and I detect the finishing sequence of pulses and flashes. Always the same, I sign off with a checksum to validate that the message was successfully sent and received. I wait a few more seconds for dramatic effect, then take off my ear protectors and motion to all to follow suit. I pull back the curtain on the box and 072 is exactly where we last saw him, sitting patiently in the middle of the box. He sniffs at something invisible, then moves to the back.

"Now, we set the code in the treat box."

I walk over to a bench where a large wooden structure waits. There are six little wheels connected to a bell and an electrical switch. The guinea pig will go into each wheel, and rotate it the correct number of turns to match the code that was programmed into his brain. After successfully entering the code, he will receive a treat. Simple. I don't know if he can count, in so many words, but he knows from his memory how long he should walk in each wheel to trigger the code. The bell and switch are more for our and the electronic circuit's benefit, rather than the subject.

I flip the switches on the back of the test box and enter the code, 8-0-0-8-1-3. The zeros require no effort on the part of the guinea pig.

"And now we move 072 into this box." I pick up the little chap from the FSMI box, carry him over, and place him inside.

Everyone crowds around and waits as 072 wanders around sniffing for a moment, then taps his nose on the wheels. For a moment, it looks like he wants to get into the fourth wheel first, and I hear Spencer inhale sharply and then hold his breath, but I have faith, having tested it thousands of times now. 072 doesn't fail me, and he shuffles over to the first wheel, climbs in, and starts to walk and turn the wheel. The bell chimes as he rotates once, twice, and then speeds up, quickly reaching eight revolutions. A display above the box shows the first number changing accordingly. 072 shuffles out of the first wheel.

"Impressive." Doctor Davidson seems awe-struck.

"Thank you."

There's some more held breath as the little chap sniffs at the second and then third wheels, but he knows he doesn't need to touch those, and he moves to the fourth wheel and repeats the eight spins.

"This is incredible!"

Ms Payne peers at the mechanism of the box. "Is this connected to the computer system?"

"No, this is an independent circuit."

She nods.

072 carries on his mission and hops into the next wheel, spinning it once, then jumping out, and climbing into the final, sixth wheel. He doesn't hesitate and spins three revolutions, and the display now shows the code that Doctor Davidson childishly chose. 8-0-0-8-1-3. A latch opens, and it dispenses a guinea pig treat into a bowl at the end of the run. 072 snuffles around, and seems delighted with himself as he grabs the little nugget of food.

"Well, I must say, I am impressed, Ms Greenwood. That is truly incredible."

"Is it repeatable?" Ms Payne, still poker-faced, enquires.

"So far, my latest data suggests a 98% success rate with this particular experiment."

"And the subject will survive?"

"Oh yes, no worry about that."

"Will he remember the code again? What if it changes, can he re-learn a new code?"

"He will remember this code until I program a new one into his memory."

"Fascinating."

"Thank you. We are still a long way from the desired outcome, but I am happy with the progress."

Spencer, with a huge grin on his face, interjects. "The project is well on track to move to more complex subjects and tests very soon." He looks to me for acknowledgement. I nod.

"We'll need circuit diagrams, drawings, component lists, a printout of the program in full, and any papers you have written on the FSMI process." Ms Payne delivers this message with a stony poker face. "And we'll need ongoing updates as you progress and develop the process further."

"This is outrageous!" I complain, but I already know my efforts are pointless. "On what authority?"

"Prime Minister Margaret Thatcher's. If you have a problem, please do take it up with her."

I turn to Spencer. He shrugs.

"Ms Greenwood, you have spent over fifteen years and considerable amounts of taxpayer's money on your Project Flash Gordon, and the Prime Minister would like to be sure that the ongoing investment is worth the effort."

"Now, Ms Payne, we have discussed this …"

"Be quiet, Spencer."

"Yes, sorry." He cowers like a beaten dog.

I trust these people about as far as I could throw them, and Ms Payne even less so. There's something so cold about her that chills my very core. For a moment, I wonder if I could reprogram her brain, but I'm not sure the FSMI process would work on solid granite.

"Very well."

"We'll be back tomorrow to collect the documents. Now, I'll bid you a good day, you have much to do." She turns to go but then doubles back. "And don't forget those papers you were trying to hide when we first came in."

Ms Payne and Doctor Davidson leave the room, and I wait a full minute to be sure they won't come back. Spencer is quiet and has sat down at my desk. I approach him, arms folded, a scowl etched onto my face.

"I'm sorry, Evelyn, there was very little I could do."

"You could have given me fair warning, Spencer!"

"I did try … anything more would have caused suspicion. They have connections in high places."

"Clearly."

I pout and glare at him. In all the years we've worked together, I would never have thought he could be so cowardly. Beaten down by two children. I may have lost all respect for the man.

He bows his head and stares at the floor. "Sorry."

"Well, never mind that, now. You can help me get all these documents together." I turn to face him. "And which bloody Department are they from, anyway?"

Spencer puffs out his cheeks and sighs. "My dear Evelyn, I honestly don't know."

CHAPTER
SEVENTEEN

I WAS DULY EJECTED from the artificial warmth — both in temperature and emotion — of Cherryoaks Lodge by nurse Rosey at the end of visiting hours yesterday. Evelyn was visibly wilting and tired anyway, and at her age, she is entitled.

I vaguely remember making my way home in a daze. Evelyn told me to come back for more of the story the next day.

My mind was racing with what she'd said so far. Am I some kind of superhero or Bond-like spy now? Able to speak a multitude of languages, win fights, think fast, interfere with the vibrations of things, and who knows what else. I'm truly stunned. This is the sort of thing you dream about as a kid, waking up one day with actual powers, able to fly or shoot lasers from your eyes. I don't think you ever believe it could really happen. What do you do when it does? I don't have any precedent of feelings to pull from. I'm numb and confused, but also the nine-year-old in me is thrilled by it. I half expect to wake up from a dream at any minute.

I went to the gym in the middle of the night, because sleep was not an option. My circadian rhythm is still in flux, and the questions and thoughts burning through my mind refused to be dulled.

I tore my muscles to shreds on the machines, trying to burn away the confusion, and force some sense into myself through violent exercise. It didn't work. Instead, I focused on the little computer display on the stationary bike, the speed ever-increasing, and I let my mind tune in to the frequency of the electronics behind it. I probed my way through the screen, into the copper traces, synchronised my brainwaves with the processor's pulses, and let chaos loose into the tiny current of electricity. The screen flickered, showed an error message, and then turned off completely. I blinked, relaxed, slowed down, and the display came back to life. What use is that?

It must be true. My brain has been reprogrammed, and I'm now some kind of Cold War military experiment. If only I knew what to do with these skills.

So many questions run around my head like frightened rats looking for safe shelter. How did Evelyn's Project Flash Gordon code get into the servers at BioDigi? Is the process she mentioned, 'FSMI', possible? I suppose it must be. How else do you explain my newfound abilities? What other things can I do that I don't yet know about?

I grab a light meal and flick on the TV, hoping it will distract me from my thoughts while I'm waiting for the care home visiting hours again, but the opposite happens. I can't focus on the show, and all I can do is churn through all the questions racing around in my head on repeat. I run a bath, and soak in the hot water until it's time to go, and with any luck get to the bottom of all my unanswered questions, and perhaps understand my fate.

I'm expected at the reception desk today. A different nurse, but I'm shown through to see Evelyn without fuss. She's back in her chair looking out at the garden. Enigmatic and frail.

"I do appreciate a punctual fellow." She doesn't turn but I sense a smile in her voice.

"I've been waiting all day to visit."

"Ah, so nice to be wanted, again." She turns with a grin and motions for me to sit. "I used to be in high demand, back in my youth."

"I can imagine."

"For my brain, you understand, not my beauty." She gently taps the side of her head, her hair again neatly braided and white as a sheet.

I smile, awkwardly looking away. From what I saw of the photos from Bletchley Park in the Turing and Enigma days, Evelyn was a pretty enough girl. Well-groomed, always smiling.

"Well then, where were we, young man?"

I glance around the room, and a few more families are visiting today. The weekend I suppose. I have lost track of days. The noise level and distance between us and anyone else, are enough that we should be able to chat without being overheard.

"Well, you were telling me I'm some kind of Superman, now, because I was zapped by your secret government experiment."

I hear the words come out of my mouth and genuinely laugh at myself. It sounds so ridiculous.

"That's right. So, I was." She points at me. "But, Flash Gordon, not Superman."

"Right."

"And zapped isn't the right word. Gently altered would be more appropriate. The process takes about seven hours."

"Really?"

"Oh, yes. You can't dump that much information into a man all at once. It takes time to sink in. Too quick and it caused … well, problems, shall we say."

I raise an eyebrow.

"Don't worry, by the end it was quite safe. I should know." She smiles and holds up her hands.

"Oh?"

"I'm living proof, young man. One hundred years old and still sharper than the rest of the care home, staff very much included." She chuckles and waggles a finger at me.

"You ran the … err, Project Flash Gordon process on yourself?"

"Well yes, of course. I had to test on a human subject. Never got around to trying it out on anyone else."

"That must have been scary. Very brave of you."

She waves a hand. "By then, I knew every line of code inside and out. I had no doubts." She pouts. "But, I will admit, I was nervous."

"So, you, and now me are the only two people in the world to ever have run the Flash Gordon thing?"

"Correct."

"But, if it was meant to be a military application, how come it never got deployed on anyone?"

Evelyn frowns. "They cancelled the project before I could complete it."

"Oh?"

"Yes, much to my annoyance, but that's another story. I'd still like to know how you came to have the code."

"So would I," I admit.

"When did you say the incident happened?"

I shrug. "A couple of weeks ago, I think."

"Can you be more specific?"

I pull out my phone and open the calendar app, scrolling back through the days. Then I remember, it was all the 2's — 22:22:22 / 22/2/22 "It was the twenty-second. I remember now, the system clock froze, all 'twos' at the command prompt."

Evelyn looks puzzled, then freezes and turns white as a sheet. "Oh, goodness … Oh, dear me."

"Are you okay?"

"Yes, but, please, would you fetch me some water?"

"Of course."

When I get back, Evelyn is agitated. She takes a drink of the water and then looks up at me. "I must apologise, Toby."

"For what?"

"Well, I never imagined the code would be run, you see. I had to hide the real program away from prying eyes, and disk space was a precious thing in those days. I hid the executable with a nonsense filename, my birthday of course. The twenty-second of February, 1922. Ten-twenty-two and twenty-two seconds. I was born in 1922, but the code ran in 2022. All 'twos' as you say."

"What?"

"Disk space was expensive, memory was sparse. The year in the filename should have been '1922', but I truncated it to only '22', so the system ran the code one hundred years later. An Easter egg, if you like. A hidden program. A bit like the Y2K issue that happened at the turn of the millennia."

My mouth drops open, but no words come out. "I … wow."

"It seems that your systems somehow accidentally triggered the program, probably a spurious cron job, I'd wager, and you, dear boy, are the unfortunate recipient."

Stunned, I stare for a moment while this information sinks in. "But, it's a good thing, isn't it? I mean, I'm now 'Flash Gordon' or something."

"Yes, but with great power comes great responsibility."

"I see." I don't see, but I don't know what else to say.

"Still remains the question of how your company came to have the code in the first place." Evelyn tilts her head.

"Indeed. I don't know, but I do know we, sorry, they, had acquired various companies over the years. I remember someone mentioned once they had to transfer a truckload of data, literally, from mainframes they got in a buy-out. It was an enormous pain, and a meticulous and complicated process to upload everything from ancient disks, tapes, and even some punch cards. Management wanted every scrap of knowledge they had paid for, so it was all ingested into a massive database, which was then hosted in the room where I was working."

"That seems likely to be the cause. You see, I had to branch my code, hiding the real version in a 'safe place.' The Department was watching me closely after I made a breakthrough in progress, and I had no intention of letting them have the genuine product. I dread to think what nefarious use those fools would have put it to."

"Safe place?"

"I found a back door link on the ARPANet to a database big enough to store the program. Completely illegal of course, but squirrelled away where no one would ever find it, or so I thought. I think it was in Boston, IMC or MCI perhaps?"

"MCI? Massachusetts Chemical Industries?"

"Yes! That's the one."

"BioDigi acquired them in 2004."

"Ah. Well, then. Mystery solved."

"Wow."

"Wow, indeed." She smiles. "I do apologise, Toby. Please understand, I did not intend this to happen. I could never have predicted the code would be transferred to your systems and then accidentally run. This was decades ago. You don't imagine a program will survive that long."

"Of course. I understand. I think I need a drink as

well." I go to the vending machine for water, but wish there was a bottle of whiskey in the thing.

"You say you were hiding the code from some department?"

"Yes, but not 'some' department, 'The Department'."

"Sorry?"

"That's all I ever found out. They were highly connected and didn't feel the need to elaborate further. 'The Department' is what they said. A Doctor Ian Davidson and a Ms Cynthia Payne were the only two I ever met. Either both together or just Cynthia. Never Ian alone; I don't think she trusted him not to accidentally give away some secrets." She shakes her head. "Anyway, they both vanished along with the end of the project. Never heard of again."

"They were government agents?"

"So it seemed, but you never know with these things."

"Could they have been military, or a private company?"

"Perhaps. But trust me, Toby, I have had decades to ponder on this, and I'm still none the wiser. All I know is I didn't trust them from the moment I laid eyes on them, so I hid the actual code and only showed them a fake branch, where progress was far, far slower than on the real version."

"So let me get this straight." I pause and take a breath, looking around in case anyone has been eavesdropping. "The government commissioned or summoned you to create this project back in 1965, and you worked on it for a rather long time. Decades?" She nods. "But then another Department got interested once you started seeing progress. You didn't trust them, or their intentions and so you hid your proper code and research on a random server far away, and only showed this 'Department' a fake set of code, where presumably all the good stuff was omitted?"

"That's more or less the better part of my life, summarised into one short statement, yes."

"Wow," I repeat, lost for more substantial words.

"Quite so."

For a moment, I look down at the patterns in the carpet, flowing and swirling, my mind seeing faces and shapes where none exist, the pattern seems to animate as I focus on a segment, slightly nauseating. I shake my head and pause to let the information seep into my brain, absorbing and processing, churning through possibilities and outcomes. The chess game of life.

"Did they do anything with the other version, this 'Department'?"

"I don't know, Toby, but it was very basic compared to what you experienced. Barely useful unless you wanted to teach rats how to find treats in a maze."

I nod. "Can you tell me all the, err, abilities I down-loaded, or inherited. Gained? Whatever the term is? I mean, aside from what I have found out so far. The languages, the thing where I can somehow manipulate energy or frequencies or something?"

Evelyn sighs and looks me in the eye. "I can tell you, Toby, that the project was never finished."

"Sorry?"

"I said they cancelled it before I completed work. I

was ejected from my labs and sent to retirement with a healthy pension. Ousted without rhyme or reason. No explanation, just one day gone."

"Oh. I'm sorry to hear that."

She waves a hand. "Water very much under the bridge, now, but what it means for you is that you don't have the full package." She smirks and looks me up and down. "Huh?" Eyes wide, I stare at her in shock. "Am I going to keel over or something?"

"Lord, no. You'll be fit as a fiddle. The program will take care of that, but you lack some upgrades I had planned for future development."

"Right, well, I suppose that's a relief." I raise an eyebrow. "Can you tell me what those were?"

"Are you sure you want to know?"

"Err, I think so?"

"You might not want to."

"Why not?"

"Well, because I believe that if I had been allowed to finish my work, these things would have been possible, and I know I have regretted not having these capabilities myself."

"It is what it is." I shrug. "And I'm keen to learn all about this project."

"Very well. But we had better go somewhere more private to discuss."

I fetch a wheelchair and push Evelyn out into the garden, wrapped in her crochet blanket. This time we trundle over the trimmed lawn, and park next to a Koi pond with a fountain that spills out white noise to fill the air. Evelyn suggested it as extra protection in case anyone heard us talking. There's no one around, save a couple of kids on the other side of the garden running around with a frisbee. I think she's just accustomed to the paranoia.

"So …" I raise my eyebrows at Evelyn.

She takes a deep breath. "These things may seem outlandish to you, ridiculous even, but given that you seem to have already accepted the other 'features' you've gained, I'm hoping that you can trust me when I tell you none of this is a lie or even an exaggeration."

I nod. "Go on. I most certainly do trust you."

She laughs. "Of course you do, that was part of the code."

"Err, right."

"You benefited from the frequency harmonising. It's a nice little feature I found when digging into some obscure research that was, err, made available to me, shall we say?" She pauses and ponders for a moment, then an idea seems to wash over her and she perks up, looking over at me. "We all have a wavelength, a frequency, a rhythmic pattern to our electrical output. It fluctuates over the course of the normal day, sleep patterns, periods of energy bursts when you digest foods, that sort of thing. All that is normal. Some people would call it an aura, claiming they can see it. Well, this paper, part of a Russian program I believe, postulated that we humans had the capability to manipulate that energy output. Focus and direct it. The research was based on studies of people who naturally had this ability. Turns out it was true, and the result, after much tweaking, is that we," She points to her chest and then to me, "Can cause things to happen in objects and people close by."

My eyes wide, I stare at Evelyn who rattled off this revelation in a matter-of-fact tone. "People?"

"Oh yes. To varying levels of success, I might add. Don't go assuming you can just flip on emotions in any cashier at Tesco. The situation has to be just right. But, I've had some fun with it, I must admit." She grins.

"I didn't realise. That's very interesting."

"Indeed. Well, now you know." She glances around again. "Well, on the back of that achievement, the next level was to try telekineses." Evelyn pauses for dramatic effect. It works.

"Seriously? You mean, moving physical objects with just the power of my mind?"

"Don't get too excited, Toby, now we are into the realm of things I didn't get working. So yes, that's what it means, but sadly, no. You can't do that."

"Ah."

"And telepathy, too. I was sure it could be done, given enough time and study, the elements were there, but it was just ever so slightly out of reach."

"Mind reading?"

"Yes."

"You think telepathy and telekinesis are possible?"

"Oh, yes, quite sure."

"And, if you had more time to work on the project, those things could have been transmitted with the other abilities?"

"Do keep up, Toby, yes. The remit of Project Flash Gordon was to take an ordinary man and make him extraordinary."

"That certainly would have done that. I mean, I

think what has already happened to me is extraordinary. Don't get me wrong."

"No, I share your frustration. I wasn't finished and to be honest, Toby, and do pardon my French, but I was bloody annoyed at the time when it was all cancelled."

"I can imagine."

"I was so close!" Evelyn clenches her fists. "Sorry. I mustn't get riled up or Nurse Rosey will be nagging me about blood pressure."

"Sorry. Do you want to go back inside now?"

"In a moment. I haven't told you all yet."

"Oh?"

"We covered telepathy, telekinesis," She counts off on her fingers, "What else? Let me see. Well, there were a few more languages I was trying to learn, Chinese, Japanese, that sort of thing ... and oh, yes. Total memory recall."

"Total recall? Like the Schwarzenegger movie?"

She rolls her eyes. "No, as in a photographic memory."

"Ah, right. Cool."

"Indeed. All of those things would have been cool, but I'm afraid you didn't get them."

"Right."

"I did say you might not want to know."

"No, no. I'm glad you told me. The whole thing is fascinating."

"Isn't it?" Evelyn smiles and then frowns at me. "Needless to say, I should hope, but even now after all these years, you cannot tell anyone about what I've told you. Understand?"

I nod. "Yes, I understand." If it was anyone else

telling me these stories, I'd have an extremely hard time believing a word of it, but coming from Evelyn, I know with every fibre of my being that she's telling me the truth.

"Good. Now, I'm cold, let's go back inside."

Back in her warm comfy chair, Evelyn sips at a cup of tea that the staff delivered from a trolley. She looks so frail, yet somehow strong with it. Certainly more agile and aware than anyone else around us in the large sitting room.

"Evelyn, if you don't mind me saying, you look great for your age."

She laughs. "Well, thank you, young man."

"Is there something in the code that helps with that?"

She pouts. "Your body is a complex thing, Toby, but the brain runs it. Keep the brain alive, stimulated, agile and keen, and your body will follow. Keep that in mind, pardon the pun."

"Good to know." A thought occurs to me. "Did you say that the program would keep me fit?"

"Ah, yes. You may feel compelled to change your eating habits, and get into some kind of training regime."

"Right. The gym … and yes, I have found myself craving different food from my usual junk."

Evelyn nods. "No point in being Flash Gordon, if you are out of breath when chasing down a baddie, is there?" She laughs.

"Suppose not." I shrug. "So, what do I do now?"

"Ah, well, whatever you like, I imagine. I'm not your mother."

"No, but, this is all your project. Wasn't it meant to, I don't know, benefit the world somehow?"

"I was never told exactly what it was for, Toby. But my guess is that the Cold War ended, and so did the need for a superhuman spy."

"But shouldn't I try to do some good with it?"

"Yes, if you like. Totally up to you, dear boy. But remember not to give away your secrets. Trust me, you'll be tempted, but for your safety, stay in the dark, out of sight, out of mind. The last thing you want is the wrong people to get wind of what you can do. Good or not. You aren't immortal and for all I know, the Department are still out there somewhere, monitoring things." She shudders. "You don't want them on your back."

"Right. Okay, then." I stand up to go. "Thank you, Evelyn, your work has quite literally changed my life. I don't know what I'll do, or where I'll go, but I think it's going to be incredible."

"Of that, you can be sure, Toby."

"I THINK you are going to enjoy this."

A tiny smile blossoms on the face of Spencer, tired and rather quiet of late, I suspect due to the constant badgering from Cynthia Payne-in-the-backside. He hasn't visited my lab for months, so it was a pleasant change today to entertain. We took lunch in town at the fanciest restaurant Spencer has found, but I think he still laments the lack of the London food scene here. Always one for the luxuries in life is Spencer.

I believe Cynthia has more or less taken up residence in Spencer's office in Cheltenham, much to his annoyance. Every expense is checked and noted, every encrypted email is intercepted and analysed. My code updates are a torturous weekly event, conducted over the phone, for the most part, but they have occasionally dragged me to Gloucestershire, or come down to the labs themselves. Consequently, I dread Friday afternoons.

Progress on the project has been slow. Painfully slow, according to the Department. So much so that they are threatening to cut off funding. Well, today Spencer is going to find out precisely why that is.

We got the monkeys about eighteen months ago. I was cautious at first, but now we seem to have bonded. Kong, a young female Rhesus macaque, and I are close friends at this stage. We share meals and even watch television together sometimes. She's rather sweet, in her way. Sharp as a pin, too.

I kitted the labs out with facilities for the monkeys. A big upgrade from the guinea pigs. I had exhausted all avenues of experimentation on those chaps, and so we moved onwards and upwards. A bigger FSMI booth was constructed to fit them in, and suitable cages, even with some natural habitat tree branches for them to climb on. I don't like that we have to do this to the poor fellows, but I make sure they are well tended to. We don't use chemicals or any kind of medicine. So they are better off than most.

Kong is waiting for her act to start, lounging on the bench seat of the Cray. Spencer tentatively walks over to the monkey.

"Go on. She won't bite."

Kong stands up and offers a hand to shake. Spencer takes it and laughs.

"What a marvellous little creature."

"Isn't she?"

"Have you made some progress, with the project?" Spencer turns to me, hope in his eyes.

"What I'm going to tell you, Spencer, is for us only.

Do you understand? This is absolutely not to be repeated to those fools, Ian and Cynthia."

"Evelyn, my dear, I am constrained in what I can promise. They have the authority …"

"Never mind that," I interrupt, "we'll keep our little findings to ourselves. Don't worry, I have a different set of results to give you so you can report back to Ms Payne. Far less interesting, of course, but oh, well."

"Do you mean to say that you are hiding the actual progress?"

I fold my arms and stare at Spencer. But remain silent.

He laughs. "Well, aren't you just a woman of mystery!"

"I'm a woman of necessity, Spencer. I won't have my life's work given over to these people for God knows what nefarious use. I'm too old and tired to be caught up in all this politics, but here we are. Now, do you want to see the real project or not?"

"I most certainly do."

"Then we agree to be silent?"

He nods.

"I'll take that as confirmation."

"This is between us, Evelyn. As you wish."

"Good." I walk over to the Cray terminal and sit down. "Kong. Come here."

Kong hops off the bench and bounces over to me, perching on the desk next to the screen. "Good girl. Are you ready?"

Kong chirps a response.

"Good lord, Evelyn, can she really understand you?"

"Of course."

"That's incredible."

I snort a laugh. "Wait until we start the show." I turn to the monkey. "Kong. Hör genau zu. Eins, fünf, sieben, drei, null, neun, vier, zwei."

Kong squawks and hops off the desk, quickly scampering across the lab to the test area. There's a number keypad connected to a screen on a low table. Kong sits down next to the keypad and then punches in the digits. One, five, seven, three, zero, nine, four, two. Each number appears on the screen as she does. She squeals and claps once finished.

"Very good girl!"

Spencer's mouth falls open, and he stares at the monkey and the screen.

"My German is rusty, but, those are the numbers you told her?"

"Yes, of course."

"My God."

I turn back to Kong. "Kong, manger une pomme."

She chirps loudly and dashes over to a basket of fruits on another bench, carefully plucking an apple from amongst bananas, pears, berries and some cut slices of pineapple. She joyfully munches the apple.

"Amazing! How many languages does she understand?"

"Well, it's mostly just a few keywords, not fluency, but five, so far."

"I'm rapidly running out of superlatives here, but, that's amazing. How?"

"I'm getting to the 'how'."

"I had no idea of any of this."

"Of course not. The official reports are empty in comparison."

"I'm stunned, truly."

"A lifetime of hiding almost everything I do will have this effect." I have to admit, I am rather enjoying showing off to Spencer. I've been so caught up in the work, that the results are even shocking to me, now I think about it. "Ready for the next demo?"

"Absolutely."

"Think about an object and define some characteristics about it. For example, 'A red ball, with white stripes' or something like that. Don't say it out loud, write it down." I hand Spencer a notepad and pen. He ponders for a moment, then scribbles something on the paper.

A blue car, with four people inside, on a rainy day.

"Very good. Now, I'll record the memory." I take the sheet of paper into my recording booth. Soundproof, and connected to various delicate and sensitive machines, that will translate my thoughts and voice into a pattern that the computer can analyse. Spencer can watch through a glass window, but it will be rather boring. Takes about half an hour. I change my mind and exit, rushing to the bathroom first.

Back in the booth, I put the helmet on, flick some switches and wave to Spencer. A red light comes on over the door and I begin the process.

. . .

"You could have chosen something simpler, Spencer." It took a bottom numbing forty-five minutes in the end to record the thoughts. It occurred to me that Kong has never seen a car before, so it was necessary to envision that concept, first, at least to a bare minimum. Once established what a car was, I visualised the people inside, and the colour of the paint, then the weather conditions outside, and a long, empty road through lush countryside for extra effect.

I stop the recordings and set off the task to flow this data through the Cray for processing. The process taking longer than it should, because of the need to store this information in my secondary hidden database, which I think is somewhere in Boston, Massachusetts, rather than locally. Spencer is getting bored, so while the task is running, I suggest we leave the lab and find a cup of coffee.

Spencer tells me he is planning a holiday soon, somewhere far away from Gloucestershire, he says. Anywhere distant from the probing eyes and ears of the Department. India, the Australian outback, or the remote highlands of Scotland. So long as there are no phones or communications of any sort, he will be happy. I don't remember Spencer ever taking a holiday before in all the years we have worked together, but perhaps he has and just not told me. I suppose there have been periods of many weeks when we haven't spoken in the past.

He seems different over the last few years. Not himself at all. I know it is down to the interference of Cynthia and Doctor Davidson, but Spencer won't directly admit it.

Hence my demonstration today. I need to keep him on my side, and with all the lack of official progress, I felt it would do him good to sample the real taste of success. The forbidden fruit of Project Flash Gordon that the Department will never find out about, if I have any say.

We take a walk around the grounds and breathe in some fresh air. Spencer points out his new vehicle in the car park. A Rover, where once an opulent Bentley would have stood. Dejected, he tells me that the car gets him from A to B, and that's all that matters, in the end.

I never thought I'd say it, but I feel sorry for the chap.

We amble back to my lab, where I hope the complicated processes have finished.

"Ah, good. We can now implant these memories into Kong."

"Evelyn, I don't think I say it often enough, but you are an amazing woman."

"I don't think you have ever said it, Spencer. But thank you."

"It was always implied."

"If you say so." I flick a smile. "Kong, go into the booth."

Kong chirps from her open cage and jumps out, then bounces along to the wooden cupboard where all the equipment is strapped to the top and sides. Dozens of strobe bulbs, mixed in with these tiny new light-emitting diodes. They use barely any power and don't blow like normal bulbs. A wonderful invention, but fiddly to wire up. I have a bank of them in a large array that can flash very fast, and even show patterns like a dot matrix display. I see great things coming from this technology. For my FSMI process, it adds functionality in that I can project a waveform at the same time as the strobing lights, emphasising the frequency and allowing for quicker downloads into the subject.

Kong settles down onto the perch inside the booth. The various lights pointed at her face, with a bank of ultra-high frequency capable speakers all around. They gently ramp up a tone that is inaudible to humans, and even Kong's delicate ears, but the wavelengths still penetrate the subconscious, delivering the memory. At the back of the booth is a huge woofer speaker that rumbles out a very low-frequency tone, again inaudible to us, but can be felt through the chest if one stands too close. This tone delivers a baseline carrier wave throughout the process. Without that drone, I found that the subject can be distracted, and the memories don't get downloaded. I've honed this process over many, many years and tens of thousands of tests. It all seems normal to me now, but I still find it to be remarkable. It makes me wonder what natural events have accidentally caused memories in people over the millennia. Perhaps our deep subconscious instincts are influenced by things like volcano erup-tions, earthquakes, or even the waves of the oceans. All these things emit sounds and frequencies of their own. There's simply too much of it around to avoid. No matter where you live on the planet. If you have ever stood out on a silent night, with no background noise or wind, and just stopped to listen, you might hear the frequency of the earth, just ticking along as it does.

I suppose it stands to reason that we, evolved from the earth and the stars before that, would be strongly influenced by the functions of the planet. I think people tend to forget that we are nothing more than a gathering of particles that were once inside a distant star.

"It will take about twenty minutes," I wave to Spencer to come and see the setup, and he gawks into the booth. Kong ignores him and focuses on a piece of food lodged in her teeth. She's been in the booth many times now, but I do still worry a little, even though I know it is safe. There's always a chance it could blow up halfway through, or that my code has a deadly bug in it, or that Kong could become agitated and smash the bulbs. So far none of that has happened, at least in recent times. The first tones initiate a dulling anaesthetic effect with a sort of paralysis, to stop the subject from moving out of range. Harmless, but frightening, so there's also a strobe pattern that promotes endorphins and a feeling of comfort. As I say, honed over the decades, I should know what I'm doing by now.

"Do we need to wear ear protectors?"

"Worse than that, I'm afraid. We will have to cram into the soundproof booth." I point to the tiny cupboard I sat in to record the memories before. One seat in a space not much bigger than a telephone booth. I don't relish the thought of being so close to Spencer for twenty minutes, but the only other option is for him to leave the room. I can't trust him not to sneak back in or go sniffing around places he shouldn't, so here we go. "No smoking in there, for obvious reasons."

"Ah. Right."

I close the door and curtain on Kong's booth, and then take the chair out of the soundproof cupboard to make a little more room for us to stand, hook up the helmet and cabling into the nooks provided by my amiable carpenter chap, and beckon Spencer in with me. "It does get a bit warm, after a while. Can't be helped."

"Enough oxygen, I presume?"

"If you hold your breath, yes," I smirk. "Of course there is."

Spencer shuffles in and I stand back so he can move around me. I need to be at the controls and look out of the single window to initiate the FSMI process. "Ready?"

"As I'll ever be." He leans up against the back wall.

"Touch nothing, don't panic, don't move around too much at all, if you can help it. Oh, and above all," I turn to look him in the eye. "For the love of all things good and holy, don't fart!"

"Noted." He grimaces and probably curses the extra helping of pasta he had at lunch.

"Kong, ready?" I shout out and receive back a muffled chirp. I close the door and flip the large red switch labelled 'Gordon's Alive!'

From here, coddled in our booth, the scene outside is extremely dull. There's no sound and no visible light through the thick curtains. I do have some sensors inside the FSMI booth, that show ambient temperature and noise level, mainly so I can monitor that the process is working. Other than a few meters and pulsing lights, we have nothing to do but stand and wait. I turn to

Spencer who has his arms folded so as not to accidentally brush against a control dial. "I suppose now is as good a time as any to ask for a pay rise?"

Spencer bursts out a laugh. "Certainly, I'll ask the treasurer in the morning."

I smile. "Joke." But then I feel a frown appear on my face. "What do you think they want, Spencer? The Department. I mean, honestly."

He shakes his head. "Even after, what is it now, three years? I haven't got the foggiest, Evelyn. They come and go as they please, spend money, and go off around the globe, seemingly untethered from any reports or accusations. I know they have an office or laboratory somewhere, but it could be on the moon for all I know. They are a mystery, and I thought I knew everything that went on."

"Is it Thatcher?"

He blows out a puff of air from his cheeks. "Perhaps. But I'm not sure. Could be Reagan for all I know."

"Americans? What would they want over here?"

"Yanks want their finger in all kinds of pies, don't they? I'm sure they have agents all over the world." He sighs. "No, perhaps not. But I'm going to make it my mission to find out exactly what this Department is up to, one way or another."

"Better you than me."

We stand in silence for a moment; I pretend to adjust some dials and monitor the sound meters.

"How are Gerald and Anthony doing now?"

I turn back to Spencer, and now it's my turn to puff out a sigh. "As infuriating as ever. Gerald has some kind of problem with his heart. Says it's nothing, but I do worry." I shake my head. "Told him to give up smoking and drinking, and he told me to stick my head back into my lab and mind my own business."

"Oh, dear." Spencer frowns. "Can we help? Hospitals, doctors. We'll find the best."

I wave a hand. "I've told him umpteen times to see someone, and he's as stubborn as a donkey. Most days, I get more sense from Kong."

"Anthony?"

My son dropped out of university, lost a succession of jobs, crashed our car into a post box, broke his nose, and was arrested for trying to break into Stonehenge with his hippy friends, and all that is just this year.

I shake my head. "Don't ask."

"Understood."

We wait the rest of the time in silence, and thoughts of my family life roll through my mess of a brain. I know that I've neglected my son, and my husband over the years I've been working on this damn project, but what else could I do? This isn't a nine-to-five type of job. I'm usually here from six until nine, at weekends, too. The work has been all engulfing and my personal life, such as it ever was, has suffered. I blame myself for Anthony's harebrained actions, and Gerald for his stubborn attitude.

A light turns on, and a bell chimes, indicating the FSMI process has finished. Thank heaven.

We exit the booth and go over to Kong, opening the curtain and letting her out. She chirps at me and slowly gets off the perch. The paralysis can sometimes take a moment to wear off.

Within a minute, Kong is bouncing around again and is eager to show off her new skills.

We move to another bench at the back of the room, where there are various objects set up.

"Now for the fun part." I motion to Kong to jump up onto the bench. She does. I turn to Spencer. "Remember your note?"

"I do."

"Very well." I look at Kong. "Kong, do you know the car?"

Kong chirps and bounces up and down, excitedly.

"Good. Combien de personnes sont dans la voiture?"

Kong squawks and spins around, then finds the number keypad on the bench, tapping at the '4' button.

"Très bien!"

Kong squawks again and comes back to me.

"A jaka jest pogoda na zewnątrz?" I turn to Spencer. "I asked her what the weather was like, in Polish." He nods.

Kong looks around on the bench. We haven't done weather before, but I'm confident she will adapt.

Kong sees a sink at the far end and scurries over to it, hitting the tap a few times, before turning the handle. A spray of water falls into the sink, and Kong chirps, dancing around in a circle.

"Bardzo dobry!"

Spencer looks at me, open-mouthed. "My God. This is amazing."

I walk over and turn the tap off, petting Kong on the head and handing her a little seed treat.

"Last one. Kong, welche farbe hat das auto?"

This one is easy. Kong jumps across the bench and finds the colour sheets we use all the time. She shuffles through them and finds a shade of blue. The exact dark blue that I was thinking of when I made the recording. She gives it to me with a squawk and sits down.

"Wunderbar! Du bist sehr klug."

"Evelyn, this is truly stunning. I could kiss you!"

"Please don't."

"I … I don't know where to start. You have done it, really done it! You've managed what I was beginning to think was the impossible, but no, I always had faith. When can we start human testing?"

"Spencer, I told you. This is just for our eyes. I can't tell the Department about this. They will ruin everything. I know it."

"But we must. This is groundbreaking, you've cracked it and now we can bring in more equipment, funding, and military testing."

"Spencer. No."

"Evelyn …"

"If you so much as think about telling them, I will delete the entire database. You'll never find a trace of it."

"But …"

"We made an agreement."

"Yes, yes, we did. Very well. But I think you are making a mistake."

"No, I'm saving the world from what could turn into a disaster."

Spencer looks at me, dejected, but nods. "You are probably right, as always."

Kong bounces back onto the bench, and I hadn't

even noticed she was away. She holds a magazine in her tiny hands and drops it down in front of us. She must have picked it up from my desk, and she points and chirps at the page. There's a full-spread advert of a blue car, driving through a lush mountainous landscape on a long, empty road. Exactly the image I had in mind when I recorded the memories. The slogan on the page; **'Vorsprung durch Technik.'**

Lead by technology.

CHAPTER
NINETEEN

THE WISE WORDS of Raymond the security guard echo around my brain; "People are scared of difference. Petrified. You show them you have something they don't understand, and they will fear you, feel threatened by you."

He's right, and so is Evelyn. Say nothing, keep the secret, or no matter what good I do, I'll be the one hunted down and torn apart. If not physically, then online by the raging mobs of people who desperately seek out some kind of conflict or argument every day. You can't fight the masses, no matter what special abilities you have. There are too many of them.

So I'll be quiet. Hide my powers. Maybe I should move somewhere else. Mainland Europe, perhaps, where speaking multiple languages isn't weird and would be extremely useful.

Or somewhere sparse. I think Norwegian is one of my languages. It feels weird, and I have to focus, but if I do ... 'En øl, takk' ... I think I'll get by. Bit cold, though.

Another part of me wants to stay here, show the

arseholes who's boss now. Plus, moving costs money and I don't have that much when all said and done. I'm good for a few months. Then I'll need to find something else to make a living. Staying where I am also costs money. Why not capitalise on my newfound skills? But, what can I do?

My phone pings with a text message, and I glance at the screen. Philippa. Shit. I forgot about her with all the drama. I grab the phone.

Hey.

Hi, how are you? Everything okay?

Yeah, just made some dinner, wondered if you were hungry?

Yeah, I could eat.

Come over then. :)

On my way!

Interesting.

On the drive, I realise Philippa is going to ask me about Evelyn and the care home. What do I tell her? Not the truth, if she'd even believe me. I'll need to use my 'enhanced' brain to come up with a reasonable story that doesn't give away that I'm now Flash Gordon or something.

I'm hit with a waft of delicious smell and heat as Philippa opens the door to me. She's looking delicious and ripe herself, and things twinge all over my body. We hug and cheek-kiss, and I'm led into the living room and told to make myself at home. I haven't been here for a while. When we were an item, we mostly spent time either out, or at my house. Philippa's house is neat and clean, clinical sometimes, but there's a subtle undercurrent of her heavy metal vibes, too. A skull here and there, black candles, a frame on the wall with gig tickets inside. I notice that quite a few of them are gigs we went to together. I didn't know she kept memorabilia. Sweet.

From the kitchen, she shouts through. "Beer or wine?"

"Beer, please." I wander into the kitchen and notice all kinds of pots and pans on the stove. "You didn't go to any trouble, did you?"

Philippa hands me a cold beer from the fridge. "No, just fancied cooking." She smiles. "And, you know, wanted to say thank you for the other night."

I grin. "Thought you already did." I wink.

She prods me in the ribs. "Hey, that was just … I don't know. But a one off."

"If you say so."

"I do, Toby." She looks at me with stern eyes, but they quickly fade into a grin. "No, I mean. I'm a mess now. I need to get myself together." She points at her pregnant belly. "Got other priorities."

"Fair enough. Oh, speaking of the other night, what happened with matey-boy, Jason?"

"Ah, yeah. I was going to get to that. He's in hospital, still."

"Oh, shit. Did I, err, cause damage?"

"No, no," She waves her hand. "It was the drugs. Apparently, he came to shortly after we left, and found all the powder, heard sirens, panicked and just stuffed it all into his stupid mouth, had an adverse reaction, and the cops found him having a seizure. It was probably cut with some junk, could be drain cleaner for all we know. When he's better, they want to have a few words with him. Serves him right. Fucking idiot."

"Oops. Did the police talk to you?"

"Yes, and I told them what happened, but minus your intervention. A friend came to the house and picked me up is all they know."

"Thanks, Pip."

"No. Thank you, Toby. I don't know what would have happened if you hadn't come."

Philippa hugs me, and I gently squeeze her. "What are friends for, eh?"

She pulls away and I notice a moistness in her eyes as she looks up at me. "You ready for food?"

"Yeah." I smile. "Need a hand?"

"Nope. All covered. You sit down and drink your beer."

I do as I'm told.

The food is great, and I didn't have to make it. Not only that, but a beautiful woman brought it to me. You can't beat those odds. Even if she had brought me a Pot Noodle, it would have been better than anything I made myself at home. I could get used to this.

Over dinner, I change the subject and ask her about the baby, the nursery she's putting together, and what she's going to do with work and stuff. She has thought little about the latter, because she had sort of assumed that she and Jason would be together, but since that has all changed in the blink of an eye, now her life is in turmoil. She'll get plenty of maternity leave, of course, but after that, then what?

I feel like we're in similar boats. Not the same, of course, but my life has also been upended in the last few weeks. Lost my job, turned into a circus freak, and started beating the crap out of people. It wasn't long ago that I was plodding into work every night to my extremely dull night shifts.

Philippa is happy, though. I can tell. It seems like a weight has been lifted from her, with Jason out of the picture. I feel her vibrations are lighter. She's going to be fine.

"Oh, yeah. What happened with that old lady, Evelyn?"

I couldn't avoid it all night, I suppose, and despite trying to come up with some plausible story, I reckon it's best in the end not to lie. My Dad always said, if you are going to be a liar, you better have an excellent memory, and according to Evelyn, I didn't get the total recall photographic memory upgrade. Shame.

Instead, the truth with some omissions is easier to manage in the long term.

"Well, it was a bit strange in the end. She didn't know me, I didn't know her. She's a lovely old dear though. Told me all about the work she used to do. Fascinating stuff."

"Where do you know her name from, then?"

I shrug. "Must have been the documentary, or maybe the museum at Bletchley. News or something. Dunno."

"You seemed so sure you knew her."

"Yeah, weird. I think I was just a bit messed up, you know, after losing my job and stuff."

Philippa rests her hand on mine. "You'll be okay, Toby. I know it."

I smile. "Cheers, Pip."

Dodged that bullet.

After dinner, we move to the couch, and another beer appears in my hand. Philippa isn't drinking of course, but she snuggles close to me as we flip around Netflix and Prime, trying to find something vaguely entertaining but not too taxing.

"Oh, my poor feet." Philippa takes off her shoes and puts her feet up on a beanbag, strategically placed for the purpose.

I turn to her with a smile and pat a hand on my lap. She grins and swivels her legs onto mine, then lies back on the arm of the couch with a soft sigh.

I say nothing and start caressing her feet, not tickling, because I know she hates that, but gently massaging. She makes encouraging noises, and I put down my beer and use both hands. Soft, but firmly squeezing in what I think are the right places.

"Toby …"

"Yes, Philippa?"

"Mmm, nothing, just keep doing that."

"Yes, Philippa." I grin.

A naughty thought pops into my head, something that Evelyn said about being able to cause 'things' to happen with people, as well as objects. I wonder …

I focus my mind on her energy, closing my eyes, visualising the emotion of the woman laying on me. Then, I remember the night we had together recently, and the fiery passion of it. Calm, but deliberate and uninhibited. I project those feelings through my hands as a frequency of energy, slowly at first, but building up. I feel her quiver in response. Heat pulses through her skin and she curls her toes as I massage.

"Toby … Mmm."

I turn the intensity up a notch and focus, running one hand along her legs.

"No, we shouldn't. Toby, oh, God."

"You want me to stop?"

"No, just … I think the heating is on too high."

She slides her skirt up her legs, and I follow along her soft skin with my hand, magnifying the energy up as high as I can manage.

"Jesus, Toby." She moves her hand to my groin and squeezes. I feel myself inflate under her touch.

"Mmm." She grins at me and grabs my shirt, pulling me down to her.

A crippling thought suddenly jolts through me. I did this. I made her horny with whatever weird energy I can output. I shouldn't have done that. It feels wrong, like spiking a drink or taking advantage of a drunk woman. Holy hell, I don't want to become the sort of bloke who would do that. I blink and stop the flow. Philippa kisses me and I kiss back, but after a long, passionate moment, she stops and pushes me away softly and slowly.

"I don't know what came over me there, but Toby, we can't. I'm sorry. I'm just, all over the place, and I don't want to end up hurting you."

I sit back up and adjust my jeans. "It's okay, Pip. I understand."

She smiles coyly. "You can keep massaging my feet, though, if you want."

I nod and go back to my duty, without the enhanced sexual energy. Philippa smiles and finds the TV remote, pressing play on some rom-com movie.

Another thing Evelyn said to me pops into my head. 'With great power comes great responsibility,' and once again, the old girl is right.

CHAPTER
TWENTY

"DEAR EVELYN. My word, you are looking wonderful." Dickie opens his arms for an embrace.

"Don't patronise me, Dickie, I know I look like a haggard old witch." I allow him to give me a bear hug but pull away when he tries to plant a kiss on my cheek. Saucy old sod.

Dickie chuckles, "Well, you have me under your spell, for sure."

I flash a smile. "Thank you for doing this, Dickie."

"My pleasure. But, I don't suppose you want to tell me what this is all about, hmm?"

"I can't. Sorry, but it's for a good cause, you understand."

He holds up his hands. "Ah, fair enough. I shan't ask again. You and your secrets."

I flash a smile. "The equipment is all here, I take it?"

"Yes, set up as you specified."

"I better check it, those buffoons have the grace of a baby elephant. That stuff cost an absolute fortune, and it's as delicate as eggshells."

"I don't know what it all is, but I made sure they were careful, Evelyn. Panic not."

"Thank you. Temperature set to seventeen degrees?"

"Yes, as you specified."

"Good. I calibrated the equipment for that. One degree too cold or hot and it's all buggered."

Dickie snorts a laugh. "We will accommodate your every whim, Evelyn."

I flash him an evil eye but melt into a smile.

Richard 'Dickie' Bligh and I go back a long way. We worked together briefly at Bletchley, and then we bumped into each other a lot while I was at the MRC. He went on to great things, reaching the rank of Commander, and seeing action all over the place, including Northern Ireland and more recently in the Falklands. Now retired from the ocean waves to do battle at a desk, pushing paper. He's a solid chap, but I won't ever tell him that to his face. His head is quite big enough as it is.

He's been a tremendous help getting this recording session set up, and I can't even tell him what it's for. I feel guilty, but I'm sure he has secrets of his own. All for the good of the country and whatnot.

We've commandeered a small theatre room, kitted out with a cobbled-together portable version of my brainwave recording system. A projector so I can show the subjects film footage while I capture their reactions. Tape machines, a minicomputer, and of course the wave helmet and connected paraphernalia. It took forever to package it all up from my lab and bring it here. If anything gets damaged, I don't know what I'll do.

I recently found that I had reached the limits of my

experience and knowledge when it came to populate my Flash Gordon database. I may have helped win the war, but I was never in close combat battle, captured by enemies, tortured, punished, or pushed to my physical limits. I've lived a quiet life of research, for the most part. Hard work though it was. I needed a fresh set of brains and experience for my next phase. All this without the Department finding out. Spencer is in on it, but he's told Cynthia I'm away for my Christmas break. I know I can trust Spencer and Dickie, but there are always some unknowns who could accidentally spill the beans. Still, needs must and all that. I won't progress the project without taking a few risks.

I'll start with Dickie, but I'll also be interviewing several younger chaps from the facility over the coming weeks. People who have excelled at the training and seen action. Been awarded medals and accolades. The cream of the military who were available to help at short notice. I need their frequencies.

"How's Gerald?" Dickie jolts me from my daydream.

"Hmm? Oh, dead."

"Good grief. I am sorry, Evelyn, I had no idea." Dickie puts a hand on his chest.

I flash a weak smile. "Last year. Heart problems. I tried to tell him to go to a doctor. Stubborn fool."

"The poor fellow. Poor you." Dickie moves closer. "And Anthony? How is he taking it?"

I scoff. "I'm not sure he's even noticed yet. He's away around the world on some kind of 'finding himself' rubbish. I can't keep up."

"Dear me. You must come for dinner, while you are

down here. Jane would love to see you again. She makes a splendid roast."

"Yes, of course. Thank you, Dickie."

"Well, where do we start?"

"We should start with a hearty breakfast. It will be a long day of calibration, interviews, recording sessions, and sensory stimulation."

"Ah, that last part sounds interesting." He grins.

"Don't get your hopes up. It's going to be boring as hell."

"I'll go first, show the troops it's all safe and harmless. Err, it is all safe and harmless, isn't it?"

"Yes, of course. I've been through the process myself hundreds of times by now. Maybe thousands."

"Very well, to the mess hall we go!"

After breakfast, where I met the other volunteers who all seem a jovial bunch, Dickie and I go to the theatre where all my equipment is set up. I fuss over the connections and run some tests, but thankfully, it has all survived the journey and is functional. I have a good hundred hours of inch-wide magnetic tape to fill, with the compressed and filtered frequencies from the subjects. This is going to provide a much-needed boost to the Flash Gordon database. Teaching monkeys to count is one thing, but for the project to have any practical use in the intended way, I need real data.

"If you need the loo, go now."

Dickie nods then runs off towards the bathrooms. At our age, you take every opportunity you can.

Strapped into the chair, with electrodes connected

on his chest, arms, legs and hands, the wave helmet on, and a special set of glasses that can be blacked out or shine lights directly into the eyes, Dickie looks the part. I can't help but chuckle. He's agitated but does a wonderful impression of someone who is comfortable.

"I owe you one, Dickie."

He waves a hand but is somewhat limited by the cables. "Glad to be of help."

"Let us begin."

I start with a calibration process. I show a film of a benign journey from the front window of a train. Pastoral countryside passes at a relaxing pace. Dickie relaxes in his chair and watches the projected image. I take measurements and make notes on my computer terminal. The tape starts to spin and record progress. After a minute or so, the train film speeds up, and the countryside now turns to grey city tower blocks, the tone overall becomes darker and a soundtrack of deep drones will play into the earphones of the helmet. I watch as the various sensors report a very slight increase in heart rate and pulse. Very good. All seems to function correctly.

Another two minutes pass and the speed of the train gently increases. I had this tape specially made, using loops of film that are run at different speeds, with filters applied as needed. The fun part is yet to come.

While the train seems to fly along at a good hundred and fifty miles per hour, the onslaught of imagery is hard to focus on. I notice Dickie remains mostly calm, but he is blinking more than previously.

Now in the film, there are some spliced-in frames of what people may consider disturbing images. Nothing too outlandish, but scenes from war films with bodies strewn across battlefields. These are single frames and you'd need to be paying very close attention to see them in the traditional sense, but the mind notices everything. They trigger subliminal reactions. I notice another slight rise in pulse rate.

The next phase is calming. The train slows down and moves back to lush green countryside. I must say, they have done a marvellous job with the edits. There are barely any noticeable flickers between the scenes.

Thirty seconds pass, and Dickie's pulse slows down to a normal slow rate. That's all going to change, though. I can't resist a grin as I know what's coming next. Spliced in at the end of the reel, there's a little surprise.

Dickie watches the film, the helmet recording a steady rate of brainwave patterns to the tape for future processing into the Flash Gordon database. I didn't know it at the time, of course, but my work at the MRC all those years ago came in very useful for this project. Measuring wave pattern fluctuations after traumatic events was fascinating, but now I'm doing it in real-time. I watch Dickie's face and check all the measure-ments once again.

Suddenly, the lush green countryside on the screen goes to pure black, and there's nothing for an unsettling moment. Silence and darkness all around. Then, a chaotic scene unfolds. A blast of loud screeching metal as the train slams on brakes, but there's no chance it will stop in time. An equally fast train comes towards the camera on the same set of rails. A crash is inevitable, and Dickie's

pulse rate rapidly increases. I notice his hands are grip-
ping the arms of the chair so his knuckles become white.
He pushes back in his chair as much as possible, flat-
tening himself away from the oncoming disaster. But the
scene progresses. The trains power towards each other,
increasing speed instead of slowing, now only seconds
away from impact. The sound in the helmet is now a
grinding, throbbing low frequency wave of doom. I
watch as the readings all show that poor Dickie is on the
verge of needing new underwear. The oncoming train is
now so close that you can see the driver's eyes.

Of course, there wasn't a real crash. The film is
vastly speeded up, and they shot the actual footage on
two very slow trains that were carefully shunted
together. No damage was done. But Dickie doesn't
know that.

The trains touch and the screen goes completely
black. At the crucial point, there's an almighty crash
sound that reverberates through the steel of the helmet
so much that I can feel it in my control station. Dickie's
pulse rockets up and the helmet shows major activity
all over the brain, especially the pre-frontal cortex.
Excellent.

I wait a moment for the adrenaline to subside, and
then flick on the room lights and release Dickie from his
chair.

"Good lord, Evelyn. You might have warned me!"
He stands up and shakes his head.

"If I had, the calibration would be useless. You'd
have been expecting the crash."

"Ahh, I see. You are too clever for your boots,

madam! Very good, very good. I must say, an enthralling experience. Invigorating!"

"Glad you enjoyed it. Will you be needing new trousers?"

"No, but I am glad you told me to go before the train left the station." He winks and chuckles.

We spend the next hour or so conducting an interview. I ask Dickie many questions about how he would react in various situations while the many devices record his answers and mental state. I'm going to have my hands full for a long while, correlating all this data and feeding it into the database, but it will be invaluable. Now I know I can transmit knowledge via the FSMI process, there are no limits as to what I can include in the database. I could interview a chef and gain all the techniques and recipes, or a mechanic and the knowledge of how to repair a car engine. In fact, both of those are extremely good ideas. Why not fill the brain with useful, solid information? Far better than the useless junk that most of us seem to carry around in our vast spongy memories.

I make a note to follow up at a later date with some more practical skills.

I also recently found some hidden research, by slightly unconventional means, I must admit, that suggests that humans have the power to transmit their thoughts out of their bodies. A fascinating topic, and I shall delve into the possibilities soon. A lot of these papers are dead ends, written by people of questionable reputations, but this one had some credulity. Russian in origin, collected by the Americans in a dump of data, squirrelled away on a military computer in Alaska, of all places. I must say, this global computer network is amazing, and I predict this will become an enormous part of society, given time to mature. The possibilities are endless if every man, woman and child has access to a vast world of information.

This particular paper is attributed to a chap called Ivan Pravdich, and alludes to research he has carried out with people who claim to have this power naturally. They can influence objects with their minds, and he has measured their bodies while it took place. The conclusion he came to was that all mammalian brains have this ability, but it is suppressed by nature, stagnant, undeveloped and unused. The people he studied who had this skill usually were in some way mentally disabled from birth. The paper of course is wildly controversial and would likely be dismissed by any western body. But I pick through these ridiculous details and ask myself, what if it were true? Could it be trained into a mind, and would it be useful for my Flash Gordon to have? Here, I'm leaning towards a 'yes' for all those points. Quite fascinating.

After a brief lunch, I wired Dickie back into the chair and we begin the good stuff. I will show him war footage and measure responses. Pausing to ask questions about the scenarios, and what he would do if he was actually in the situations himself. There are graphic scenes of battle, as well as interrogations, enemy captures, terrifying aeroplane flights from bombers, and even footage from a parachute jump. I trawled archives for weeks to pull this all together, with some help from unwitting assistants, frequently switching from duty to duty, so no one can piece together the real reason for all my work. This work is exhausting, but now forms a huge part of my life, and I want it to be done. Finished, and handed over to someone to implement and use, otherwise I've wasted decades of my life on a worthless cause.

CHAPTER
TWENTY-ONE

THE ENDLESS DARKNESS. Comforting, warm and embracing. Natural. I thrive in its midst, but so do the scumbags of the world. They hide away in the nooks and crannies, the puddles of shadows, the edge of the normal-people daylight world.

With all our advancements and technology, all it takes is the lack of sunlight to lure out the undesirables among us. We are simple animals when all said and done, but without our technology, have we advanced much from the cavemen? The panic that ensues if Wi-Fi is down, or power is off in most people's homes suggests not. How quickly we revert to base instincts. I'd argue that some never rise above those at all. Eat, fuck, sleep, repeat. Not necessarily in that order.

Well, maybe I can do something about the evil night walkers, in my small way.

I spent the day pondering my circumstances, and what I should do with my new life. If I'm going to use my powers to do good in the world, somehow, and maybe make a living while doing it — and, why shouldn't I? Then I'll need some practice. I'm not even sure of the limits of my reach. Can I fend off multiple villains at once? Can I shut down approaching tanks? No idea. I feel like I should at least try some basic stuff and see what happens. If I do nothing, then I'll always wonder 'what if?' Will I live to one hundred and then some, like Evelyn, and if I do, will I look back on my life with emptiness and regret? If I pass by a crime scene and do nothing, am I no better than the criminals?

Tonight, for all anyone knows, I'm just a dude out for a walk in the dark. It happens, nothing strange. I could be walking back from the pub, or a girlfriend's house, work, or the gym. I'm invisible to the humans. Just another bloke living his boring life. Except, tonight I'm out looking for trouble. It seems a bit clichéd, but you have to start somewhere.

Armed with nothing more than a sturdy metal high-powered LED flashlight, my phone, heavy boots, a long black leather coat, and my wits, I patrol the dark town. Sodium orange drizzle mist surrounds me as I pass under the streetlights, mostly quiet in the town now, people will be in their beds, or heading to them via a dose of bedtime propaganda from the television.

I start with some pubs around chucking out time. There's always some trouble when you mix desperation with alcohol. But, on a Monday night, all I see are a few quiet loners making their way back to whatever they call home. No brawls, no damage done. I carry on. I walk to the beat of my headphones, spilling melodic heavy metal into my ears, fuelling my confidence, and keeping me at a steady pace. I pass a twenty-four-hour supermarket and pop in, grabbing a bottle of energy drink and a packet of peanuts. There's no drama though, no fights, no one stealing anything. I move back into the night. It occurs to me that the whole of the UK is saturated with security cameras, and this surely has some effect on the level of casual crimes being committed. Why would you bother when it's almost certain that you'll be caught in the act? I suppose in the loss of our freedom and privacy, we've gained some semblance of safety. At least perceived. It probably means that the crimes have moved from the streets to behind the closed doors of homes. Like my phone thief friend who had his work-from-home business shut down care of Evelyn's Project Flash Gordon.

I keep walking, passing closed shops and restaurants, heading out of Main Street, passing the quiet railway station, and onwards out of town. I pop into a petrol station and walk around, but none of the over-priced junk or stacked-up chocolate catches my eye. There's no one trying to rob it or drive away without paying, and there are at least eight cameras that I can see around the premises. I think they are covered. I go back out and continue walking.

This is a route I sometimes take on the bike, and I walk on for another fifteen minutes or so. Tonight's venture is proving fruitless. I witness no crimes and don't even receive an evil eye stare from anyone. There aren't many folks around at all. I turn back and head towards home. This method will not work.

What was I thinking? I'm one man, wandering around one town on one evening. The chances of literally bumping into some bad stuff happening are probably at lottery-winning levels. I need a new plan.

I check my watch. 1:03 am. Packing up time I reckon, plus my tummy is rumbling. I should be having my lunch about now, according to my vague biological clock.

I cut across an estate that will get me home a few minutes quicker, and ramp up the music to fill my brain and keep me at a steady pace.

I look down at the ground to keep my footing, dimly lit with sparse street lights, wet and cold with the endless mist, cracks in the paving measuring the distance with their regularity.

Something makes me look up, a flash of colour amongst the grey. A guy approaches me on the pavement, gaunt and decked in a bright yellow hoodie and soggy white tracksuit pants. His face is hidden in shadow from the hood, pulled tight into a narrow circle, and his gait is that of a creature not from this world. He bounces with every step as if he's not used to our gravity level. He sees me and moves to the inside of the pavement so we can pass. I do the same and shuffle over to the kerb edge. I look back down and carry on, but as I approach the man, no more than a kid, really, I feel a sickness stir in my guts. I look up when he's within a few feet away, and there's a ghastly aura around him, shimmering in the misty haze with a deep browny-green tinge over a core of black. The dude is stricken. I catch a glimpse of his eyes deep in the shadow of his hood, and they are barren of any life. I never knew what the phrase 'piss holes in the snow' meant until now. He looks down and away from me and passes without comment.

I stop and turn. As he walks away, I can still sense the torture and pain that he's oozing out from every pore in his skin. It's like his soul is diseased and fighting a losing battle to keep him awake.

He's on drugs. Of that I'm sure, but which kind I don't know.

An idea lands in my mind like a pigeon swooping down onto a town centre statue.

I pluck out my headphones. "Hey."

The gaunt man doesn't flinch, and keeps on walking away. I follow, increasing my speed so I catch him.

"Hey!" I repeat from right behind him. Maybe he has headphones in as well and can't hear.

"DUDE!" I raise my voice, but nothing. Much as it pains me to touch this afflicted being, I reach out and tap him on the shoulder. This has an effect. He jumps so hard that he barely stays standing, and has to lean on the hedge to keep up. The hedge, being of some variety of soft coppiced conifer, doesn't offer any support, and the dude falls straight into it. I shake my head and watch as he tumbles in slow motion. I don't want to touch him again, but his awkward freak-out leaves me no choice. I grab his arm and yank him back to an upright position, then pause for a second to allow kinetic energy to subside, and let go, leaving him standing, shocked and tense.

He moves his hands up to his ears and pulls out earphones.

"Sorry, pal. Didn't mean to scare you."

"WHAT THE FUCK!" He spits the words at me.

"I just wanted to ask you a question."

"Fuck off, mister." He backs away, but there's terror in his dead eyes now.

"Where do you get your stuff?"

"Eh?" His eyes now shift around, looking for an escape path. I'm not blocking his way, he could just run if he needed to.

"Your stuff. Your gear. Whatever you want to call it. Where did you get it? I'm trying to find the dealer around here. Got lost." I flash a grin.

"I ain't got nothing."

"Didn't say you had it on you. Just need a little help to get my bearings. I'm not from here. Someone told me directions to the place, but I've been walking around here all night and I can't find it."

I raise my palms in a gesture of peace.

The dude calms down a notch. Still suspicious, he eyes me up and down, and the greasy feel of his stare makes me want to throw up right there. But I keep it together.

There's a battle going on in his head. He doesn't want to admit he's just come from the drug dealer, but the sliver of human decency at his core, seeping through from his childhood, tells him he should be polite and give directions.

"Twenty quid in it for you if you can show me?"

He looks up, scratches at his face, and then seems to make a decision. "Givvus the cash first." Now cocky, his stance changes. He thinks he's got the upper hand.

"Now, that wouldn't be a very good strategy on my part, would it?"

The dude shrugs and moves to walk away.

"Ten quid now, ten quid when you show me the place. Deal?"

He hesitates, then shrugs again. "Fuckin' whatever." He sticks out a hand.

I pull a tenner from my pocket. Careful not to take my wallet out in view. I slap it into his grimy hand. He turns back the way he came, and heads off at an unnatural pace without a word. I follow.

We walk on for about forty-five seconds, and then he ducks through a gap in the hedge into the grounds of a block of flats, that was more or less hidden behind the tall conifer. He follows a worn, muddy path in the grass that is a shortcut for the residents here. The proper paths are concrete and straight and connect the exits to the street, but the designers didn't factor in the apathy that would exist in the residents. Of course, they are going to forge their own shorter paths. Better to have made those in the first place.

The sickly teen heads for a gap between two blocks that's in shadow from most street lights. For a moment I think he might lead me into a trap, and would turn on me with a knife or something, but he passes through quickly and out into a clearing between more blocks of flats behind. They probably thought this gave a sense of community to the people unfortunate enough to live here, but it is more likely to be the arena for a burning car, than a street party for the coronation.

He turns left and points to the nearest doorway into one of the buildings. Then without a word sticks out his hand for his other tenner.

"In there?" I ask, for some clarity.

"Yeah."

"What number?"

"Twenty-two. Thought you was told directions?"

"Yeah, and I got lost like I said."

"Whatever. Money."

I fish out the other tenner I had in my pocket, and offer it to him, but then pull back. "What did you get from them?"

"I ain't got nothin'!"

"Right, so you said. Well, if you were going to get something, what would you get from here?"

"Fuck off, mister. Give me my money."

Worth a try, I suppose. I look at the emaciated skeleton under the hoodie, and try not to feel repulsed by his poisoned mug. I toy with the idea of trying some harmonising on him to get more information, but decide he isn't worth the hassle. I give him the tenner and he snaps it away, then turns and trots off, looking back three times to make sure I'm not following before he vanishes into the alleyway. Poor fucker.

I was going home, but now I have a drug dealer's home address, and I should at least scope it out. There's no one else around and I suspect security cameras sparsely cover this estate. There's likely some on the streets nearby, but in here, they leave the rats to play alone.

I bash open the door with a boot and head into the concrete corridors, ill-lit with fluorescent tubes, cold with the night air that seeps in through several broken wire-mesh windows, yet not washing away the stench of stale piss.

I pass quietly by several doors on the first floor, and

the numbers only seem to go up to six, so I take the stairway up, not wishing to chance the lift, even if it functions it's probably the source of the stink. The second floor yields another six numbers, so I climb another two floors to the fourth and exit back into the corridors. There's a distinct smell here, like acrid burning plastic. I find number twenty-two quickly, but even if I didn't know this was the drug dealer's den, it is pretty obvious. The door has a camera mounted above it, and another on the doorbell. There's a hefty lock that isn't on any of the other doors. It looks like it could be electronically controlled with a phone or passkey, but I can't see the make and model.

I stay away from the view of the cameras and back away, walking around the circle of the corridors until I get to the other side of the dealer door. There's a flick-ering fluorescent tube light above me, which is not ideal, so I reach up a hand towards it and focus my mind on the electronics inside, feeling my way through copper and lead solder, through capacitors and into the ballast, then I feel for the frequency of the materials inside it, and I burst out a pulse of energy. The light above me flickers once more, then glows brighter than it ever did for a few seconds, before going dead with a quiet 'ping'. I am left in a pool of darkness. Nice.

I back away into a doorway that probably leads to a maintenance cupboard. It is locked, but I can flatten myself against the door and without the light, I am more or less invisible.

I wait.

I don't have a plan, and a glance at my watch confirms my now grumbling stomach. Two in the morning and I am hiding in a doorway, in a skanky block of flats, staking out a dealer. Why? I could be at home, enjoying a meal with a beer, watching a movie, or soaking in a bath. I chose to come out and wreak havoc among the ne'er-do-wells, and I should at least see it through to some kind of conclusion.

I wait some more.

I'm sort of hoping that someone will come and knock on their door so I can confirm I'm at the right place. A thought occurs to me that the yellow hooded guy could have sent a message to the dealers, informing them of my arrival, but I haven't heard a peep or seen any signs of life from the place. I think I'm as unexpected as I am myself. They could be asleep. Closed for business, but I find that hard to believe. A bleak, wet Tuesday in the wee small hours should be exactly when they are at their busiest.

If I concentrate, I can hear the sounds that resonate around the building. No, 'hear' is the wrong word. I feel it in my bones. A television blaring in one home, a washing machine spinning in another. Flushes and drains spill effluent into the sewers and snores from many more rooms. A cocktail of human life, concentrated and unfiltered. Disgusting.

I wait, I wait, I wait.

An echo floats up from the stairwell. Steps approach. Finally.

I press myself flat into the doorway and peer out towards the door, hoping someone is coming to buy drugs. The steps grow louder, but they are meek at best. Light, dulled with rubber, but I'm guessing the person is a girl or a very small dude.

There's a pause, then a patter of feet towards me. I shrink more into the shadows. The footsteps stop and I peer out. A girl is standing at the dealer door. Tiny, blonde fuzzy hair pulled into a ponytail. Again a hoodie, but over pink leggings. She looks towards me in the gloom, peering into the dark, but I don't think she can see me. She doesn't knock, but after a second she turns and waves at the camera. There's a phone in her hand, and it lights up. She pushes the door, and it swings open. She disappears. A moment later, a head sticks out from the door and looks towards where I'm standing. An ugly head, sweaty, black stubble and flapping jowls. It grunts a curse, then vanishes back inside. The door slams closed.

I wait.

No more than four minutes pass, and the door opens again. The girl quickly comes out and pulls the door closed behind her. She glances back towards me and the darkness with a shudder, then patters back the way she came. Her steps fading as she goes down and back out into the chilly night.

Well, if that isn't proof enough, I don't know what is. She came for some gear, or whatever the colloquialism is, and got sorted, then left. Why else would anyone be coming to this shit hole in the middle of the night?

I form a plan.

I pause for about fifteen minutes, all the while keeping an eye for any more patrons of the twenty-four-hour pharmacy, and then I slide along the wall towards the door, staying away from the dead eyes of the cameras as I do.

Both of the cameras prove simple to disable. All I had to do was short out a few connections in the shell of the enclosures. Tiny wires and circuits, so close that it takes very little to burn through the copper. Their red lights die with them, and I'm confident the screens inside the flat are dark. The door still has a peephole in it, so I bang at the door and then slide to the left so I can't be seen.

I wait for a few seconds, then thud at the door with more force. No doubt the ugly head is watching some crap on TV, not expecting a traditional knock.

A faint click inside the lock, and the door creaks open a crack.

"Good evening," I cheerily announce.

The head stares at me from behind a chain. He's taking no chances.

Confused, the head cracks open a foul mouth. "What do you want?" An Eastern European accent, but I can't tell if he's Polish or something else. I don't think I have Romanian or Czech in my list of tongues. He could be Russian, and then we'd be in luck.

I try Polish first. "Szukam narkotyków"

He's taken aback. The head disappears from view and the door closes, re-opening shortly without the chain, but still cracked.

"Who the fuck are you?"

"Does it matter? I'm looking for gear."

He comes out into the corridor, and a waft of heat pours out with him from the flat, and a stench of stale sweat with it. He's wearing a grey wife beater vest, of course, and the obligatory sweatpants. Bare feet. He looks up at the camera above the door, then swings the door back and checks the one there. They look like they always did. The damage is inside.

"You mess with camera?"

I shrug and shake my head.

"Where you come from?" He looks again at the dark corridor where the light should be on.

"Not from here. A guy in town told me you had good stuff."

"Shut the fuck up, okay?" He flinches and raises a fat finger to his lips and motions me inside the flat. I follow.

"No text?" He pulls a phone from his pocket and glances at the screen.

"Sorry?"

"Meant to text first."

"Oh, sorry, didn't know." I shrug again. "Well, are you open or not?"

"Open? What the fuck. Not a shop."

"Przepraszam," I pause for a reaction. "nie znam twojego systemu."

He looks up at me with screwed-up eyes. "You fucking speak English. You not Polish. Fuck you."

"Fair enough."

"Kurwa, how you fucking know my language?"

"Long story."

"What do you want?"

"Well, what have you got?"

He tilts his head. "What you say? What the fuck you think I got?"

"Well, can I see the menu?" I look around the room, sparsely decorated with a vast television taking up more or less all of one wall. There's one armchair in front of it, with a mess of beer cans littered around it, and an ashtray on the floor, overflowing with fag butts. The room is stifling hot. It must be at least twenty-seven degrees. Perhaps he's also growing weed somewhere.

"Menu? You taking the piss?"

"Yes. I am."

The fat man reaches behind the chair and pulls out a baseball bat, and swings it into the palm of his fat hand with a greasy slap. Ah, here we go. The old favourite. "You want some of this?"

I step backwards, holding up my hands. "Chill out, dude. Just kidding."

"What the fuck you want, you got one second, or you leave, or you eat this."

"Well, if you don't have a menu, perhaps you can recommend the house special?"

"Okay mister fucking joker, I don't need this shit. Get out." He points the bat towards the door.

"I mean, what's good, any special offers? Oh, do you have a loyalty card scheme I should sign up for? Can I use my Tesco Clubcard points here?"

He swings the bat, aiming for my head, I guess, but I laugh at the snail's pace of his move, and snatch it out of the air and fling it to the floor in a single fluid motion. He cries out and clutches his wrist. I may have broken it with the snap. Oops.

"You fucker!" He doubles over with another cry, then tries a head-butt by running towards me. I dodge his advance and he runs straight into the door with a hefty thud, then another as his limp body hits the bare boards. K.O. What a twat.

"Well, thanks for doing the hard work for me, mate."

I glance around the flat again, and head through a doorway behind the chair. There's a small room that probably should be a bedroom, but instead, there are three tables pushed against the walls, each one with neatly laid out packets of powder, pills and resin. A cornucopia of medical supplies on a shelf, and a large wad of cash in a Chinese takeaway box.

I leave it all untouched, then go back to sleeping beauty, find his phone that fell to the floor with him, and dial the emergency services.

Now then, I'm bloody starving, and Chinese takeaway sounds like an excellent idea if there's one still open.

TWENTY-TWO

———

CONFIDENTIAL MEMORANDUM
TO: Evelyn Greenwood
SUBJECT: PROJECT FLASH GORDON
DATE: 15 JUNE 1987
MESSAGE:
Project FLASH GORDON is hereby
CANCELLED with immediate effect. Discontinue efforts and destroy all code, documents,
research and notes. TOP SECRET status remains
in effect until further notice. You have 24 hours
to shut down all operations.

———

I STARE at the paper in my hands for a full minute
before it registers as reality. I've been doing a lot of late
nights, preceded by a lot of early mornings lately, and

reality is hard to keep a track of. My candle, as it were, is burnt down to a tiny nub in the middle. I'm exhausted, but I'm not hallucinating. The document that was casually delivered to my desk, amongst the usual administration and letters, is real, and is sealed with the stamp of the realm. I read the words again.

Project FLASH GORDON is hereby CANCELLED with immediate effect

Bile and rage flare up in my chest. I slam my fists down on the desk and immediately wish I hadn't. Pain spurts in pulses down my arms and fuels my rage even further.

"How bloody dare they?" I shout to no one but the animals in their cages. "How BLOODY DARE they!"

I pick up the phone on my desk and hit the quick dial button for Spencer. The phone rings for much longer than usual, and I notice some clicks as someone finally answers the call.

"Good morning," A voice on the other end politely says. "Switchboard, How may I help you?" A female voice in the tone of a front office receptionist. I assume my call has been redirected.

"Spencer Jenkins, please. I called his direct line."

"One moment, please." There's a pause and the clacking of some typing in the background. "I'm sorry, there's no one by that name working here."

"What? Yes, there most certainly is. Check again."

"Yes, Madam." Again the pause and typing. "Can you spell the name?"

Reluctantly, and through clenched teeth, I spell the name out, letter by letter, clearly and with phonetics.

"Yes, I can confirm, no one of that name works here. Is there anything else I can help you with?"

The phone handset drops from my hands down onto the desk as I realise the truth. My God. They've got to Spencer as well. He's gone. Just vanished? I only spoke to him last week, and everything was normal and fine, at least he said nothing. He wouldn't keep this from me, would he? An icy, shivery feeling floods my veins. My work … twenty-two years of work, all for nothing?

I spend another useless hour trying to find Spencer, then Cynthia and Ian, being put through to one person, then another, and another as all of them claim not to know what I'm talking about. They asked me 'what department' on more than one occasion, and had to stop myself from throwing the phone out through a window. If I knew what Department they worked for … Gah!

According to official channels, none of the people I have worked with for all these years exists, at least in the world of government intelligence. Or lack of.

What am I going to do? The memo doesn't say where it came from, which agency or department sent it? On what authority is my project being cancelled?

I curse myself for never having taken any personal contact details for Spencer. It was never important before. We kept in touch all the time. He knows how to find me, so I can only imagine that he either isn't allowed to, or doesn't want to, or worse, that he's been 'eliminated'. I'm sure the official message for anyone privileged enough to know is that he took retirement. True enough, neither he nor I are spring chickens, these days. Even so, he had a good few years in him yet.

I walk down to the post room and ask where the memo came from. They don't know. However, I am informed by the security desk that I must vacate my labs by nine tomorrow morning. Where did that instruction come from? 'Downing Street' is all they will tell me. Never been very communicative, the security chaps.

I'm stunned. Numb with the shock. I've given my life to this bloody project and now ... what?

I walk back towards my lab, slowly, thoughts running wild in my brain. Was it because of the slow progress I was showing to the Department? Even artificially slowed down, it was still quicker than my first ten years or so. I've made great strides of late towards the final goal, but there's still so much more I can do. What will they do with the equipment, the animals? They want me to destroy all notes and research. Surely they wouldn't waste so much effort in one sweep like this? No, perhaps that's exactly how it goes. The Prime Minister has already done much worse. Who am I compared to the thousands already made unemployed? At least I have savings and a healthy pension. I'm sixty-five years old, in reality, could I expect this to go on for much longer? That isn't the point, though. I wanted to plan my retirement on my agenda, not be forced into it like this. I wanted to finish my work.

I haven't even begun testing on human subjects yet.

Oh … the obvious drops into my mind like a lead balloon.

I know what I have to do. I dash back to the lab and begin preparations immediately. I have little time.

The real 'Flash Gordon' database is split at the moment into multiple tests. Dozens, or maybe hundreds. I've lost count. Each is focused on a particular skill that the various creatures have been testing for me. I need to sort them into stacks, concatenate them into a single seamless routine, compile it all and then undergo the procedure myself. There's no other way. I'm not going to leave it like this. I can't. After twenty-two years of work, what sane person could just walk away from it? No, I have to run the program on myself. It will be fine. I know each line of code like the back of my hand. Of course, it will run from an illegal hack halfway across the world, but that's a minor detail. The equipment can handle it. I'm sure of it. Kong and the other subjects have tested this all for me thousands of times now. It works. It just isn't finished.

I also need to do what they have asked me. Destroy all the local code, documents, paperwork and whatever else I can find lying around. Dismantle the recording headset and the test chambers. Remove all evidence that I was ever here.

Kong hops onto my desk with a look of worry.

"Kong, sweet child. It will be okay. I promise."

They had better take care of the animals. "Perhaps I can sneak you home with me?"

Kong chirps and hops from foot to foot.

"First, you can help me sort this mess out. Yes?"

She squeals in acknowledgement.

"Very good. Now, gather all the papers from, well, everywhere and drop them into this basket. See here?" I tap on the side of a huge bin. We'll have to take them down to the incinerator room later.

Kong chirps and eagerly gets to work. It's incredible, but I'm sure she can understand every word I say.

I leave her to it, and get stuck into the actual work.

―――――

"Ms Greenwood?" A nervous voice comes from the doorway. I look up.

"Yes, hello."

"May I come in?" A woman lingers at the entrance, peeking around my lab as if the very walls would reach out and bite her.

"You may."

She steps in and tentatively walks over to me at the Cray terminal.

"I'm Jana Scully from personnel." She sticks out a limp hand. I ignore it.

"Oh, hello, Jana."

"Congratulations!"

"Sorry, on what?"

"On your retirement." She beams a smile. "You've made it!"

"Ah, I see." I turn back to my terminal screen.

"I just have some paperwork for you to sign, and

then you're all set. So exciting! Are you having a leaving party?"

I raise an eyebrow. "No." Jana seems disappointed. She's not the only one.

"Oh. Well, can we spend a moment and go through the documents?"

"Very well, if we must."

"Won't take a jiffy." She drops a wad of papers down on my desk.

Much to my surprise, I'm being sent off with a bang. My retirement package is significant, and I'm being awarded some kind of generous military pension by the looks of it. I'll be set for life. I suspect this is my 'keep shtum' money. Good. I'll take the money and run, but I'm also taking the program. They don't need to know about that part, though.

Jana doesn't seem to have a clue what it is I do here. She furtively peers around at the cages, and flinches when Kong passes by. Clearly, she can't wait to leave this hellhole and get back to her safe personnel desk.

"Do you have any plans for your retirement? Travel the world, soak up the sun on a tropical beach? Oh, I'm so jealous!"

Jana seems to have more of a plan for my life than I do.

"Well, I hadn't given it much thought, to be honest."

Maybe I will take a holiday somewhere. Or maybe I'll try to find Spencer and ask what the bloody hell is going on.

"Sorry, Jana, you don't by chance know if my colleague, Spencer Jenkins, also retired, do you?"

"No, sorry, Never heard of that name."

I nod. "Never mind, then." I flash a disarming smile.

Jana leaves with all her paperwork signed. I'm to be out of here by the end of the day. But we'll see about that. My memo said I had 24 hours, so 24 hours is what I'll take. I need time to get everything ready.

Thankful for my stash of food in the freezer with the animal supplies; I heat a frozen meal in a microwave. I had once toyed with the idea to use a magnetron and the microwave frequency range in the FSMI process, but that didn't work out well for the unfortunate subjects. I quickly put that idea to bed. Still, handy for heating food.

The day has been another long one. Nothing new there, but I didn't come in this morning expecting to re-compile all my code and optimise it for human brain-waves. However, after a monumental effort with much hair-pulling and cursing, I think I have a functional system. I can't test it, of course. There's no time for that. I check my watch. Midnight.

The FSMI should take about seven or eight hours to run, and I imagine security guards will be at my door, waiting to escort me from the premises in about nine hours.

The clock is ticking.

It will be cramped in the new chamber, which was built for the likes of Kong, crammed full of lights, computer screens, speakers and all the mess of cabling. But I can just about squeeze in. The colour screens were a massive improvement to the efficiency. With those, I can display shifting patterns, animating and swooping around, which increases the data transfer rate immensely. They are quite beautiful in themselves, mesmerising and calming, a bit like the screen savers you get on modern home computers, but far more complex, and one hopes the home systems don't project spurious memories into one's brain. If they did, they could reprogram the brains of every schoolchild in the country over the course of afternoon computer class. Now there's a thought.

It will be hot, too. I crank the cabinet fans to maximum and flick on all the switches.

I'm nervous, to tell the truth. This could either work perfectly, as I'm sure it will, or I could wake up in the morning as a vegetable. If the signal is corrupted, it could wipe my memory completely, or worse, do some actual damage and I'll be screaming in pain from headaches for the rest of my presumably brief life.

It's a risk. I've seen poor subjects over the years writhe in torment after a bad download, but that was a long time ago. The process is proven now. Tested many, many times. Admittedly, not on a human, but I'm confident it will work. It will be fine. It has to be.

"Kong," She pads over to me and I stroke her head. "I need you to guard the door for me. Understand? Don't let anyone come in."

Kong squeals and hops from one foot to another then runs over to the door, turning the lock and then holding onto the handle.

I laugh. I'll miss her if I can't sneak her away somehow. We'll cross that bridge in the morning, assuming I survive.

"Very good. I'll see you soon."

Kong chirps in reply.

I climb into the chamber and sit down. I've rigged a remote trigger on a little box connected to the computers with a long length of wire. I shuffle to get comfortable, glance around at the various displays, convince myself it will be worth it in the end, and flip the switch.

A drone of bass bursts from the huge speakers around me, throbbing at my core. A squeal of high-pitched sine waves pulses out from the smaller speakers mounted around the top of the cabinet. All the screens flicker on with what looks like a snow pattern detuned signal, but in fact, the pattern is a kick-start to the process. A deep brainwave trigger that lulls one into a sense of calm and soporific state. I let the machines do their work, and feel my pulse slow. Don't panic, Evelyn. All will be good.

Patterns evolve on the screens, coming out from the mist and gradually undulating around. Growing, shrinking, merging and twisting. Colours fluctuate and flicker as the sounds change to a frequency I can't hear. I can feel the bass through my bottom, rising through my body. Pressure in my ears tells me that the high-frequency sounds are equally present. The patterns increase speed, spinning and zooming in and out. I lean back and let it all wash over me.

Minutes pass, and by now my limbs should be paralysed. I try to move a finger, and then an arm, but nothing happens. The process triggers a sleep state to prevent the subject from breaking out halfway through, which would be disastrous and possibly fatal. It is working. Everything is going exactly as it should. My eyes are fixed on the screens and the patterns sway and shake, spin and shiver, burning decades of work and research into my memory as I sit here. All I can do now is wait for the morning to find out what my fate will be.

TWENTY-THREE

SOME THINGS ARE UNKNOWABLE.

For example, there's no person, no computer, and no calculation that can precisely give the exact number of grains of sand on the planet right now. I don't mean an estimate, or a fairly accurate average, based on the amount of coastline, the approximate tonnage of a square kilometre of beach, and then divided by the weight of a single grain. No, I mean, **exactly** how many grains of sand are there on Earth right now? It isn't something that can be discovered or predicted. It might be something that a deity could tell you, but last I checked, they don't tend to communicate very often, and if they did, I'm sure there are more important questions we could ask them. Effectively, there are questions about the world to which we simply cannot know the answers. See also the number of blades of grass or oranges, or insert your chosen natural phenomenon.

It follows, then, that we can't expect to know the answer to other things. Things that seem more important, like for instance, why some people are absolute scumbags and why they are far more prevalent than you'd imagine.

But, in the grand scheme of things, from the perspective of a universe, grains of sand versus scumbags, it's all the same. All are born from the same source. All came from nothing, and will one day go back to nothing. So what does it matter?

The problem is that like grains of sand, the scumbags seem to be never-ending. If you take one out of the picture, another one will replace it almost immediately. I read something once about snails, or was it slugs? There has to be a certain number of them for a particular area. If you wipe some out, more will just appear. The same is true of drug dealers, thieves, abusers and general arseholes. There are too many to fight, and so overall, the situation doesn't change, ever.

After I took out that first drug dealer a couple of weeks ago, I read about it in the local paper. They said he was found unconscious after he made a call to emergency services from his phone. The police then found about £150,000 worth of drugs stashed in his grotty little flat, and at least £10,000 in cash. He was put out of business, and sent away to spend the rest of his days doing a lot of nothing in a small cell. To be honest, that's pretty much exactly what he was doing anyway, and I'm sure he can find a way to shift pharmaceuticals in jail, too. The difference now is he'll have hot meals provided courtesy of the taxpayer.

Have I done any good? I tell myself I have, but what it really means is that the kids who went to him will just go somewhere else for their fix.

Since then, I've done a nightly patrol of the town,

picking different areas where I thought there could be bad stuff happening, but aside from a few drunk fights on a Saturday night outside a club, I haven't struck lucky again with a nice neat package like the dealer. At least I'm getting my daily step count.

Perhaps, and I'm open to being wildly wrong on this, maybe being a vigilante server of justice isn't as great a job as it is cracked up to be.

The pay is terrible, too. Non-existent. In fact, it cost me twenty quid to find the dealer. I should have helped myself from his stash, but I didn't want to touch his filthy money.

I need to rethink my plan. Not that I had much of a plan in the first place. But this just isn't working.

I'm startled by my phone ringing. I grab it from my pocket and check the number. A local landline, but I don't know it. Curious, but also worrying. It could be someone who's traced me to the various incidents that have happened recently. I realised I haven't exactly been very careful in hiding my identity or fingerprints, and I've damaged several people now in ways that the police would most certainly want to discuss with me. I have worried about this, but not for too long. I harmed no one who didn't deserve it, and far less than deserved a beating. I have since invested in some gloves, at least.

I answer the phone.

"Hello?"

"Toby?"

A familiar voice in my ear changes my mood instantly. "Yes, is that Evelyn?"

"It is."

"Oh, hello. How did you get my number?"

"Never mind that, now. I need you to come to the home immediately."

"Right, of course. What's the matter?"

"My granddaughter is missing."

———

Outside of visiting hours, I need special approval from Nurse Rosey at the door to get into the care home. I think the staff are all secretly scared of Evelyn, and they probably should be. I'm guided into her room where she is sitting in the huge comfy armchair. So vast that it makes Evelyn look like a toy doll sitting in the middle of it. When the nurse leaves us, after checking if we need anything, Evelyn turns to me.

"Thank you for coming so quickly, Toby."

"No problem." In truth, I had no choice. Evelyn appears to have power over me. I felt a rush of adrenaline as she said the words, 'My granddaughter is missing.' And I immediately drove to the care home as fast as I could. I suspect this is something to do with her programming living inside my head. I reckon she baked in a formula that means I have no choice but to do her bidding. Plus, she's a lovely old lady, and why wouldn't I help her? She's changed my life. So, here I am. "What happened?"

"I don't know, and that's why I called you."

"Okay, well, what can you tell me?"

"She always, without fail, phones me on the twenty-second of every month for a chat. This month she didn't. Now it's the twenty-fifth, and she still hasn't been in touch." Evelyn motions to a phone on her bedside table. That is probably how she rang me earlier. I suppose the mobile phone revolution passed her by.

"Oh, well, perhaps she's just busy or something? It's only a few days?"

Evelyn shakes her head. "No, she always rings, no matter what."

"Did you try to call her?"

"Of course. It won't connect."

"Can I try the number?" I reach into my pocket for my phone.

Evelyn nods towards her bedside table, and a note-book that is on top. "Hand me the notebook, if you will."

I do. She flips through and finds a page, then hands the book back to me. "Here." She points to a number, handwritten in black ink.

I dial the number. A mobile, of course. A long pause while I wait for the connection, and I check my screen to make sure I have a signal. Eventually, a tone chirps out, then a recorded voice. "The number you have dialled is not in service." Then the call ends.

"Oh. Is it possible she got a new number or a new phone? Perhaps she lost it."

Evelyn looks at me with a mixture of anger and terror, then she takes a deep breath. "Toby, she is miss-ing. I want you to find her."

"Of course. I will."

"Very good. I knew you would."

"Can you tell me something about her? How old is she, what's her name, and home address?"

"I was getting to that. Her name is Cassie. Cassiopeia Andromeda Wright. She's thirty-two, …"

Something jolts in my brain, and I interrupt Evelyn. "Sorry, did you say Cassiopeia Andromeda?"

"Yes, her parents … well, they are hippies or something."

"No, it's just. I know her."

"What?" Evelyn looks up at me in shock.

"I met her once, in a pub. Well, an inn here in the town. She was staying there. We talked for a while." A stray beam of light casts a glimmer over a dark part of my memory. "Ah," I slap my forehead. "She told me she was visiting her gran who was one hundred! I mean, there can't be many other Cassiopeia Andromeda's who were visiting their one-hundred-year-old gran here, can there?"

"I shouldn't think so, no."

"Amazing! Small world."

"Indeed, but you don't know where she is?"

"No. I didn't even get her phone number, she told me she had a boyfriend, and that was that." Of course, now I have her number, but it doesn't work.

"A boyfriend?" Evelyn's eyes widen.

"Err, yes. Sorry, maybe I shouldn't have said."

"We need to find her, Toby, and any information is valuable."

"Yes, of course. I think his name was Brian."

"What else did she tell you?"

"Err, well," I scratch my head. "She works in some kind of environmental services company."

"Renewable energy, yes."

"Oh, yes. She said Brian worked with her at the same company. That's how they met."

"Hmm. She never mentioned this to me."

"Oh, well, perhaps she wasn't ready yet. I think it was early days."

Evelyn shakes her head. "Cassie is like the daughter I never had, but also a great friend. She would tell me. There's something sinister about this."

"When was the last time you heard from her?"

"Well, apparently just before you. My birthday. She came to visit for a few days."

I nod. "Right. Where does she live?"

"King's Lynn."

"Oh, yes. She said she lived far enough away." I check the distance with the map on my phone. About ninety miles. Less than two hours drive, on a good day.

"Do you have any other numbers for her, family, or friends?"

Evelyn shakes her head. "No."

"Where are her parents?"

"Australia, last I heard." She sighs. "Anthony, my son, ran away there a long time ago."

"Oh, funny. My brother lives there."

She raises an eyebrow. "Sydney?"

"No, Melbourne, I think." She nods, knowingly. "Have you gone to the police?"

Evelyn scoffs. "Of course, not. Bunch of chocolate teapots." She looks away and down at the carpet.

"I'm sure she's fine," I try to reassure the old lady, "Presumably, she hasn't just vanished. She has a job, they would look for her. I'm sure there's just a problem with her phone, something silly like that."

Evelyn seems to break from her trance, staring at the patterns on the floor. "Yes, you are probably right. Still, I would like you to find out. I'm far too old to be gallivanting around. You must be my eyes and hands."

"Yes, of course. I will do my best." A thought occurs to me. "Do you know the name of the company she works for?"

"Oh, yes. It will be in the notepad." She picks it up again. "EverGreen Power."

I tap the name into my phone and immediately get their website. I scroll down, find the 'Contact Us' link, and twenty seconds later, I'm connected to their receptionist on speakerphone so Evelyn can hear.

"EverGreen Power, how may I help you?"

"Hello, can you put me through to Cassie Wright, please?"

"Certainly, who shall I say is calling?"

Ah, what do I say now? I told her my name in the pub that day. If she remembers me, she'll assume I'm a stalker or something and not answer. I fluster. "Mike." I shrug and make a face at Evelyn. "Mike Wazowski. She was working on an energy quote for me."

"One moment please, Mr Wazowski."

Evelyn smiles at me, "Very smart, Mike."

The voice returns to the phone. "Hello, sorry to keep you. I'm afraid Miss Wright is out of office at the moment. Can someone else help you?" Evelyn's face turns stony.

"Oh, out of office? Do you know when she'll be back?"

"I'm afraid not."

"Okay, thanks. I'll call back another day."

"No problem, thank you for calling EverGreen Power."

I hang up and turn back to Evelyn. "Well, seems like Cassie took a holiday."

"She didn't mention that to me. This is most unusual."

"Well, perhaps it was a spur-of-the-moment thing. Maybe she went off somewhere with her new chap?"

"Dear boy, I don't think you understand. Cassie simply would not do that. But if she did, she would tell me. I brought her up, cared for her, taught her everything I know." She pauses. "No, not everything. Some things I couldn't tell anyone," she points a finger at me, "except you, Toby Steele."

I nod. "I remember Cassie telling me you taught her. She thinks extremely highly of you."

"As I do her. So, believe me when I tell you, this isn't right. There is something amiss and you must help me find out what."

"Yes. Of course, I will." A stray memory returns to me, like a tiny bird who flew away and now lands back on my finger, pecking at a palm full of seeds. "Ah, I may have sort of mentioned to Cassie about the frequency stuff." I sheepishly grimace.

"What?"

"Well, I had no idea what was going on, and she seemed … er, well, she seemed the type who would listen."

"Were you chatting up my granddaughter?" Evelyn scowls.

"I … sorry, I mean, she is very beautiful." I hold up

my hands. "She wasn't interested if that makes it better?"

"Men!" Evelyn chuckles. "Always the same. Never mind. How much did you tell her?"

"I was trying to figure out what had happened to me, I said something about being able to 'feel' frequencies." I shrug.

"Hmm, well, never mention it again. Cassie doesn't know about my work. No one does. No one could."

"Tell me all the details you know. Address, what car she has, what food she likes, where she likes to shop, anything that may help me find her, and I will go immediately." I pause. "I will find Cassie for you, and she will be safe and fine. You'll see."

Evelyn slowly nods. "Toby, you are the one person on the planet I can trust to do exactly that."

CHAPTER
TWENTY-FOUR

14:37, THURSDAY, JANUARY 18TH,
1990. ALL SAINTS MATERNITY
HOSPITAL, GLASTONBURY.

"SHE'S BEAUTIFUL!" I stare down at the tiny face born only minutes ago, swaddled in towels and blankets, and held in my arms, barely weighing anything at all. Innocent and truly amazing. My eyes are wet with joy.

My granddaughter. I never imagined I'd be able to say those words, but here we are. Finally, Anthony did something right. No doubt, by accident, but nevertheless.

Her mother is still out of it. I thought being a 'child of nature' or whatever it is they call themselves, that she'd go natural, but apparently, she always prefers drugs to reality. Can't say I blame her.

"Isn't she?" Anthony comes back into the room. After the birth, he immediately went outside for a smoke break. Said he needed to chill out for a bit because it was all a bit too hectic. I could wallop the boy sometimes.

"Have you chosen a name?"

Anthony hesitates, "Yes. We have."

"Well, spit it out. What is it?"

"Cassiopeia Andromeda." He pauses for effect. "And Wright, of course, for Dad."

I can see in his eyes he expects me to be shocked by this choice, but no, I think it's a lovely name. "Beautiful. Cassie, for short?"

"Yes. Cassie."

"Conceived under the stars?" I chuckle. "No, don't tell me."

Anthony smirks. "Some things are better left unknown. May I hold my daughter, mother?"

"Have you washed your hands?"

"Yes, of course."

"Very well, then." I stand up and reluctantly pass the little bundle over to my son. Her father, for better or for worse. "I'll go check on Susan. Don't drop her."

"Don't worry, I know what to do." He smiles, and for a moment, I feel the warmth and love of family. "Sue will be out of it for a while yet. Go get a cuppa or something, if you want. You've been here all day."

"Right, yes. Good idea. Stretch my legs."

Walking the hospital corridors takes me back to my days at the MRC all those years ago. They always smell the same, don't they? So much emotion tied up in these walls. Makes me wonder, yet again, what could have happened to Spencer. I tried to find him, scoured and searched, and even filed a missing person's report with the police, but of course, that was fruitless. They told me that no information was available, and that as a grown man, he could vanish if he wanted to. I'm sure that if they really made any investigations, they were quickly and quietly put to bed by invisible agents working above the law.

Perhaps Spencer finally got his wish to go off-grid. Maybe he's in a log cabin in the mountains, or on a beach in Tahiti. Or, maybe he was 'taken care of' and he sleeps with the fishes. It seems like I'll never know. Cynthia and Ian, too. No sign of any of them.

A triple disappearing act, pulled off nicely by Her Majesty's Government. I suppose I should be thankful they didn't make me 'go away' as well.

I should also be thankful that my FSMI process didn't wipe my brain or kill me. But I have only myself to thank for that, and Kong of course, who kept watch over me as the computer programmed my memories. Poor Kong. I often wonder what happened to her. I tried to take her home with me that morning after the process, but they wouldn't let me. Said she was the property of the facility. Property, indeed! She's an intelligent being. I should have set them all loose, but how would they have survived? I miss that tiny creature.

The process worked. It worked bloody perfectly, even though I do say so myself. I'm rather proud of it, not that I can tell a soul. Project Flash Gordon, after all those years of research, testing, trial and error, mostly error, long, long hours and sacrifice, all for nothing in the end. But I know it worked. If I could just have added the finishing touches, the world could be a very different place now.

Of course, I already knew a good chunk of the database, all the languages and general knowledge came from my brain in the first place, but the rest, well, it was quite an eye-opener. The input from Dickie Bligh, and the other military folks who gave their knowledge to my database, was fascinating to capture, but even more so to have that experience now available in my brain. It doesn't surface much, but in times of need, I've greatly benefited from that knowledge. I'm an old woman, though, not a fighter. I'm hardly going to fend off a group of assailants, and thankfully, in my relatively sheltered life, I've never had to. However, I was once mugged walking through London a couple of years ago. The chap picked the wrong old lady to steal from. He found himself pinned to a wall, arm twisted up his back, and the pathetic little knife he was wielding held to his gasping throat, until someone called for the police. Self-defence classes, I told them and a cheer came from the crowd of onlookers.

The practical skills are one thing, but the more esoteric functions that I built into the program are quite something else. Based on nothing but speculation and reading between the lines of a Russian paper, hacked and stolen by the Americans, stashed away on a hidden database, then stolen again by me. I wondered if it would really work. It wasn't something I could give to Kong for testing. How would she have explained the experience to me? No, this required a human test subject, and that started and ended with me.

More than a sixth sense, this is a two-way thing. A transceiving effect. I receive the feelings, but I can also send them to people, and even some objects with differing results I haven't been able to fully categorise yet. Quite amazing, really, and it raises so many questions about the human brain. Are we all naturally capable of this function? Have we just lost the ability over the millennia? What other skills do we have the potential for that we now lack? I had planned various other programmes for testing that I didn't have time to implement.

If we had retained all these skills, the world would be a different place now. Would it be better or worse? I don't know. Ironic that it was likely the progress of technology that eroded our brain functions over time, and now, with the application of technology, I could bring it back.

When I picked up little Cassie just now, I could feel her frequency. Her unique, new, vibrant and clear energy. I know she will grow up to do great things, and I intend to make her my protégé. Anthony and Susan won't teach her anything useful. I could never make him interested in the sciences. I think he resented my work, and no doubt that was my fault. My son grew up without me, because I was always too busy working. Even when I was at home, my head was always in a bundle of papers, books, and documents. I missed every school play, sports day, parents' evening, and his entire childhood. Gerald, may he rest in peace, took care of all that. I'm not sure I ever made it clear how grateful I was that he did. A fact I remind myself of daily.

I have so much regret that I don't know what to do with it all.

I didn't choose my career. Government agents coerced me into it. However, I suppose they didn't force me to work all hours God sent. That was my choice. I could have taken more holidays, spent the weekends away from work, or left it at the office doors, but no, I had to be brilliant. I had to make it work, and for all my sacrifice, in the end, they just flicked a switch and turned my project off. All traces of it were deleted, wiped, and put to bed. Project Flash Gordon never officially existed, and yet I wasted my life on it. Who is the fool, at the end of the day?

Little did I know back in those huts at Bletchley, working with Turing to decode the war, that the rest of my life would be so defined and coloured by my actions there.

Well, no more. I'm free of the burden of work, I have adequate funds and God knows I have plenty of time to fill. I will make up for all my years of neglect by making sure little Cassie reaches the stars that she's named after. She will be my saving grace and my second chance at a family. I may be old, but I'm not done yet. There's plenty of fight left in this old bat, yet.

CHAPTER TWENTY-FIVE

SOMETHING OCCURRED to me on the drive to King's Lynn; what do I tell Cassie when I find her? How can I explain that suddenly I know her grandmother, without telling her the whole complicated backstory of Project Flash Gordon, which I have been told clearly not to ever tell anyone, and let's face it, she probably wouldn't believe me if I tried.

A lot has changed since I met Cassie in that bar. Back then, I worked night shift tech support, and did not know that I'd just had my brain upgraded courtesy of Evelyn. Now I have no job, and I've committed a variety of what some might think of as crimes, but I prefer to define them as justice.

Cross that bridge when I get to it, I suppose. First, I need to find her.

I'm armed with some details that Evelyn could tell me. The address, which is where I'm heading, the type of car she drives, and a bit more about the work she does. Other than that, Evelyn wasn't aware of any particular friends, and certainly didn't know about the boyfriend. As I said to Cassie that day, he can't be anything special, but he's first on my list to question. Brian from her work. Can't be too hard to find?

I'm going into this as a total newbie. I've never done an investigation like this, and I haven't got a clue where to start, so I'm hoping that my Flash Gordon database has something to help me.

My phone informs me that I have arrived at Cassie's house. She lives in a nice enough suburban area. Not ostentatious and not a slum. Nicer than my area, for sure. I park on the road outside and get out of the car. Stretching my legs after the long drive, I glance up and down casually to see if there are many folks around. Thankfully not, but I nod a hello to a passing jogger and then walk up the path to the house.

I knock on the door, because what else should I do? I wait a long minute and knock again. No answer.

I know she's not at work, and now I know she's not at home. I can see through the frosted glass front door, that there are quite a few items of junk mail littering the hallway. Obviously junk, because genuine letters don't come in colourful envelopes.

Her car is here, too. She didn't drive anywhere. I wander up to it and peer through the windows. Nothing strange as far as I can tell. Clean and tidy.

I reckon the art of not looking suspicious is not to try too hard. Without glancing around, I casually go through the little gate to the back garden and go straight to the wheelie bins, opening the lids. Half full, both of them. I go back out to the street and look up and down, but I don't see anyone's bins out. I make a mental note to check the schedule later. I return to the back garden. There's a little shed at the bottom, not locked. I go in and look around in the gloom, but it's your common garden shed. Pots of half-used paint, a stepladder, a few tools and some bags of soil, cardboard boxes from an expensive and hefty-looking desktop computer and a huge new TV, a bike that is ancient and rusty, and a stack of empty plastic plant pots.

I look back out at the house. The curtains are closed upstairs, and downstairs each window is swathed in white netting. It's pretty obvious, there's no one here, and she intended to go away somewhere for at least a few days. I exit and go back to the car, peeking at the front of the house on the way. Same story as the back.

I search for a nearby coffee shop, not least because I need a bio-break, and to pause for a moment and come up with a plan. So far, I know Cassie isn't in the two most likely places she should be, but that doesn't tell me much at all.

I drive away because I don't want nearby curtains to twitch if I linger here too long.

Evelyn asked me to ring her when I had some news, and I wonder if a lack of information is still news. I'll ponder over a coffee and toasted sandwich first. No sense in worrying Evelyn unnecessarily. I'm still sure that there's nothing nefarious about this at all, and that Cassie just went off on a break. It happens, and perhaps she wasn't ready to tell her gran the story of the boyfriend just yet.

But it is a little strange that her phone would be off. I dial it once again to be sure, and get the same message, 'the number you have dialled is not in service'. Where in the world could she have gone where there's no service for this long, or did she just forget to take her charger? No, none of that adds up. You can buy a spare charger almost anywhere now, and even if you pass through an area of no phone service, unless you are literally up a mountain somewhere, you'll be back in reach of technology soon enough.

I wonder if Cassie ever travels for work. Perhaps she went to visit a customer site somewhere crazy like an offshore wind farm. That might fit the criteria of not having phone service.

Something to think about.

Sandwich and coffee acquired, I do what everyone does these days in coffee shops, and open up a laptop in front of me. I connect to the free Wi-Fi and open a browser in anonymous mode, then search for Cassie. I start with social media; the obvious place to start with any person search. The bulk of the world's population are all quite happy to share their entire life story in a public open forum, often with photos or even videos. 'I've got nothing to hide', they would tell you, but imagine going up to a stranger in the street and asking them 'Where did you go for your birthday night out?' or 'When is your wedding anniversary?' or even 'Can you show me a video of your kids playing?' You'd be arrested in minutes, and yet all of that, and much, much more, is freely available online. Strange behaviour.

Not so with Cassie, however. I find her Facebook page quickly. You'd think there wouldn't be many 'Cassiopeia's' on Facebook, but I'm surprised that there are a good few dozen. Still, I could narrow her down quickly from the profile photo. Tiny and probably a few years old, but unmistakable regardless. Trouble is, her profile is set to private. I can't see anything apart from her photo and an empty page. I'm not her 'friend' so I'm stuck behind this wall of white space. I wonder about sending a friend request but decide against it. She may or may not remember my name from the pub that afternoon, but again, I don't want to seem like a stalker, even if that is now exactly what I am. For a good cause, though.

I try Instagram and find the same situation. A different photo, this time, better quality, probably more recent and zoomed in on her smiling face. Quite beautiful, as previously noted, but I can't glean any data from this source, either. Cassie must be savvy about her internet use, and good on her for that. Doesn't help me, though.

A search on Twitter shows she doesn't have an account, and Google fares no better. Back to the same empty bucket of information that I found when I previously searched for Evelyn. It used to be much easier to find people, but these days it seems the data is better hidden.

I'm left scratching my head and waving down a waitress for more coffee.

Thirty minutes of fruitless googling later, and I'm no further forward than when I came into the cafe. I get up to leave with no plan on where I'll go next. I slide my laptop back into my backpack and go to the counter to pay. I can't just sit here all day.

I'm distracted by a loud laugh behind me. I turn as two suited businessmen enter, mid banter, overly testosterone-fuelled, slicked-back hair and obnoxious as only salespeople can be. They sit down at a table and carry on their conversation, opening up laptops and notebooks as they do. A 'face-to-face' meeting. The old-fashioned way of doing business. I turn away with a shudder, but they spark an idea in my brain.

In my car, I search for a men's clothes shop nearby and quickly find a few to choose from. I need a suit and a new pair of shoes, maybe a shave, too, while I'm at it.

———

"Hello, my name is Paul Underdown. I've been working with, err …" I pause and look at my phone screen, pretending to look up the name. "Cassie Wright, yes that's her, on an energy proposal, and I was just passing by town so I thought I might pop in and say hello." I smile at the receptionist "She's been so helpful, you see, I wanted to say thank you."

"Do you have an appointment?"

"No, no. I didn't think to make one. Sorry, I expect she's busy, I should have called, first. I'm all over the place!" I wave my phone around then shrug and grin like a fool. "We're very casual at my office. I forget other companies are more rigid."

"No, that's fine Mr Underdown. Let me see if she's available. Please, take a seat."

Three hundred quid later, and I feel like a total dickhead in a brand new suit and shoes, stubble gone and neatly shaved in the Sainsbury's bathrooms, hair brushed and tied back, and an unhealthy amount of aftershave splashed all over. But I look the part, or at least I seem to. I went for dark navy blue trousers and a jacket with a white shirt and a deep green tie. Subtle elements of authority and earth tones. If I had shown up at Cassie's office looking like my normal self, I probably wouldn't have got in the door before they called the police.

"Thank you." I smile and look around, finding two low chairs in front of a large TV showing some promotional crap about the company, EverGreen Power.

The video is an emotional loop of wind generators out at sea, and a drone zoom over a field of solar panels, then school kids, animals in fields, flocks of birds, all that sort of thing. Very inspiring.

I chose my pseudonym from a random person on Facebook, and my reason to be here is based on a mythical conversation that Cassie obviously hasn't been having, about moving the power usage at BioDigi Pharmaceutical to be one hundred per cent renewable by 2028. A laudable goal, but I'm not convinced there's anyone there who cares enough to pursue it. You never know, maybe this will spark them to look into it.

"Mr Underdown?" The receptionist girl calls me over to the desk again.

"Hello, yes."

"Miss Wright isn't at work today, I'm afraid."

"Oh, that's a shame." I look downhearted. Of course, I knew this to be the case already. "Well, I've come a long way. Is her manager around, perhaps, or someone else in her department? I wanted to ask some questions about the proposal, you see." I flash a smile and a hopeful look.

"Let me check. Err, sorry what company did you say you were from, again?"

"BioDigi Pharmaceutical."

"Right, please take a seat again and I'll see who I can find for you."

I nod a polite thanks and sit back down on the low chairs staring up at the TV, while the reception girl makes a call. No one wants drama in their workplace, and if you are overly polite, you can schmooze your way through all manner of corporate bullshit.

"Someone will be down to meet you shortly, Mr Underdown."

"Ah, lovely, thank you so much."

Who will they send out? I'm hoping it will be Brian, the boyfriend, but although I know he works here, I don't know if he is in the same department as Cassie. I don't have much of a plan past this point. I suppose I didn't even think I'd make it this far before being caught, or just told to piss off, so from here on in I'm winging it. I do know some details about BioDigi, of course, but if anyone goes digging too deep, I'm screwed.

At least two security cameras are visible as I look around the foyer.

"Hello, I'm Rachel Hazlewood, Cassie's manager. How can I help you?" A woman approaches me from a doorway behind the reception desk, hand outstretched to shake. I stand up and walk towards her.

Time slows down, and the distance between our

outstretched hands seems infinite. We stay frozen mid-stride while a tsunami of thoughts crashes against my brain. Rachel, a woman in her mid-forties, brunette, laughter lines, nothing on her ring finger. A simple silver heart-shaped necklace that hangs over minor work-friendly cleavage. Deep red fingernails, muted lipstick and a perfume that's light and fruity for day use. Slight heels, black tights, a business suit that can't be comfortable. A skirt that seems too tight, and a jacket with slight shoulder pads. Are we doing shoulder pads again, or did the 80s call? A plan fizzles into existence and then slides to the front of my mind. I have to schmooze this woman and extract information from her. She won't be expecting this, I need to know where Cassie is, and there's no way that I'd get that information asking for it straight out. I need to call on my powers. She's a manager at a green energy company, so she's, therefore, likely to be all about the environment and saving the planet. I can use that information.

By the time our palms touch and our eyes make contact, my plan is created, checked, extrapolated and saved, ready for action. I deploy my skills immediately as I squeeze Rachel's hand and shake. I focus on warmth, comfort, passion and spontaneous actions based on random chance. We just met, and this is crazy, but you're going to tell me everything, and I don't mean maybe.

"Paul Underdown. Pleased to meet you." I continue shaking for a little longer, noticing a gentle blush on Rachel's cheeks. I focus more, and feel a burst of energy flow through my hand into her. Sex bomb deployed and target hit.

"Lovely to meet you, too, Paul." She smiles and I sense her pulse increase and pupils dilate. I play to it and move closer to her. "How can I help?"

"Well, I just wanted to ask some questions about the energy sources and things."

"Certainly. Err, gosh, it's warm in here, isn't it? Perhaps we can go for coffee somewhere?"

"Sure." I shrug. "That sounds great."

"Cassie didn't mention she was working with you, or your company, BioDigi Pharmaceutical, did you say?"

"Yes, that's right. Err, well it's very informal so far. Nothing is decided. I'm just sort of trying to gauge the lay of the land, as it were. We're hoping to implement a total renewable carbon-neutral energy supply. Early stages yet."

I take a sip of the coffee I didn't want, having had a bucket of it already today. We went across the road to another little cafe near the office. Rachel insisted she paid.

"Wonderful, well I'm sure we can assist with that. Do you know your annual energy usage?"

Shit. Of course I don't. "Well, it varies, we don't do any manufacturing here, anymore, but there are various research labs and data centres." I change the subject. "Cassie mentioned another chap, err …" I snap my fingers as if trying to remember. "Brian, something. God my memory. I can't think of his name now."

"Oh, Brian Sullivan?"

"Yes! That's him. I think he works with her?"

"That's right. Were you talking to Brian as well?"

"No, she said he would look at some calculations though. Maybe I'm getting mixed up."

"He's new in the team. Just joined us a couple of months ago. Quick, though. I'm sure he'll be able to help you with your numbers."

"Great. Is he in the office today?"

"Ah, no, sorry he's on holiday, too I'm afraid."

"Oh!" I laugh. "Did they go together?"

Rachel nods then leans in and whispers. "Yes, I think they are an item, but don't say I told you." She grabs my arm, and I take the opportunity to burst out a little more passionate energy in her direction. "Brian organised it all as a surprise for Cassie. Very romantic." Rachel varnishes the word 'romantic' with a heavy dollop of sweet syrup.

"Oh, right." I tap the side of my nose. "Hope they went somewhere nice?"

"Spain, I think."

"Lovely. Do you know when they'll be back?"

"Week on Monday. They took two weeks off."

"All right for some, isn't it? Can't remember when I had two weeks' holiday."

Rachel laughs much too hard. I think she's a little drunk from the frequencies I'm pumping out. Maybe I should pull back a little, in case things get out of hand.

"Are you in town for long?" She looks me dead in my eyes, brushing a strand of hair away from her face.

"Just passing through, today. I might pop back a week on Monday, though and tie things up with Brian and Cassie."

I stand up to leave. "Thank you for the coffee, and look forward to working with your company."

"Oh, yes. Absolutely. Do let me know if you need anything, Paul." She grabs my arm again, squeezing a little harder, this time. Then she reaches into her purse and pulls out a business card, handing it to me. "Do you have one?"

"Oh, thank you. No, I'm just getting some new ones printed, but I'll drop you an email when I get back to my office. Thank you so much."

"Please do." She smiles and looks at me in a way that's hard to misinterpret. For a moment, I wonder if I should go for it, but I may yet need her help again, so best to save it for another time. Leave them wanting. I make my excuses, say my goodbyes, and get the hell out before she starts panting.

CHAPTER TWENTY-SIX

"HELLO, Evelyn. Toby here. Cassie is in Spain."

"Spain?"

"Yes, that's what her manager told me. Two weeks' holiday in Spain."

There's silence on the phone. I called Evelyn from the car as I headed back home. It seems like this case is cut, dry and solidly closed so I don't know what else I can do here. Cassie has been whisked away for a romantic break by her new boyfriend. Lucky her.

"She'll be back at work a week on Monday, so I'm told." The silence continues for a little too long. "Hello? Are you still there?"

"Yes, I'm thinking."

"Right. I'm heading back now. I'll check in again next Monday if you like? Make sure all is well."

"Hold on, Toby."

"Okay …" I'm glad I changed back into my normal clothes in the supermarket toilets. I couldn't stand to wear a suit all day, every day. No idea how people do it.

"Did you check at her house?"

"I did. She's not there, obviously."

"Nothing suspicious?"

"No." I shrug, but then remember Evelyn can't see me through the phone.

"Spain …" Evelyn seems to be talking to herself. "Why would she go to Spain?"

"The boyfriend, Brian, organised it as some kind of surprise."

"Who is this Brian?"

"Brian Sullivan. I got his name from the manager." I'm hoping Evelyn doesn't ask me how I extracted the information. Not my proudest moment, using my horny projection skills to bend a woman around my finger, but I'm sure plenty of people have done much worse. "I know little else."

"How long have they been together?"

"Well, Rachel, the manager lady, said Brian was new. A couple of months. I'm guessing around that long at the most."

"Seems quick to be rushing off to Spain for two weeks, doesn't it?"

"Well, I mean, a little, but you know how things go … with, err, romance, I mean."

Evelyn scoffs. "A long time ago, Toby, dear boy. What surprise? It can't be any kind of anniversary."

"True. I don't know, to be honest. Spontaneity, perhaps?" Evelyn mumbles something I can't hear. "Well, anyway …" I can feel the awkwardness building up through the phone. "I think it's fairly clear all is well, don't you?"

"No, I don't."

"Oh. Right."

"Don't mobile phones work in Spain?"

"Ah, yes. I wondered that, too, but maybe she forgot her charger, or it broke, or something silly like that."

"No. I don't like it one bit. Did you go in?"

"Into her house? No, of course not."

"Go back to the house, get inside, look around. Find what you can."

"Sorry, what? You want me to break into her house?"

"I don't have a key, so yes, you must gain entry somehow. You ought to be perfectly capable."

"But, why?"

"I don't know, Toby, but this isn't right. Trust me on this. Don't worry, I will pay you for your time and expenses."

"Oh, I …"

"I know you don't have a job, and I feel responsible for you now you are, well, Flash Gordon … and I've asked you to do a job for me, so of course, I should pay you."

"Right. Well, thank you."

"We can work out the details later, but don't concern yourself with expenses. Whatever it takes, you will find my Cassie."

"Yes, of course." I sort of thought I had, but apparently not. I pull into a petrol station and turn around, heading back to King's Lynn the way I came with a silent sigh.

"Find out everything you can about this Brian. I

don't like the sound of him at all. Spontaneity, indeed!" She spits the words out.

If I'm honest, I don't much like the sound of this Brian chap, either, but my reasoning is different. "Cassie is a grown woman … I mean, she knows what she's doing."

"Toby!" Evelyn's tone changes and I feel a shiver go down my spine. "Just do as I say."

"Right, yes. Of course."

"Find a hotel for the night, wait until after dark, check the house and look for anything strange. There's something very fishy about all this, and I promise you we will get to the bottom of it."

"Okay, understood. It will get dark soon. I'm going to find a hardware shop and buy some tools and things, then."

"Very well, keep the receipts. And for heaven's sake, don't get caught, Toby."

"I'll do my best."

———

The average door lock is barely more than an ornament when it comes to providing home security. An illusion of safety and protection. Of course, we all still use them, because it is a step up from leaving the door wide open, but if someone wants to get into your house, a small metal puzzle isn't a challenge.

I furnished myself with some basic tools at the local hardware superstore; a can of WD40, a packet of paper-clips, an Allen key and screwdriver set, as well as a hammer, wire cutters, and a hacksaw, just in case.

Another flashlight, because I left my usual hefty one at home, and a pack of rubber gloves.

I also did what Evelyn suggested — found a local hotel, and booked myself a room for the night. Then I went back to the supermarket and acquired basic toiletries and a change of underwear. No sense in being unhygienic.

Over dinner in a pub next to the hotel, I applied the same social media searching techniques on 'Brian Sullivan', but this came up with nothing useful. There are many such people, but I couldn't narrow any of them down to King's Lynn. I think I'll need to look elsewhere for some clues before I can gather anything useful on this chap. I know he's worked at Evergreen Power for about two months, and that he's booked flights to Spain recently. That's about it, so far.

I'm hoping to find something around Cassie's house, assuming I get in, and assuming I don't get caught.

I park my car a few streets away and walk to her house at just after midnight. Not too late to attract attention, and not too early to be busy.

I go straight to the back of the house without looking around or up at any neighbours' houses. A light comes on and I feel a pounding in my chest, but it's an automatic sensor lamp over the back door. I shrug it off. It will help me see what I'm doing, and everyone has lights. Nothing strange here, move along.

I have the equipment stashed in various pockets. First the rubber gloves, then I pull out the little can of WD40 and spray a generous amount into the lock. Then I jam a tiny Allen key into the keyhole, wedge in a straightened paperclip and wiggle it just so. Somehow, well not somehow I suppose, but I seem to know exactly what I'm doing as if I've done this hundreds of times before, even though I don't think I've ever tried to pick a lock before in my life. A strange feeling. I'm quite shocked when the lock turns open in less than thirty seconds. I must remember to thank Evelyn again for all these talents. I chuckle as I push open the door and quietly close it behind me.

I'm in the kitchen.

I wait for thirty seconds, listening intently in case there's an alarm, but there is nothing but silence. The house is dark, and I wonder if I should turn on the lights or wander around with my torch. If someone sees a torch light beam, that is surely more suspicious than just normal room lights. There is a blind in the kitchen window, so I pull it down slowly, but it clashes against a pot of wooden spoons which falls over into the sink, clattering loudly, sending adrenaline pounding around my body. I freeze and wait another minute, but nothing happens. Christ, I need to be careful.

Blind now down, I flick on the light and blink as my eyes adjust. Nice clean kitchen; everything is as normal as you'd expect. Kettle, microwave, toaster, bananas in a bowl going brown. I open the fridge and find an assortment of food and half a carton of milk. Cassie left in a hurry.

I go through into the living room, pull the curtains and then flick on a standing lamp. There's a dining table at one end, cluttered with ornaments and a candle-powered scented oil burner with some liquid on the top. I bend down to smell heady lavender perfume. There's a burned-out tea light candle inside.

A single chair pulled out from the table and a space clear in front of it. Presumably where Cassie eats her dinner. On the right, there's a stack of clean beer mats, and one of them is next to it alone, ringed with coffee stains.

I look around the room, a vast television at the other end mounted on the wall. Looks new. A couch in front of it and a small coffee table. A bookshelf and another selection of candles on top. Nothing strange. I move on through the hallway, lit by the streetlamp outside through the frosted glass. The pile of junk mail accumulates under the letterbox. Downstairs toilet, clean and empty. I go upstairs.

I'm feeling increasingly weird as I do this. This is wrong. I shouldn't be poking around someone's house like this, but I'm just doing what Evelyn asked, no, told me to do. I still don't see evidence of foul play, but who am I to say what is wrong or right? Evelyn obviously cares for her granddaughter; if she thinks this is abnormal, then I suppose she's correct. Still, I can't help feeling like a creep. I go into the bedroom and the creepy feeling increases exponentially. I'm not going to rifle through her knicker drawer, but I may as well be. As I look around the room, I feel my cheeks redden. A bed, a dressing table, bedside table with a phone charger cable sticking out from behind it. There's something. I guessed she may have forgotten a phone charger in the hurry to go to Spain, but everyone has more than one phone charger, these days. I have at least four in my house and one in a travel bag. Probably means nothing.

I open the wardrobe and something else strikes me as a little odd. A suitcase is tucked into the bottom. A good one that looks a little worn, but hard-case and solid. Why didn't she pack her luggage in that? Don't know if I should read anything into this, maybe she has a better one, or maybe it was too big for her trip. I move on.

The bathroom is clean, which is more than I can say for my house. I open a medicine cabinet and a packet of contraceptive pills falls out into the sink. Checking the prescription date reveals it was issued about three weeks ago. I open the box and slide out the plastic sheet. There's two weeks' supply left, meaning she was taking them until about a week ago. Weird, wouldn't she want to take those on a romantic trip, or maybe she changed her mind and wants to get pregnant?

There are two other rooms upstairs. One with some gym equipment in it; a static bike and a rowing machine, a wooden floor, and a Bluetooth speaker, shelves on one side with some more books, mostly text-books of physics and chemistry. Maybe she's been studying for a degree or something?

The last room is a guest bedroom. A small bed pushed to one side, a bedside table and another wardrobe which contains a few dresses, some shoes and a box marked 'Xmas decorations'.

Cassie is extremely organised, it seems.

I go back down the stairs, remembering to turn off all the lights.

Well, aside from some minor inconsistencies, there's

nothing obviously untoward. What did Evelyn think I would find here?

I go back to the kitchen, turn the light off and pull the blind back up as it was when I got here, then quietly open the door to leave.

A glint of light reflects from something at the end of the garden. I freeze. Did it move? I squint and wait a moment for my eyes to adjust to the night. The shed, of course. A lamp post is reflecting on the tiny window of the shed. Nothing to worry about. I move to pull the door closed behind me.

Hang on … the shed.

Before the kitchen door is fully closed, I stop and open it again. I go back into the house. A quick circuit of the entire house confirms it. There's something significant missing here.

I prop the kitchen door open with a chair from the dining table, and then slip down to the shed. Inside, I shine my torch around and find what I'm looking for. The computer box. An enormous lump of a thing. I slide it out and open the lid. Empty, of course. Who would keep a computer in a shed? I look around the sides and find the shipping label. It was delivered here last year, on November 30th to C. Wright, at this address. Checks out. So, where is the computer?

The PC box tells me the model number, and a quick search online tells me this machine would be a powerful beast. A gaming desktop machine with a crazy expensive GPU in it. Cassie is a gamer? I take a few photos of the box and the label details for reference. There's another box that's slimmer for a 4K monitor to complement the PC. Same delivery date.

I go back to the house again and do a slow, thorough check of every room. Even poking around the big TV and all the shelves near it. There's no sign of the computer. No cables, no mouse and keyboard, and no game controllers anywhere, either.

She wouldn't have taken this with her? It probably weighs a ton. You take a laptop on a holiday, not a massive tower PC.

Okay, now something is solidly fishy.

The only place in this house where a giant desktop computer could have sat was at the dining table.

I sit down at the table in the empty space and imagine how Cassie might have sat here. The screen could have been on the table, keyboard and mouse in front of it, and the tower would likely have been underneath. I get up, pull out the chair and get down on the floor, shining the torch under the table, but find precisely zero computers. There is a four-way surge-protecting power extension lead with nothing plugged into it, and some indentations in the carpet, like alien crop circles where the feet of the computer likely would have sat. I snap more photos of the scene. Coffee ring-stained beer mat, a table that was used as a desk, and no sign of the powerful gaming computer that should be under it. Has it been stolen? It certainly would have been valuable. Maybe four or five thousand for the full set-up.

Aside from me, there's no sign of a break-in here. If someone nicked the PC, they likely had a key, or the skill to pick a lock as cleanly as I did. Someone who knew it was here, not a chance robbery.

I go back to the front hallway. There's a network

router plugged in on a low table next to the door. Tiny green lights flash on and off. She has a broadband internet connection. Of course, she does. I pull out my phone, connect to her Wi-Fi, read the password from the back of the router and hope she hasn't changed it from the default. She hasn't, and I'm quickly connected. I then open a browser on my phone and log into the router maintenance screen to check the uptime; ninety-eight days. Connected devices; three. My phone and two smart plugs. They are named 'living room lamp' and 'bedside lamp' so no ambiguity there. She probably has those things turning on and off on a schedule, controlled over Wi-Fi. There aren't any computers that I've somehow missed, hidden away in cupboards. No cameras, either. There are no static rules set and no open ports. In other words, this network was plugged in months ago by the installer and has never been touched since. I disconnect from the box and put it back how it was on the table.

I check the time; after one in the morning. Too late to bother Evelyn now. I don't want to wake her up and worry her, but this is certainly something strange.

I leave the house quietly, walking casually back to my car and then head to my hotel, wondering how I should explain this to Evelyn tomorrow morning. She will have to know about the computer. I suppose there's a chance that Cassie could have sold the PC recently to make money for something, but that seems unlikely. It was only five months old. Maybe it broke, and she sent it back to the manufacturer? However, in both cases, you'd think she would have put it back into the original packaging. Why else would she keep that in the shed?

I run a hot bath and pour in all the freebie shower gel tubes from the hotel, then lie down and let the heat soak through me, pondering on the strange day I've had.

TWENTY-SEVEN

I DON'T KNOW WHY, but I always forget about the existence of the worky social network, LinkedIn. The Facebook of the corporate world. I used it occasionally when I was looking for a better job, at the start of my night shift era. However, I quickly found that the site is just a virtue signalling and oneupmanship network, rather than anything useful, so I deleted the app from my phone in a fit of disgust. I shudder at the thought of scrolling through all the repulsive posts of my ex-colleagues fake positivity spam.

Through gritted teeth, I download the app again, and after a forgotten password reset, I'm back in. I search for 'Brian Sullivan' at EverGreen Power and find him immediately.

His profile picture is a professionally taken headshot, slicked back blonde hair, neat, clean, and sharp. Dead, judgemental eyes. What does Cassie see in this dickhead?

I scroll through his resume which is a sickeningly perfect list of achievements and qualifications. He's got a heap of prior jobs at other green-focused companies, that goes back to before his university graduation, yet he's also got a long list of countries visited as a backpacker, charity volunteer work, climbing mountains, sailing, and running marathons. He's the sort of prick who never has a hangover, and is revoltingly enthusiastic while eating a bowl of dry twigs for breakfast at five o'clock in the morning. Bastard. I hate him already.

Before EverGreen Power he was working for a company in New Zealand that installed solar arrays, and before that he was in China working on a proposal to reduce smog in cities.

It almost feels like his current job; Renewable's program manager at EverGreen Power, is a downgrade from his previous life. At age thirty-five, he's achieved more than most will in their entire lives, and the smugness comes across in his cold eyes. His posts are erratic; the last one was a few weeks ago about yet another charity event he was participating in.

I scan through the rest of his profile and it's all the same. If I was a cynical bastard, which I most certainly am, I could almost say that his resume is a bit too perfect. Too neat. It feels off.

No contact phone number, but there's an email address, @EverGreenPower.co.uk.

I search for Cassie and also find her quickly. But as with her other profiles, this one is locked so only approved contacts can see the details.

I try her manager, Rachel, and find that profile open. I read through her resume and posts. She's less of a bragger than Brian, and her last posting was well over a year ago, at some green conference in London. She's been working at EverGreen Power for six years, but there's no mention of what she did before.

I stroke my chin and wonder what I should do next.

I woke up early, but haven't left my hotel room yet.

I decide to call Evelyn with a status update. The phone rings for a while and she answers just as I am about to hang up. I imagine they have nurses doing rounds all the time in the care home, and I wouldn't like to be interrupting.

"Hello?"

"Hi. Toby, here."

"Ah, good. I was wondering when you would be in touch."

"I didn't want to wake you, so waited for a while."

She snorts a laugh. "I barely sleep, Toby, especially while Cassie is missing."

"Right, sorry."

"Never mind, what do you have?"

I dive straight in, assuming that Evelyn doesn't need a preamble about how we both are, and the weather. "Do you know if Cassie has sold a computer recently?"

"No idea, I'm afraid. Why?"

I recount the story of the computer box in the shed, and the lack of a hulking great tower PC in her house. I also mention the suitcase, but out of embarrassment and modesty on my part, and Cassie's, I don't mention the contraceptive pills. Some things are meant to be private, even to close relatives.

There's a pause. I wait.

"Was there any sign of a break-in? I imagine it would be worth something?"

"No, unless they were professionals and nipped in

and out. I don't think anything else was taken. No damage, no smells, no mess. I can't be sure, of course. Is Cassie a gamer?"

"A what?"

"You know, does she play video games?"

"No, I don't think so."

"Okay, well the PC was highly specified, very capable. Either used for games or some kind of software that needs a lot of computing power. Does she make videos?"

"No." Evelyn sighs. "She hates her photo being taken."

"Then I would venture that she's using it to create models of some kind, 3D maybe."

"Hmm." Evelyn ponders. "She was excited about something she was working on the last time I saw her. She wouldn't tell me what it was, though. Something amazing, she said."

"Something on the computer, you mean?"

"Possibly."

"That's interesting. Could this thing be significant, something valuable?"

"It could, I suppose."

"Could it be so important that she'd take a big, heavy computer with her to Spain? Maybe to keep working on it?"

"Seems unlikely. How big?"

"Bigger than a large suitcase, for sure. Plus a huge monitor. Keyboard, mouse. Other peripherals, backup disks, all that sort of thing."

"No. Why wouldn't she take a laptop? Isn't that what everyone uses nowadays?"

"Yes, true. But her computer had a powerful GPU in it. That's a graphics chip, but it can be used for other things. Intense computations, bitcoin, or modelling. Hard to cram that into a laptop. If whatever she is doing required that kind of power, there aren't many choices."

"Well, far be it for me to comment, the machines of my day filled a room, and then some. But I can't see Cassie taking such a thing on what should be a romantic holiday."

"No, probably not. Which makes me think that it was stolen. But it was likely someone who knew of its existence. Knew the value of it."

"What did you find out about the chap, Brian, wasn't it?"

"Yes. I did some digging and found that his resume is impeccable. He's worked all over the world on various green projects. Bit too much, if you ask me."

"What do you mean?"

"Where I found it, everything there is so fake. Hyped-up positivity. Everyone is always 'thrilled and excited' to be doing whatever it is they are doing. I can't stand it all. Corporate bullshit, if you ask me. Pardon my French."

"Fake?"

"Yeah, you know. Exaggerated and over the top. Someone posts a mediocre business quote that means nothing, but sounds poignant, and it gets thousands of 'likes'. It's all so plastic."

"You didn't get the resume from his workplace?"

"No, an online social network."

"I see. Well, what if it is fake? This Brian, you say he's worked all over the world?"

"Yup, according to his profile. New Zealand, China, USA, Greenland."

"Places that would be hard to verify and easy to fabricate."

"Now you mention it. I suppose so."

"Is that all you found?"

"Yeah, couldn't find him on any other social media site."

"But you met the manager, at her work?"

"I did, yes."

"A woman, if I recall correctly?"

"Yes, Rachel Hazlewood."

"Talk to her again. Get more information on Brian. Sleep with her if you need to. You know what to do?"

Blushing, I take the phone away from my ear for a moment, and double-take. "Err, I mean, yes. But … What?"

"How else do you propose to gain her trust and extract information?"

"Well … I don't know, I just … Sleep … with her?" I stammer, embarrassed.

"Toby, I didn't program those skills into the Flash Gordon database for fun. They were there for a good reason, and this is that reason. Espionage, intelligence, deception. You know how to manipulate someone and get what you want from them. Use it. Don't pretend you haven't always wanted to."

"Right. But, isn't that a bit, I don't know, immoral?"

"Is it immoral to kidnap my granddaughter?"

Evelyn raises her voice. "And I'll wager she isn't anywhere near Spain, either. Spain! Of all places."

"Kidnap? Hold on, who said anything about kidnapping?"

"Cassie wouldn't just leave like this, and now with her computer missing, I'm sure there is something fishy going on here. So yes, kidnap. Something she was working on caught the wrong people's interest." Evelyn pauses, then takes a sharp intake of breath. "My God. The Department."

"The Department?"

"It's all happening again."

"What is?"

"Never mind. Just find her, Toby. I know you can."

"I'll do my best." I end the phone call and turn on the shower. Need to clean up for this.

———

"Hey, thanks for coming." I stand up and greet Rachel as she comes over to my table in the same coffee shop we were at yesterday. Same table. I rang her number on the card she gave me, hoping it wasn't a work-only mobile, or if it was, that she kept it with her on Saturdays. She did, apparently, and after a moment of awkwardness when she couldn't remember who I was, she agreed to meet me for a coffee. Why? Well, because my work plans had changed, and I found myself back in King's Lynn with nothing else to do until Monday. Not much of a story, but it doesn't pay to complicate a web of lies with detail. Hold back. Be mysterious.

Rachel looks different. She's in jeans, a long pale

pink knitted jumper, her hair loosely tied back, and minimal makeup. Bit of a MILF, actually now I think about it. However, she was available on a Saturday lunchtime at short notice, so I doubt she's a mother.

"Yeah, no problem." A glint returns to her eyes, and she casually embraces me in a light friendly hug. I take the opportunity to flood her with some of my potent sexual energy frequencies, focusing on warmth and passion, relaxation and pleasure. In my head, I hear a Barry White song play. Good grief. I can't believe I'm doing this. Then the harsh tone of Evelyn rings in my memory, and I'm compelled to do whatever it takes to help find Cassie. I take it easy with the frequency harmonising and pull away, noticing a blush on Rachel's cheeks as she sits down opposite me. "I wasn't doing anything much, anyway." Her eyes widen as she looks at me.

I smile. "What would you like?"

"Hmm?" She grins, then looks confused. I nod towards the coffee menu. "Oh! Sorry, yeah. Flat white, please."

"Coming right up."

I furnish myself with a black coffee, and whatever a 'flat white' is for Rachel, then pick up two pastries as a spur-of-the-moment decision, reasoning that she'd want one, but would never admit it.

"Oh, thank you. Those look lovely. I shouldn't though." She pats her tummy and rolls her eyes.

"Course you should." I grin. "Bit of sweetness never hurt anyone."

She laughs. "My scales would disagree."

"Nah," I look her up and down. "You've got that

Marilyn Monroe figure going on there. Very attractive."
I point a finger at her as I sit down. She blushes even
more and looks down at her coffee. She isn't used to
attention or the straight-down-to-business flirting I'm
layering on. To be honest, I'm not either, but this comes
from Evelyn's code, not me. Toby Steele of old would
never in a million years have said that.

"Thank you." She takes a sip of her drink.

"My pleasure," I say, emphasising 'pleasure' with
my eyes. Christ, I'm smooth.

"So," she clears her throat, "Paul, what did you
want to talk about?"

For a moment, I have to think who Paul is, but of
course, it's the name of the pseudonym I perhaps ill-
advisedly chose. Well, I've made that bed, now I have to
lie in it. The question is, will Rachel Hazlewood lie in it
with me?

I can't just blurt out that I want to gather information on her employee, Brian Sullivan. I need to ease into
the conversation, schmooze my way into her trust and
confidence, and gradually extract the information, so
subtly that she won't even know she's given it away.

Time to test my abilities.

I glance down at the table, "You probably don't
remember, but I was at the Green Energy conference in
London last year. I came to your stand."

Her eyes light up as I look back up into them.
"Really?"

"Yeah, and it was you who got me interested in the
subject of switching to renewable in the first place. Then
I must have subliminally found your company when I
was doing some research later, but I ended up talking to

Cassie Wright about it. It wasn't until I met you yesterday that I put two and two together. I had forgotten the name of the company at the stand, but I remembered you." I let that hang for a moment with a sultry glance.

"That's so random. What a coincidence." Her eyes are wide.

"Sure, if you believe in coincidence." I smile.

"You don't believe in them?" She tilts her head.

"Maybe … but I also believe in destiny. In the universal forces that guide us all, if we know it or not."

"Destiny?"

"Yup. What if we were destined to meet?" I think I'm going to need a sick bucket here, and I wonder if I've stepped over a cheesiness line, but she seems to go for it. I emphasise the point with a blast of warm, radiating frequencies in her direction just in case. "Don't get me wrong, Cassie is awesome, and she's been very helpful, but I think I need you to help me from here on." I raise my eyebrows in a 'you know what I mean' gesture. I'm aiming to get her back into the office, which is just across the street, where I might get my hands on Brian or Cassie's work computers. A bit of hacking, and I'm sure I can get through any weak security they have. Then I can look through emails and documents and find out some more information. Maybe see what Cassie was working on, or if she had made any flight bookings. Same for Brian. How I will distract Rachel so I can do this, I don't know yet. Play it by ear.

Rachel is pretty when she blushes, which she's been doing a lot since she arrived. "I'm sure I can help you,

Paul." She reaches across the table and grips my arm, then runs her fingers down my hand.

"Excellent. I know it's the weekend, but could we maybe get my files from your system now? I think Cassie had some numbers done up for me, but I never got a copy."

"You want to go into the office now?"

"Well, I have to be back on Monday, so if we could, that would be awesome." I flash a smile. "You'd be doing me a massive favour," I add, this time I reach over to touch her on the arm.

"Yeah, sure. Why not." She seems reluctant, so I focus my thoughts on a wonderful evening. Wine and dinner, a night of steamy passion, long hot kisses, caresses and grasps, and direct that energy through my fingertips to her. Melting and buzzing its way into her subconscious, overriding any doubt or confusion.

"Thank you, Rachel. I'm extremely grateful."

We finish our coffee and walk across to the office. It's closed, but Rachel has a pass to get in. She leads me through to her domain and I keep up a gentle trickle of energy towards her. For the first time, I'm feeling drained from the effort of it. I had assumed this power was infinite, but I suppose energy has to come from somewhere, and I haven't eaten today, aside from that pastry. This is good, though. I need to know the limits of my skills.

Rachel takes me to her office, which is a semi-open room off the main area. Empty, of course, apart from us. Nice enough. A window looks out over the car park at the back of the building, but there is some green in the distance, and there's a bicycle shed that seems to be covered in solar panels, presumably producing power for the building.

"Well, here we are." She spreads her arms and spins around. "Welcome to my world."

"Not bad. Bigger than my office." I don't have an office at all now, so this technically isn't a lie.

She laughs. "Take a seat and I'll see what we have on file for you."

"Thanks."

She has a laptop on her desk, and she switches it on and waits for it to boot up. "Can I get you a drink while we wait?"

I don't want more coffee, but it might help with my energy drain situation. "Sure."

Rachel gets up and heads deeper into the building, towards a small kitchen at the back. I follow.

There are six desks in the room, most of them have small monitors on them, and one has two huge screens connected to a tower computer.

"This is where Cassie sits." Rachel points to a desk next to the front window as we pass by. I scan the area. She has a monitor and a laptop docking station, but there's no sign of a computer.

"Cool. What about Brian?"

"Oh, he's over here." Rachel points to another desk opposite.

Same situation, monitor, docking station, no computers.

Shit.

I look again at the desk, but aside from a small

cactus in a pot, nothing is interesting. Clean and neat. There's a single drawer under the desk which I'd love to nose into.

We reach the kitchen, and Rachel fills the kettle and finds two cups in a small dishwasher.

"Not as fancy as over the road, I'm afraid."

I nod. "No worries." I wave back towards the desks. "Do people normally take their laptops home, or lock them in a drawer or something?"

"No, not really. Unless we're busy, maybe."

"I just notice there's no computer on some desks."

"Oh?"

"I was in IT for a while, I notice these things." I laugh.

Rachel walks over to Cassie's desk and then looks back towards Brian's. "Strange."

"Would they be locked away in an IT room or something?"

"No, we don't have one."

"Maybe they took their work on holiday with them?"

Rachel scoffs. "Hardly. No, probably just forgot them at home or something."

"Right, yeah."

This has screwed my plan completely. But it certainly adds to the suspicion. Cassie's home PC, and now her work laptop are both missing, and Brian's with it. I know her laptop isn't at her house, so unless she dumped it into a river, she must have taken it to Spain with her, if that's where she went. I need Brian's home address, but I'm unlikely to get that no matter how much schmoozing I do with his boss.

Rachel hands me a cup of instant coffee, and we walk back to her office.

"Now then, let's see." She finds a pair of glasses on her desk and then taps at her laptop. "What did you say your company was called?"

"BioDigi Pharmaceutical."

"Ah, yes." She taps some more, then screws up her face. "That's weird. There's no record of an account for you."

"Oh, maybe Cassie didn't get around to setting it up yet?"

"Maybe. We would normally create a new customer file on the database. Could it be in any other name?"

"I don't think so. Perhaps it was just on her computer so far, which doesn't seem to be here." I turn and look around the office again.

"That could be it. Well, I'm ever so sorry, Paul, it looks like I won't be able to do much for you until Cassie gets back, then." Rachel flashes a grimace. "At least, not here …" She raises an eyebrow and barely runs her tongue over her lips.

I grin. "Well, what else can you do for me, Rachel?"

CHAPTER TWENTY-EIGHT

I COULDN'T DISAPPOINT the woman, could I? After all that build-up of sexual tension, she wasn't going to be satisfied with a hug and a 'catch you later,' as I exited, stage left. No, I needed to make good on the feelings and wavelengths I had piped into her consciousness, or I'd be doing the whole of mankind a disfavour.

The letdown will come later, when she inevitably finds out that I'm not who I said I was. That is a river that I'll drive thousands of miles to avoid crossing anytime soon, if at all possible. A woman scorned, and all that.

Still, Rachel is currently satisfied, as far as I can tell. Back in King's Lynn feeling like an attractive woman again, so she said. Five years since she was in a relationship, and she wanted to make up for all that time in one wild night. Consequently, I was like a rag doll on Sunday.

All that effort was to no avail, however, since I'm no closer to finding any information on Brian, Cassie or the missing computers. I tried searching for Brian's home address using the electoral register database, and what used to be the phone book, now online, but all of that came up with nothing. He's not listed. Ex-directory, as people used to say. I found out from Rachel that Brian doesn't have a car, either. I had wondered if perhaps the missing laptops could be there. She said he uses public transport. Naturally. I should have guessed. Short of just blurting out the question; 'where does Brian live?', I couldn't come up with a way that didn't seem extremely suspicious.

With nothing left to go on, I came back home on Sunday night. I can't stay in King's Lynn forever, especially as Cassie certainly isn't there, and for now, I have run out of leads.

Equally, I can't comb the whole of Spain looking for her. I'm going to need a new strategy, and I prefer my home base for that sort of brainstorming. Not to mention the sudden need to be far away from Rachel Hazlewood. Not because I'm the sort of bloke who humps and dumps, but because if she pokes too deep, my thin veneer of lies will easily crack.

I should visit Evelyn and give her an update, too. I'm putting that off until visiting hours. No need to cause a scene. Instead, I'm planning to go for a bike ride to clear my head. Maybe do some vigilante work for the local community; setting fire to the odd drug dealer, breaking the legs of casual thieves, that sort of thing. Something mundane to let my brain meander and make sense of things.

My phone rings in my pocket. One glance at the screen tells me my plans may be changing.

"Evelyn, good morning."

"Toby, I have something."

"Oh?"

"How quickly can you get here?"

"Err, give me twenty minutes."

"You aren't in King's Lynn?"

"No, I came home last night. I was going to give you an update later."

"Did you … Well, never mind. You can explain shortly."

"Right, okay. See you soon."

———

Dear Gran, in case you were wondering where I ran away to, I needed a break and Benidorm, Valencia offered exceptional value for lazy days. Wish you were here, gran. See you. Write to you again soon - lost phone. Love, Cassie.

It never hurts to keep looking for sunshine.

———

I'm looking at a postcard, handwritten in blue ballpoint ink, sent from Benidorm a few days ago according to the postmark. Delivered to Evelyn this morning. She thrust it into my hand as I sat down in her room, once the nurse had left us.

"Oh. Well, that's that, then." I look up. Seems all my investigating has been in vain.

Evelyn taps a finger on her lips, frustrated. "No. There's something odd about it."

"Is that Cassie's handwriting?"

"Oh, yes. Most definitely."

"Well, then?"

"I've read it a hundred times this morning, and I don't know, there's just something not right."

"I mean, the phrasing is a little strange, but maybe she wrote it after some sangria. And she says she lost her phone, which explains the lack of communication."

Evelyn stays silent.

I turn the card over and look at the picture. A wonderful sandy beach, and azure blue sea stretching into the distance.

"You met Cassie once, didn't you?"

"Yes, all too briefly."

"Tell me, did you notice her skin?"

"Her skin? I mean, yes, I suppose. It covered her face and hands."

"Don't get smart with me, young man."

"Sorry."

"Cassie is as pale as a china teacup. Milky white. She doesn't go on beach holidays."

"Now you say it, yes, okay. Even so. Perhaps she fancied a change?"

"Perhaps."

I hand the card back to Evelyn.

"What did you find out in King's Lynn?"

"Ah, well, not very much, in the end. I got into her office, and her computer wasn't there, either. Her work one, I mean. She has a laptop for work and it was missing."

Evelyn's eyes widen. "Oh?"

"Brian's as well. Both of them gone."

"Did the manager know where they were?"

"No, she assumed they had taken them home, but Cassie's wasn't in her house. Must have taken it to Benidorm, for some reason." I wave at the postcard now propped up on the windowsill next to Evelyn.

"Why would she take her work computer with her?"

"Maybe she had to catch up on some things because it was all very sudden?"

Something catches my eye, and I look back at the postcard. The sun shines straight into the window, and there's glitter or something on the photo of the ocean, sparkling. I move my head, and the tiny points of light disappear.

"Can I see that card, again?"

"Hmm, yes." Evelyn hands me the card.

I look at the writing on the back, then flip over to the photo. I hold it up to the light and twist it until I can see the sparkles, but now I can see they aren't caused by glitter. There are holes in the card. Tiny pinpricks all over it.

"That's strange."

"What is?"

"Hard to see, but there are little holes all over this card."

"Holes?"

"Yeah, pinpricks. Barely there at all, but the sun was shining through them there on the window."

"Let me see."

I hand the card back to Evelyn and she squints at the card, then fishes for a pair of glasses around her neck, puts them on and squints some more, holding the card up to the window as I had.

"I can't see any holes?"

"They are small, but they are there. I assure you."

"Too small for my old eyes. I'll take your word for it, but what does that mean?"

"Err, no idea. Maybe something in the postal system?"

She hands the card back to me.

"Look the other way."

I turn the card around and hold it up to the light, so I can see the pinpricks on the writing side.

"The holes are on some words."

"Which ones?" Evelyn darts forward in her chair. "Quickly, man."

"Letters, actually. Specific letters have a pinhole right through the middle of them."

Evelyn grabs a pen and a piece of paper, an envelope by the looks of things. "Shout them out. Which letters have the pinhole?"

I read out the letters to Evelyn, and she jots each one down, but it seems like total nonsense to me.

C I R Y B E V O X V O Z D W G U R T T

"It's just random letters."

Evelyn looks over to me with a grin. "No, dear boy, this is not nonsense at all. This is a cypher, and I know quite a bit about cyphers."

"Cypher? Like Enigma, you mean?"

Evelyn shakes her head with a scoff. "No, where would Cassie have found an Enigma machine in modern-day Benidorm?"

"Well, I don't know …"

"No, I'll wager this is a simple Vigenère cypher."

"A what?"

Evelyn waves a hand. "It's a fairly straightforward polyalphabetic substitution encryption, using a series of interwoven Caesar cyphers, based on a keyword. Without the keyword, the text is meaningless, but if you know it, you can easily decode the cypher. Cassie is well aware of the system."

"I thought you said simple?" I laugh, "But if I follow you correctly, these letters that seem to be nonsense, identified by tiny pinholes in the card, are an encrypted message you can only understand if you know what the password is?"

"Keyword, but yes, more or less."

"Cassie is sending you a secret message inside this postcard?"

"Precisely. We just need to decrypt it."

"Why would she do that?"

"Because, Toby, as I've been telling you over and over, something is not right about this whole situation."

"I see. Right. So, what is the keyword?"

"That, young man, is a good question."

"You don't know?"

"I taught Cassie everything I know about cryptology, more or less, but that was a long time ago when she was just a child. We sometimes played games with secret messages, tapped out in morse code on glasses or plates over dinner, or written on a napkin. The fun would be in the clues. Finding the hidden message within the hidden message." Evelyn smiles as her eyes blur into the distance of memories.

I look at the card again, focusing on the marked letters, trying to see a pattern or some significance to the placement.

I read the words over and over, letting my eyes focus through the card, holding it up to the window, and staring at the pinpricks of light that sparkle and dance as I move, searching for anything that could be a clue or a suggestion. Suddenly, a beam of light from one of those tiny holes shines on a stuck brain cell, through my eyes, and something occurs to me.

"The last line, there are no pinholes in that at all. It's like an afterthought. It doesn't fit next to the first passage."

"Let me see,"

I hand the card back to Evelyn.

"It never hurts to keep looking for sunshine … where have I heard that before?"

"No idea. A song, maybe? A poem?"

"No, no. I don't think so."

"Well, the beauty of the modern world is that there's no need to wonder anymore. You can find out things like song lyrics, quotes, phrases, and almost any irrelevant fact in a matter of seconds." I pull my phone from my pocket and type the phrase into Google.

It never hurts to keep looking for sunshine

I'm immediately shown a page full of Winnie the Pooh images and quotes.

"Eeyore." I chuckle. "From Winnie the Pooh. He said it." I show Evelyn my phone screen, and a drawing of Eeyore with the phrase next to him.

"Of course! It was Cassie's favourite as a child."

"Is that the keyword; Eeyore?"

"Worth a try. I'll need some more paper and a ruler, would you fetch some?"

"Paper and a ruler?"

"Yes, I'll have to draw out the tabula recta. It will take a little while."

"The what?"

"The matrix of letters that make the cypher. Twenty-six lines shifted alphabetically, with the number of characters according to the keyword."

I shake my head. "I'm pretty sure that won't be necessary. What did you call the cypher?"

"Vigenère."

I tap on my phone again, search for 'Vigenère decoder', and get back a page of results. I tap on a link that looks legitimate, and a page appears where I can type in my cypher, then a keyword and have it decoded.

"Here we go. If I learned anything from my time in IT, it's that computers are great for this sort of thing."

"Ah, good thinking." Evelyn taps the side of her head with a sly grin. "Alan would be proud."

"Alan?"

"Turing."

"Oh, yes. Wow. I forgot you knew him."

"A lovely man. Such a shame."

"Indeed."

I tap in the letters from Evelyn's envelope note and then double check them, then the keyword; **Eeyore**, and hit the decode button.

Y E T K K A R K Z H X V Z S I G A P P

"Oh. Hmm." I show Evelyn the screen. "I don't think that worked. Looks like gibberish." I check the cypher text again and it is definitely correct.

"No. But it was a damn sight quicker than it would have taken to draw it out. Of course, I had a pretty robust Vigenère transcoder on my Cray, back at Porton Down, but those days are long gone. Anyway, excellent work. Try something else."

"Like what?"

Evelyn ponders for a moment, staring out of the window."Looking for sunshine … hurts … no, no. It's too obvious."

"Maybe it's just Pooh?"

"Too short."

"Winnie the Pooh?"

Evelyn turns to me. "Give it a go." She says with a shrug.

I tap in the keyword, minus spaces, as the field won't accept a space character. '**WinnieThePooh**'

G A E L T A C H T G A L W A Y H E L P

"Err." I look at the characters that are decoded and shrug, they look like gibberish again, but then I notice the word at the end. **HELP**. "Oh!"

"What is it? What does it say?"

I show Evelyn the phone.

She squints for a moment and then her hand flies up to her mouth. "My God. It says ... Gaeltacht Galway Help."

"What does that mean?"

"What it means is that Cassie is not in Benidorm or Spain. She's in Ireland, and she needs help!"

CHAPTER
TWENTY-NINE

THE GAELTACHT, according to Wikipedia, are districts of Ireland where people predominantly speak Irish as their first language. Several such areas are dotted across the Republic, and one of them is in the County of Galway.

However, the article also states that the Galway Gaeltacht encompasses a geographical area of almost five hundred square miles. I'm going to need to narrow it down.

I'm booked onto a flight to Dublin tomorrow afternoon, the earliest I could get. From there I plan to rent a car and head towards Galway. After that, I'm going to have to wing it. I've never been to Ireland before, and I'm not sure what to expect. I'm sure it isn't all Guinness, four-leaf clovers, leprechauns, and faery magic. You never know, though. I had pondered on getting a ferry and driving over immediately, but Evelyn pointed out that my car registration would attract attention, and I want to stay invisible as much as possible. Good point.

Sadly, Irish, or Gaeilge, is not one of the many

languages that I can speak. However, according to Evelyn, who has travelled to Ireland before, albeit many years ago, it shouldn't be a problem as everyone speaks English, except for the odd old timer in those Gaeltacht areas, and even they probably do if they want to.

I asked her if now would be a good time to involve the police, given that we have some evidence of kidnap, but she scoffed and shuddered. "If the Department are behind this, the police will have no power."

I pushed on this Department that she keeps mentioning a little, and got more confusion than answers. From what I can tell, they are a secret government agency that has power over pretty much any other in the United Kingdom. I pointed out that the Republic of Ireland is not part of the United Kingdom, but this earned me a glare and a "precisely", and I chose not to press the matter.

Their mission is unknown, but they were very interested in Evelyn's Project Flash Gordon back in the 80s, right until they cancelled the project. She has never heard from or about them since. That hasn't stopped the cogs whirring in her active brain. Forty or so years later, who knows what power they have gathered over the decades. Politics and progress have advanced so much. The Cold War might be long since warmed up, but there's always something going on in the world of global intelligence and espionage. She visibly shuddered at the thought of it.

Convinced that whatever Cassie was working on had triggered the Department to get involved, and so kidnap her and, for some reason, drag her to an Irish-speaking part of rural Ireland, for what nefarious ends

Evelyn could only imagine, she made it very clear that I must use any means necessary to rescue her granddaughter.

I am programmed with skills and expertise in just such a mission, and now is my time to shine. So she said, anyway.

The thing is, all I have to go on is that Brian, and at least three computers are likely to have gone with her, and that she's somewhere in county Galway. At least we know she's alive, but we also know she's being coerced into writing fake postcards to make people think she's okay. That in itself is something to worry about. For now, I think we have to assume that Brian is central to all this, and that he could be part of the Department. If so, that would go some way to explaining his pristine and perfect resume on LinkedIn. It is all fabricated, targeted to endear himself to Cassie, and get a job working with her. That means they planned and detailed this perhaps months in advance. A long-term project. That makes it rather more scary.

I remembered the Spanish postal mark on the card, and this only made Evelyn more anxious. They must have an agency in Benidorm to route post through. If it weren't for the encrypted message that Cassie cleverly hid on the card, I'd be headed totally in the wrong direction by now. A smooth move on the part of the kidnappers, misdirection for the cost of a few extra stamps.

Evelyn sent me shopping for clothes. Something to make me invisible, she said. A tourist, but one who doesn't stand out. In the real world, tourist camouflage means blue jeans, a faded t-shirt, a backpack, a water bottle, and maybe a chunky camera. I asked what was wrong with my usual attire and she scoffed a laugh. "You look like someone in one of those rock bands." She said, and I told her I took that as a compliment. We agreed to disagree about that.

She also asked me to get her a 'mobile telephone thing', so we can communicate easier and with text messages, photos, videos, and location information. A good idea, but I wondered if she'd be confident in how to use it. She told me she knows far more about computers than I do, **real computers**, and that she coded a system to reprogram a human's brain when I was nothing but a dream in my parents' eyes. Fair enough, but I'll still give her a quick tour of the basics before I go.

———

Now a regular at the care home, Nurse Rosey leads me straight in to see Evelyn. She looked at me a little strangely the last few visits and, as this is my second visit today, even more suspiciously this afternoon. However, Evelyn's stern glare gave that short shrift. If I'm asked questions, I'm to say I'm just running some errands for Evelyn and her granddaughter. No need for specifics. Keep any lies to a minimum so as not to complicate things. If you are going to lie, you need to have an excellent memory.

I've already changed into my travel clothes, and Evelyn gives me a nod of approval as I enter. I feel like a dork, but needs must. Against every urge and sense of fashion in my body, I even had to tie my hair back and put on a baseball cap. I shudder at the thought and barely calm my inner demons with the reassurance that this is all to save a damsel in distress.

I set up the brand-new iPhone I bought for Evelyn, and then show her the basics. I set it to recognise her face to unlock, and plug in the charger next to her bed. She seems to understand it all quickly, and I send her a few test messages with a photo, and then a map location so she understands how it works. She needs yet another pair of glasses to see the screen, but despite her hundred years, she certainly learns fast.

"Very good, young man. Now, onto matters more pressing."

"I know, I'm going to need a plan to narrow down the location."

"Yes, that. And I've been thinking …"

"Oh?"

"Actually, can this thing get into my bank?" She waves the phone at me.

"Internet banking? Yes, I expect so."

"Save me turning on the computer." Evelyn points to a chest of drawers on the other side of the room.

"Sorry?"

"I only use it for the money things. Old beast of a thing in the drawer there. Laptop, but it weighs a ton."

"Right." I nod. "Then yes, you should be able to transfer the data onto the phone easily enough."

After some mumbled swearing on my part, whilst waiting on hold for twenty minutes to Evelyn's bank, we finally got their app functioning on her bank account.

"Good. Now, where were we?" She presses her lips

with a finger. "Oh, yes. I'll need your bank account details, won't I?"

"Ah, right. Sure, but there's no rush." I feel embarrassed about taking money from her. I haven't done much to earn it.

"There is, Toby, as you are flying tomorrow. Have you forgotten?"

"No, no. But, I'm fine for now."

She sighs. "I don't know if you have noticed, young man, but I am very old."

I chuckle. "You may be old, but you don't seem it."

"Nonetheless." She points a finger at me. "There's no cheating time. Death comes for us all, in the end."

"What? You are fit as a fiddle!"

She stares me down. "I know I can trust you, Toby, and that's why I'm going to send you twenty thousand pounds immediately. You will use that money to find Cassie and bring her home. Get her to safety and make sure she stays safe. If I am not around, then the responsibility lies with you."

"Twenty grand?"

"Just in case."

"Wow."

"Promise me you will find her, Toby. No matter what it takes."

I take a deep breath. For the first time, Evelyn looks her age. Weak, weary, tired and helpless. Of course, she can't do anything about the situation herself, and Cassie must know that. She's probably expecting Evelyn to raise the alarm with the police, but if what I'm told is true, then that would only make things worse for her. I have no choice. I will find her. "I promise I won't stop until she's here, in this room, with you both safe and sound. I'll be back before you know it."

"Good." She looks relieved. "I don't intend to kick the bucket anytime soon, but we don't know how long it will take you, and … well, you get the point."

I nod. "It will be fine."

"I hope so."

"Should we tell her parents?"

Evelyn scoffs and waves a hand. "No. They are both useless, and half a world away."

"Oh, yes. I remember you saying they were in Australia, but they might want to know their daughter is missing?"

"Kidnapped." Evelyn corrects me. "And there's little point in involving them. It would only cause worry and stress."

"Right, okay, fair enough."

I flash a reassuring smile, but there's an awkwardness in the silence that follows.

There's a knock on the door, causing a welcome distraction.

"Yes?" Evelyn calls out.

Nurse Rosey pokes her head into the room. "Sorry to bother you, but we must have missed this with the post, earlier." She comes into the room and hands Evelyn another postcard and flashes me a grin. "We went to Benidorm last year, great place. Sounds like Cassie is having a wonderful time."

"Never been, myself."

"Sorry about the card, it was in the bottom of the cart. Must have got covered up or something. Anyway,

I'll leave you to it." She leaves us and quietly closes the door behind her.

"Another postcard from Benidorm?"

Evelyn puts on the right glasses and studies the card. "So it would seem."

After scanning the words, Evelyn hands me the card.

———

Dear Gran,

Location is everything, and the view from the balcony checks out. There's a great club for a bit of a mixup over on the North side.

Just down the road, there's a Jazz Lounge on the West side.

Anyway, wish you were here.

Cassie.

K ♪ ♩ ♩

———

The postmark is from a day after the earlier card. The wonders of the postal system meant it caught up to the earlier one, somehow. The stamps are the same. The handwriting also matches the first card.

I hold the card up to the light, but this time there are no pinholes.

"It has to be another cypher, look at that first word. Location."

"Yes, I saw. Then north and west, both capitalised."

"Oh, yes."

"These buildings she mentions, perhaps they correlate to places in Galway?"

"I very much doubt there's a Jazz lounge in the middle of the Gaeltacht. More sheep than people."

"Ah, take your point."

"No, it has to be something deeper."

I turn the card over to the photo side. A sprawling view of the towering hotels above the beach. Sun, sea, sand. All very picturesque. I flip the card over again, but as I do, I notice something on the photo. Bumps. I look closer, and it seems like some words have pressed through the card so hard, that the pen almost penetrated the thin sheet. Not quite, though, and it isn't all the words.

"This could be something."

"Hmm?" Evelyn looks up.

I flip the card over. "Yes, look. The word Location is strongly pressed in. It shows through on the other side."

I show her the card. "These words, as well. North, West. And at the bottom, K I S S."

"Very good. What else?"

"Well, it sort of looks like those letters are spaced out more than they should be." I sound out the letters, "K. I. S. S."

"Keep it simple, stupid." Evelyn retorts.

"What?"

"It's a design principle that I used to work by. A US Navy thing, I think."

"Right, yeah. I've heard of it."

"So that kiss isn't a kiss. It's a clue."

"Interesting." I study the card again. "There are more indentations, not full words though. Letters."

Evelyn grabs a notebook and pen. "Shout them out."

"E, C, C, B, X - North, then J, J, L - West."

"Coordinates."

"Yeah, could be. But they are encrypted. So what's the keyword? Winnie The Pooh, again?"

"No, you need numbers for a set of coordinates and Vigenère doesn't work for that. Alphabet only."

"Ah."

"Keep it simple, stupid." Evelyn repeats to herself. "Keep it sim … Ah!"

"What?"

"Simple number-to-letter swap. It has to be."

"Right. Yes, that could be it." This is getting exciting now. "So, for example, the first letter, E, would be a number 5?"

"Yes. Try it." Evelyn hands me the notepad and I scribble a number under each of the letters.

E, C, C, B, X - North. J, J, L - West.

5, 3, 3, 2, 24 - North. 10, 10, 12 - West.

"Now we're getting somewhere." I show Evelyn the pad.

"Excellent. Can you put that into the map thing?"

"I should think so, yes." I type the numbers into Google maps on my phone. "Hmm. Not found."

"What? Let me see." I show her my screen. "No, no. You'll need the symbols around the numbers. This is in degrees, minutes and seconds. Look, 53 degrees, 32 minutes, 24 seconds. You should know that?"

I ponder for a moment. "Yes, you are right." The syntax of map coordinates bubbles up in my brain from a long-term memory bank, presumably programmed by Evelyn. "Sorry. Not thinking straight."

Evelyn makes a face. "I wonder if I needed to calibrate the FSMI for a male brain, specifically."

"What?"

"Never mind. Try the coordinates again, properly this time."

I type in the numbers, formatted for degrees, minutes and seconds.

53°32'24"N 10°10'12"W

The map instantly recognises the format, and moves from my current location to a big patch of blue.

"Oh. Hmm. She's in the middle of the sea?" I pinch out the zoom. "Ah. Now we're talking." I show Evelyn my screen again.

The map shows a pin that is in the Atlantic Ocean, just off the west coast of Galway, Ireland.

"Her calculations must be a bit off, but that's good."

"Calculations?"

"I imagine she had access to a window, at least, in whatever prison they hold her in, and could measure the arc of the sun over the course of a day or two, and then she had to estimate the figures a little."

"Wow. Smart girl."

Evelyn looks up at me. "She's an exceptional woman, and she's in danger. Target your search on the area around this point, that should narrow it down considerably. There can't be many buildings or people in that area."

"Got it. If any more postcards arrive, take a photo of each side and send it to me. You know how?"

"Yes, good idea. And I'll transfer the money to you now. Prepare. Think through your plans and objectives. Don't act rashly, but do use force and your talents if you need to. Get that girl home safely, Toby." Evelyn pauses. "And yourself as well. Be careful. The Department could be extremely dangerous."

"Understood."

CHAPTER THIRTY

ONE UNEVENTFUL AND short flight later, and I'm over the water in the Emerald Isle. After picking up my car, the first stop was at the nearest camping store to tool up. I couldn't bring rope, knives, a first aid kit, fishing rods and equipment, a torch, backup power-bank battery packs, and cylinders of butane on the plane, so I'm sourcing everything locally. The next stop was a hardware shop to get lock-picking equipment, although they don't call it that; a mini screwdriver and hex key set, a crowbar, rubber gloves, two carbon dioxide fire extinguishers, three rolls of duct tape, a hefty hammer, heavy-duty wire cutters, and a toolbox to put everything in.

I don't know what I'm getting into, so best to be prepared for all eventualities. A gun would be handy, but I doubt I can get my hands on one easily.

Instead, I settled for a five-litre tank of petrol, a lighter, and a pack of doughnuts at the first fuel station. Then I drew out five hundred Euro in cash at an ATM.

My car boot loaded up with trouble, and two dull

motorway hours later, and I'm in Galway. I stop for a bathroom break and enjoy the accents of the locals, as I buy a cup of coffee at another fuel station. It's been a long day, and there's a lot to do and a good distance to cover yet.

I'm heading for a place called Clifden, as it was the biggest town close to Cassie's coordinates. I'll start there and work out in a sweeping arc. I've got photos of Brian and Cassie from their social profiles on my phone, and my plan, if you can call it that, is to ask around if anyone has seen them. They are my friends who I'm supposed to be meeting for a fishing holiday in the wilds of Connemara, but lost contact with and their phones aren't working. Vaguely plausible, and not too complicated if anyone should ask.

Evelyn showed me a 'Flash Gordon' trick that I didn't know about. Using the same brain wavelength manipulation, or frequency harmonising as she calls it, that I use for my horny thought projection, I can also shift the frequency a little, to insinuate a feeling of safety and trust towards me. Meaning, that if someone is unwilling to tell me the information I need to know, they'll be more inclined to ease up and spill the beans if I focus the energy on them for a moment. Very handy. I wonder what other skills I have in my armoury that I don't yet know about. I suppose I'll need to explore the limits of my abilities at some point.

I press on towards Clifden, guided by the car Sat-Nav. The roads become winding and narrow and seem to go on forever. I pass through miles, or kilometres, of beautiful countryside. Grey stone walls divide rich green fields, rolling hills and sweeping vistas, grazing sheep that stray onto the roads occasionally, streams, rivers and wilderness everywhere I look. As stunning as it is, I'm not here for any of this. I focus on the road ahead, twisting and bleak into infinity.

Finally, I arrive at the hotel I'm booked into. I picked the most anonymous seeming hotel from the choices available online. More expensive than some, but I don't want a guesthouse where the owners might be friendly and ask me too many questions. I need to stay invisible.

The girl on reception is obviously Polish, and I toy with the idea of speaking to her in her native language, but I decide against it. Again, that would make me stand out as someone interesting, and I want to be bland and forgettable. I am checked in promptly without complication, and given a keycard in a little paper envelope. I'm here for a week, but hopefully, I don't need that long.

My room is decent, and a welcome break from the long day of travel. I flop down on the bed and relax for a quiet moment. I send Evelyn a message that I have arrived, and she replies quickly with a thumbs-up emoji. I laugh at that. Did she know what an emoji was yesterday? She said she would ask Nurse Rosey if she had any more iPhone-related questions, reasoning that Rosey seems to spend most of her day glued to hers, so she ought to know how to use it.

I left the tools and equipment in the car boot, and parked it in the hotel carpark out of sight. My travel bag contains more of my tourist clothes, plus my laptop. I open it up, connect to the free hotel Wi-Fi, and load a full screen of Google Maps. The coordinates Cassie sent are now only fifteen kilometres away. I search for post offices within a fifty-kilometre range of it and, thankfully, there aren't many. A good start. Reasoning that Brian, or someone connected must be buying stamps to send the postcards to Spain, there aren't many other options. The drive back to Galway city is a good two hours, so I have to assume they wouldn't go to those lengths to hide the origin of the postcards, since the redirect in Spain is presumably all the misdirection they think they need.

Too late for post offices tonight. I take a quick shower to freshen up and wash away the travel grime, then tourist myself up and head out to check out the local pubs. I'm starving, too, so a decent meal is in order.

"How are ye getting on?"

A chap approaches me as soon as I get to the bar of the pub next to the hotel. Burly and hipster-looking with a groomed beard.

"Good, thanks."

"On holiday?" He gives me a sideways smile.

I guess my accent gave me away in less than a second. "Yeah, doing a bit of fishing."

"You're very welcome, so. Good man, yourself. No better place for it."

"So I've heard." I lie. I've never fished in my life, and don't intend to do any this week, not for fish anyway, fishing for information is a different matter.

"What can I get ye?" He motions to the beer taps.

"Guinness, please."

"Pint?"

"Yup, is there any other way?" I smile.

"Some ladies would take a glass, all right, but pint it is." He smiles and sets about pouring the stout. "I can tell you some good spots if you are interested. Catch ye some whoppers."

"Oh, yeah, cheers. Well, I'm meant to be meeting some friends somewhere around here, but we got a bit disconnected. Their phones aren't working, and I've forgotten where I'm meant to go." I laugh.

"Sure, there's no fecking signal up here once you are out in the sticks."

I pull out my phone and bring up the photo of Brian. It's a long shot, but worth a try.

"You wouldn't have seen this guy in here recently, would you?" I show him the photo.

The bartender squints at the screen but shakes his head. "Can't say I have."

I swipe to the picture of Cassie. "What about her?"

He raises his eyebrows. "Ah, now. I'd remember if I saw her." He gives me a 'know what I mean' grin. "No, sorry, buddy. You might try Stanleys. Fishing shop not far from here." He points to the left, then changes his mind and switches to the right. "Right out of here, then left at the cross, then keep going. You'll see it, no bother. They'll be closed now, but try in the morning."

"Nice one, cheers."

"Slainte." He hands me the Guinness and goes off to serve another customer.

I look around the bar. Cosy, old-fashioned, snug and warm. Dark wood, a peat fire burning in the vast fire-place, worn leather seats, and the aroma that can only come from hundreds of years worth of beer spillage and sweat. A proper Irish pub, not fabricated in the stereo-type of what that should mean, bought from a cata-logue and cloned all over the world.

In different circumstances, I could enjoy this. Perhaps when Cassie is safely rescued and back at home, I might plan a proper holiday for myself.

I take a sip of the Guinness. Cold, smooth and deli-cious. "That hits the spot," I mumble to myself.

"That it does, lad, that it does."

I turn to find an old boy sitting next to me at the bar. Drunk eyes, red-rimmed. A thatch of grey hair perched on his blotchy face. He grins as wide as the bar, and nods towards my fresh pint, then his empty glass.

"You here on holiday?"

"I am."

"First time in Ireland?"

"It is, indeed."

"You'll be wanting a guide then, so." He slaps his hands together. "And all it will cost you is the price of a fine glass of stout." The old man flashes a theatrical wink at me, then back at his empty glass. "Is that too much to ask?" I can take a hint.

"Fair enough."

"Ah, you're a sound lad. A hundred thousand thankyous as we say here. Wait, or is it one hundred thousand welcomes? Céad míle fáilte. Either way, you're a grand lad."

I nod to the barman and point to the Guinness tap, and then to the old chap next to me.

"Now, Seamus, don't be taking advantage of our guest here." He smiles and pours the pint.

"God. Now, as if I would do that, Mícheál. Wouldn't

the bottom of your porter barrels dry up before I would take advantage of a soul? Wouldn't the whiskey in your jars go sour before I, Seamus O'Shaughnessy, would act in anything other than honesty and goodwill?"

"Save the performance, Seamus. Just take it easy." The barman rolls his eyes at me, then winks. "Mind yourself with this one, eh?"

"Ah, he's a grand lad, really. Don't mind him." Seamus indicates the barman with the jerk of an elbow in a threadbare tweed jacket.

I laugh and hand the barman, Mícheál, a ten euro note to settle the bill.

"Don't worry, I can take care of myself."

"There you are now, he can take care of himself." He points to the barman and then to me. "Never a doubt about that, either. A sound lad, I said to myself as I saw you. A sound English lad, and I bet he can take care of himself. Not a bother on him."

"Indeed." I change the subject. "So, what can you tell me about the place, Seamus?"

"First things first, boy. Don't rush ahead of the horse or you'll lose your cart. First things first. What's your name, son?"

"Toby." I hold out a hand.

Seamus shakes my hand with surprising vigour. "A delight to meet you, Toby. A genuine delight."

"And yourself, Seamus." I grin. He's a character, for sure.

"Now we're acquainted, it seems fitting that we should take a whiskey together." He grins and looks up at the shelf of impressive-looking whiskey bottles behind the bar.

"Ah, I see where this is going." I can't help but chuckle. "But I'm not here for a session."

"Who said anything about a session, Toby? One small glass is all I'm saying. Barely a drop to wet your lips. A christening to celebrate your first time in the beautiful and green land of Ireland. It would be a crime not to, a sin. You can't come all the way here from England and not taste the very tears of the land. The drops that are squeezed from the peaty heart of our homeland, and nurtured into this heaven-sent delight." He thuds a clenched fist to his chest in reverence. The old boy certainly loves a performance, I'll give him that.

"Fine. One glass."

"That's the spirit, Toby. One glass. That'll do it."

"What do you recommend?"

"Well, now. Normally I'd say start with the Jameson and work up, but I think we're past that already. No, you are in Connemara, so you should taste the sweet Connemara whiskey."

"Fair enough. I'll go for that."

Seamus doesn't hesitate and calls over the barman again. "Two of your finest measures of the elixir, Connemara whiskey, please Mícheál. And my good friend, Toby, here will be delighted to pay."

I chuckle and shake my head, but pull a twenty from my wallet and drop it on the bar. "That's it now. I'm not having any more after this."

"Not at all, Toby. Not a single drop more. One glass, we said, and one glass it shall be!"

CHAPTER
THIRTY-ONE

"UGHHHHHH." Cold, stiff, creaky, and a relentless throbbing of pain from every nerve in my body. My eyes remain closed. "Ughhhhhh!" I groan and try to find warmth under the blankets, but none comes. Bells ring, but they come from inside my head, not outside. I can see why Ireland is Catholic. After a heavy night, you need Jesus and Mary to save you from the hangover. I clutch at my head to try to drown out the noise, but it makes no difference. I experimentally open an eye.

"What the …" Where am I? A burst of adrenaline crashes around my body, my other eye opens and I'm sharply brought home to reality. "Oh, fuck!"

This is not my comfortable and opulent hotel room, with a soft warm bed, tea and coffee-making facilities, a deep bath, a rain-head shower, a thirty-two-inch television mounted on the wall, and a view over rolling countryside. No, this is the very opposite of that. I'm in a tiny bare room, cold, stark and dismal, lying on a thin, hard sliver of a bed, covered by a stinking grey blanket with views of a tiny barred window. I'm in a jail cell. What happened?

I sit up and immediately regret it. The room sways as my brain lags on a five-second delay. My guts churn, but I keep it together by taking a deep breath. I'm parched, and my throat is a barren desert. The back of my head is a jackhammer drilling into my spine.

Jesus.

Whiskey. Lots of whiskeys. An entire shelf full, in fact. Seamus. What happened to Seamus? He said something really important, something about, ughhhh, my head pulsates … never mind Seamus for now. How did I get here? I reach into my pocket for my phone, but it isn't there. Shit.

<< Rewind.

We were outside in the street. I remember that much. Must have been three in the morning by the time we left the warm sanctuary of the pub, Seamus having convinced me I needed to try all the different nuances and flavours of the evil firewater they call whiskey. In fairness, they do a good job and some of those single malts are an entire world of taste and experience all on their own, but after the tenth or twelfth shot, I knew I was at the limit. Seamus, the old soak, seemed no worse for wear than when I met him. Eloquent and verbose as he was, he never relented, and he did give me the promised guided tour of Ireland. What I didn't know was that the tour would take a liquid form.

We hadn't strayed from the one pub; I was next door

to my hotel. A crawl at worst, and a handful of steps at best. How did I go so wrong in such a short distance?

My stomach rumbles, and I swear the sound echoes around the cell. I still haven't eaten since those dough-nuts somewhere between Dublin and Galway. All that booze on an empty stomach. No wonder I'm dying here.

The memory rushes back to me in a chaotic montage. There was a fight right outside the pub. Two lads. A young woman was watching while leaning against the wall.

Two lads fighting over a woman. How clichéd, but could it be anything else? There are only two things that start wars. Women and money. This one was very much the former. One lad was Slavic. Polish probably, but maybe Romanian. I couldn't tell. The other guy was definitely Irish. They were prodding and swearing as we came out into the cool night air, nothing more than a standoff of words, but that's just the incendiary that triggers the explosion. The fuse was lit, and the pushing started. Then after only a few seconds, the fists started flailing. Seamus tried to step in and stop it, but they shoved him aside with barely a glance. It was at that point my Flash Gordon instincts kicked in, and I grabbed the two lads by their forearms, and twisted them both around in a single choreographed move. Two arms pushed up their backs, and I slammed them up against the wall of the pub before they knew what was happening. Impressive work, if I say so myself, and that should have been the end of it.

Now I remember.

The wall wasn't a wall. It was a black painted

window, and the glass smashed and shattered with a horrific crash in the quiet street. The shock of it caused me to release the lads, and they quickly scarpered. Stunned, I stood there for a moment, trying to parse what had happened. Then the blue lights flashed, and I turned around to see a Garda stepping out of his car and rushing towards me. Seamus, the two lads and the girl were all notable by their absence. I stood there alone and held my hands up.

Shit. Shit. Shit.

Evelyn is going to kill me. I'm meant to be here saving her granddaughter, and instead, not twenty-four hours after I arrived in Ireland, I've been shit-faced on whiskey, in a fight, caused criminal damage, arrested and locked up in a cell.

This is not going as I had planned.

"Wakey, wakey. Rise and shine!"

A loud voice outside the cell shoots daggers into my throbbing head.

"I'm awake," I mumble and slowly sit back up on the low bed. I was lying down trying to let my body recover. It didn't work. I have no idea what the time is, but the light from the tiny window is harsh and bright.

"Well, now. Good morning Mr Steele."

After the clanking din of the door being unlocked and opened, a tall thin man looms above me. A police-man, or Garda as they are called here.

"Can I have some water, please?"

"You can, of course. Come on, so. Let's get you sorted out."

I stand up and follow the Garda through bleak corridors that stink of disinfectant and misery, to another room, this time with a table and two chairs and not much else. He indicates I should sit down and then leaves the room, locking the door behind him. I rest my head on my hands and try to focus on clearing my mind.

———

"Now." The Garda drops a cup of water down in front of me, and I take a gulp immediately, then quickly sink the rest. The cold water nurses my dry throat and courses through my body, dulling the tentacles of pain that are intertwined throughout every nerve in me.

"Thank you."

"Feeling better?"

"A little, yes."

"Good. Now, then." He sits down opposite me. "Let's talk about what happened last night, shall we?"

The Garda takes my statement, and jots down notes on a pad. He makes the occasional scoffing sound, especially when I mentioned the whiskeys, but allows me to finish my story. I was just trying to stop a fight. A seemingly benevolent act. It was an accident; I didn't know they made the wall out of glass.

"I checked the CCTV footage from the hotel, your story checks out."

I look up. "Oh, good. Right."

"But that doesn't excuse your actions."

"No, well, fair enough. I had a bit too much whiskey. But that wasn't my intention."

"And did Seamus bend your arm up your back to drink them?"

I never mentioned Seamus by name, I suppose he must be known to the Garda. Not surprising, given the size of the town and his loud and flamboyant nature.

"No," I admit. "Just got carried away, I suppose. I'm on holiday."

"So I see." The Garda rubs his chin. "To be honest, Toby, I can't be arsed with the paperwork this morning. I've got a missing flock of sheep to deal with, and a robbery over in Moyard. I've no time for your shenanigans."

Should I tell him there's a kidnapped woman not far away, as well? Held in some kind of prison against her will, and that's the real reason I'm here? No, probably not. I see an opportunity here, though, and I take another deep breath, blocking out the pain of my killer hangover, and summoning up all my strength. I look the officer straight in his eyes and I focus, shifting frequencies in my mind and body, pulsating and pouring out the wavelengths. Harmonising, balancing and streaming a message of trust towards the Garda. I'm harmless, just an accident, a misunderstanding. I'm the victim here. A pain in my head throbs, but I disregard it and focus, focus, focus.

"Can you pay for the window?" The Garda jolts me from my concentration.

"Yeah, no problem." I think of the money that Evelyn sent me. This isn't quite what she had in mind, but oh, well.

"Grand. Let's go sort it out with the landlord, shall we?" He stands up. "But I don't want to see you back here again, understood? There are no second chances."

"Understood."

———

Fifteen hundred euro later, and I'm free, but politely asked never to darken the pub doors again. No fear of that. I'm done drinking for a while. The price of a pane of glass seemed a tad high, but I was in no position to negotiate. I was lucky we could convince them not to press charges, and that the brother of the landlord has a glazing business and could come at short notice. The black paint will have to wait another day, but for now, the problem is solved.

Reconciled with my phone, wallet and hotel room key, I take another shower, this time to wash away the stink of booze and prison sweat. The hot water does wonders, and after a solid forty-five minutes, I'm feeling a bit more human. Starving, I'm glad that the hotel is still serving breakfast by the time I make it down. I drown my sorrows in coffee, and a full Irish fry of rashers, eggs, black and white puddings, and a swathe of buttered toast.

A message pings on my phone. Evelyn.

Any progress?

Shit. I can't exactly tell her what happened, and that I'm only just free and starting my search.

Search … the word triggers a memory that was

buried under a lake of whiskey. Seamus ... he told me something important during the evening.

Several whiskeys down, and I pressed him for the guide he had promised me. I showed him the photos of Brian and Cassie, and asked if he had seen them anywhere, that we were meant to be fishing together, but I couldn't get ahold of them. He said no — he didn't recognise the faces at all. He asked if they were English, too. I said yes. Then he mentioned something casually, "A few of you fellas around here, these days, as well as the Polish lads, of course. A couple lives up at Bally-nasióg. English couple. Both of them strange as a fish in a tree, but your people, nonetheless."

"An English couple. Are they nearby?" I asked, a flicker of sobriety tickled at my senses.

"Not far, as the crow flies, but as the car drives, even closer. Three houses down from the post office. Cynthia and Ian. The strangest couple I ever met."

It turned out that Seamus is the postman around here, so he knows exactly where everyone lives. Very handy, indeed.

I reply to Evelyn.

> Yes, I have a lead. I'm about to go look into it.

———

I buy several litres of water, and a packet of aspirin at the grocery shop near the hotel, and flood my body with both. Gradually, the life ebbs back into me and I feel reasonably good again.

I type in the village's name, Ballynasióg, into the Sat Nav and as Seamus noted, it isn't far. About a twenty-minute drive from Clifden.

My first drive-through tells me that it isn't so much a village, as a small collection of houses. No more than twenty, at a guess. There's a single building that serves as a shop, pub, petrol station and post office at a cross-roads, and one road leading away from it is home to several new-looking houses. Ostentatious and vast, but bleak in stone grey without so much as a sapling of trees anywhere near them. Green lawn gardens hedged with more grey stone and tarmac driveways. The third house away from the post office is nothing like the others. An old farmhouse. Still made of stone, but quite different in style. The house is set back about a hundred yards from the road, and there's a scattering of outbuildings behind. Sheds, and a huge open barn. The main house looks large, too. Maybe five bedrooms and there are three chimneys. One of which has smoke drifting away from it on the breeze. I drive away, not wanting to be noticed. If I stop here, I'll immediately be suspicious. There's no other traffic at all, unless you count the field of cows opposite. I drive on for a couple of minutes then find a place to turn around, pausing for a moment in a driveway to get my bearings. Cassie is in that house. I know it. I feel it. Cynthia and Ian. Those names have meaning, I'm sure Evelyn mentioned them.

I pull out my phone to send a message to her. No signal. Shit.

The cold, harsh light of day is of no use to me. I need the velvet darkness to engulf me and hide within.

The night is my friend.

I drive back past the house, slowly, but not too slow to give myself away. Someone took a wrong turn, that's all. Nothing to see here. There's no visible movement in the house, aside from the wisp of smoke from the chimney. There are five windows at the front, and at least three on one side. Probably similar on the other. The large shed behind the house could be used as a garage, with a single wide door, and there are two wheelie bins next to a window at the side. I drive on, noting the name of the pub — O'Dwyer's, and head back to my hotel in Clifden to work on my strategy.

CHAPTER THIRTY-TWO

The Department. I bloody knew it.

Pardon my French.

Be careful, Toby. These people are dangerous.

EVELYN RESPONDS to the message I could send when back in my hotel room. Cynthia and Ian are the same people she was working with — or against, all those years ago at Porton Down. I didn't get their surnames, but what are the chances it could be anyone else?

That means the Department are behind this, just as Evelyn has been saying. But, why, and why here in the middle of nowhere?

I thought about just knocking on the door of the farmhouse, and storming the place as soon as they opened it, reasoning that if they are the same Cynthia and Ian that Evelyn knew, they have to be in their sixties or more by now, and wouldn't put up much of a fight. But there's Brian to consider. He's not sixty, and he's part of the gang. I imagine he somehow got Cassie here, probably by car or van, and now keeps her locked up. She's been here for a while now, so they either have weapons to threaten her, or a jail cell inside the house. There could be more henchmen, too. The question remains; why?

No, a brute force attack won't work here. I need to be subtle and get in another way.

I grab a light dinner in the hotel restaurant, and drink only sparkling water with it. No booze for me today, or ever again, if the feeling in my guts and head this morning was any kind of deterrent.

Back in my room, I change into my normal clothes, which thankfully I included in my bag. Black jeans, a black tee shirt, and a long black coat. I throw away the baseball cap, loosen my hair back to normal and get ready for action.

The roads are more treacherous in the dark. Single track narrow and twisting, looming cavernous potholes, and on the rare occasion I meet another vehicle approaching, I need to pull into a lay-by or farm gate to let them go past. I take it easy, no need to rush. I have all evening.

I arrive at the pub, O'Dwyer's, and note there are three cars outside. Although this place is in the back of beyond, people still need a pint … or a pint of milk at the adjoining shop. I carry on, passing the new build houses, then the old farmhouse, which is now lit up in three of the front windows. Dull lights from behind curtains. I can't see inside. I don't want to go too far away, but I can't leave the car too close, either. I find the gateway I turned in earlier. It leads up to a house that's in the process of being built. Block walls, concrete base and wooden framework, but nothing substantially more. I drive around to the rear of the house and park.

The car is hidden from the road. Getting out and looking around, I can't see any other buildings. Perfect. I wait for a silent moment, listening for any hints that I was noticed, but the breeze drowns out any other sound. I creep to the edge of the half-finished building and peer around the corner, down at the road. Nothing but darkness. Just as I hoped.

Staying on alert, I move back to the boot of the car and open it. I take a torch from the toolbox and tape it to the boot lid, shining it down so I can see what I'm doing. The built-in lights in this rental car are too dim. I set about duct taping up the butane cylinders, meant for camp cooking, with two power-bank battery packs around each one in neat little parcels of fun, then I put those into a big shopping bag with the petrol can.

I stuff a fresh duct tape roll into a pocket. Rope, a camping knife, wire cutters, and one of the small fire extinguishers slide into various other pockets. I turn off the torch, shut the boot and lock the car, hiding the key on top of the front passenger side wheel, close to the wall of the house.

The walk back to the farmhouse should take about five minutes. There are no lights anywhere, save the faint glint of moonlight between clouds. I am not familiar with the territory, so I pause and let my eyes get used to the darkness, peering into the gloom that is unadulterated by human light. This place really is remote. If it weren't for the occasional break in clouds, it would be totally dark, and I would need my torch just to find the road.

I set off with my various devices weighing me down. The plastic shopping bag handle digs into my palm, but I ignore it and focus on the road. If another car drives down here, I'll be spotted, for sure, unless it coincides with one of the infrequent gateways, and I can make it into a field to hide before the headlights pick me out. The hedge is way too high most of the time, and there's an electric fence on the other side, anyway. I occasionally hear the ticking of the fence as energy pulses through it, keeping the livestock locked up. I quicken my pace, now used to the darkness, thriving amidst the power it affords me.

As I near the farmhouse, having not met another person or vehicle, I slow down and take out my phone. The screen light blinds me for a second and I turn away, shutting one eye and fumbling to find the camera app. The screen turns dark as the phone tries to focus on nothing. I point it towards the house, zooming in as much as possible. I find the dim light from the front windows, then slowly shift to the side of the house, and up a level to what are probably bedrooms. One more dim light, but nothing visible inside through a curtain. I keep walking, holding the phone in front of me and get to the driveway entrance, then stop and crouch down behind a low wall at the edge of the road.

I'm sure there are sensor lights and cameras all over the place, so I need to avoid them. I look through the phone screen, pointed over the wall and up at the house.

There is no sign of movement while I wait for a minute or two. I'm hoping to see a blip of infrared if there are any night-vision cameras. I'm probably too far away, though, and nothing shows up. I can't risk it. If my cover is blown, I lose the element of surprise and this plan is ruined. I turn back and find the gate that leads to the field next to the house. The gate is tied up with an old length of rope, as the lock mechanism has long since rusted away. I slip the loop of rope over the post, pull open the gate just enough to get through, and then close it again after me, replacing the rope. The ground is rough. Cow hooves have turned the soft mud into a churned-up mess rather than a flat field. I set off in a direction parallel to the driveway of the farmhouse, aiming for the barn that looms behind. The electric fence ticks with power, and I'm sure it won't kill me, but I'd rather not take a belt up the arse as I cross it, so I whip out my wire cutters and snip away a section of the thick wire, and step over. Sorry farmer, but all is fair in love and war. I grab the short length of wire and coil it up, slipping it into my big pocket. Could be useful.

Now I just have to climb the stone hedge, thick with brambles and nettles, and I'm into the backyard of the farmhouse.

Glad of my heavy boots, I trample down the bulk of the vicious plants, and grab onto tufts of grass to help me climb. At the peak, I can see clearly towards the back of the farmhouse. There's another door and window, this time no curtain, but dark inside.

A light flicks on from the wall above the door, and

someone steps out. Adrenaline bursts through me and I duck down, still at the top of the hedge. I freeze, silent and hopefully invisible in the night. The person — a man, doesn't look up, and instead walks around the side of the house, and towards the road. Two more lights automatically come on as he passes, and I stay frozen and silent until he is out of sight and the two lights flick off again. Well, now I know where the lights are, and that someone has gone out. To the pub, perhaps? I think my plans have changed.

I wait another minute, then jump down into the yard. The back door light is still on, so I shuffle around the edge, staying close to the hedge in the shadows.

I was planning to set off my bombs at opposite sides of the house, and then a petrol fire in the barn to give the sense of a bigger attack than just one man. Draw the occupants out, and then sneak in while they are engaged in putting out the fires, find Cassie, break her free and run back to the safety of my car. Not the most thought-out plan in the history of rescues, but it was the best I could come up with at the time, assuming of course, that this is the right house. If it isn't, then I could be heading for trouble. However, now I think there's a better idea.

Staying away from the light, I traverse the yard over to the two wheelie bins. I lift the lids. One is only half full, while the other is jammed full of crushed Amazon boxes. I guess kidnappers need Prime shopping as well as the rest of us. Into the first bin, I drop one of my butane bombs, and into the recycling bin, I perch my petrol can on top, with the other butane device next to it. I have to push down to get the lid to close, but it does without too much effort. I wait for a moment, straining to listen for any sounds, and then I take the roll of duct tape out and set about firmly taping down both bin lids.

I skulk back into the depths of the yard, over to the shed which is likely a garage. Behind it, there's another stone building that has long since eroded, and now it's nothing more than a vague pile of stones, with a sheet of rusty corrugated iron, jagged and broken, forming a roof.

I drop my other equipment here, then cover it up with some short planks of wood that are lying around. Old floorboards by the look of them, chopped up for firewood.

Preparations made, I sneak back over the hedge, into the field, and head towards the pub.

————

O'Dwyer's is certainly an Irish pub, in that it is a pub, in Ireland. There's no disputing that. But the similarities end at that point. Inside is not the wood and leather, dim lights, lulled conversation and pleasant scent of beer that you'd expect. The single room the pub inhabits is more akin to a large living room, where someone has installed a small bar they knocked up themselves, from scrap bits of kitchen. The bar itself is a black marble effect worktop, and the gap behind it is barely big enough for the man who occupies it. He vaguely glances in my direction as I come in, then looks away with a hint of disappointment.

Around the room are some old sofas that could have come from the 'free to a good home' section of Facebook, none of them matching, and two thin Argos-style tables pushed up against one wall. The focus of everything, including the barman, is angled towards a large flatscreen TV on a wall above a fireplace, where a football game plays out. There are maybe a dozen folk crammed into the place, mostly men who look suspiciously like farmers.

At the edge of one sofa, pint in one hand, staring up at the game, sits Brian. I recognise him immediately from the LinkedIn photo. He's less smooth in real life. Four-day stubble and his hair is longer, but it's him.

Bingo.

CHAPTER
THIRTY-THREE

THE CHOICES of booze here are limited. Heineken or Guinness, and a couple of whiskey bottles that I don't even want to think about. Despite my pledge not to drink, I choose a pint of Heineken and manage to avoid much discussion with the barman. He's more interested in the match than in why a random English bloke is in his bar. I'm a tourist, just passing through. Nothing interesting here. He pulled my pint, took my money and then jolted back to his game.

I sit down on the other side of the sofa from Brian. He glances at me briefly, and I barely raise an eyebrow with a nod hello; he returns the gesture and turns back to stare up at the sport. What I know about sport could be written on the back of a postage stamp with a thick marker, but I can vaguely recognise that this isn't football as I had assumed, instead, it's Rugby. The funny-shaped ball is the giveaway.

I watch for a moment, but as the commentary seems to be in Irish, I don't know what is going on. I don't care, either, but that's not the point.

"What's the score?" I turn to Brian.

"Seven nil." He tells me automatically without looking away from the screen, but then he double-takes and turns towards me, eying me up. I nod in thanks.

My accent gives me away again, I imagine. He turns back to the game.

I watch for a few minutes, keeping a peripheral eye on Brian. He sips at his beer, but otherwise just watches the TV, rarely taking his eyes off the screen.

"Well, this is fucking boring," I announce.

Brian looks over at me with surprise.

"I'm more in the mood for finding women, you know?"

"I think you're in the wrong place for that, mate." He scoffs and takes a sip of beer.

"Yeah? Well, I'm hoping to find my Miss right …" I leave that thought hanging for a moment. Brian doesn't flinch. "I just have this feeling that the stars are aligned, and today's the day, I dunno."

"Yeah, good luck with that."

"The constellation of Andromeda is aligned with Uranus, that sort of thing." I chuckle and wink. "Could use some heavenly bodies tonight."

Either Brian is stupid as a box of frogs, or he's deliberately not picking up on my references. I can't tell which. He doesn't engage.

I try another tack. "My Department recently laid me off, so I took a holiday. Get away from things. Staying in a B&B down the road. Dirt cheap, but it's not bad."

"Yeah?" Brian reluctantly replies. He seems annoyed that I'm distracting him from the game. Good.

"Yeah. Bunch of tossers, anyway, in that Department. Good riddance, I say."

"Ha. Yeah." He mutters.

"What do you do, yourself, mate?"

"Bit of this, bit of that." He shrugs.

"I'm in green energy, myself. I help companies find renewable energy sources, instead of relying on burning coal or gas."

This wakes him up. "Oh, yeah?"

"Yeah, well, I was until I got laid off."

"Right."

"You know anything about that?"

"I do, as it happens."

"Yeah? Any jobs going in your Department?"

He shakes his head. "No, don't think so."

There's a glimmer of confusion on his face. I continue pushing.

"I met a girl once at a seminar who did similar work. Can't think of her name, now." I look up at the ceiling for inspiration. "It was something like Sandra, or Clarissa," I make a show of thinking hard, and focus on emitting an aura of trust towards Brian. "Gorgeous, she was. Wish I'd got her number." I look Brian dead in his eyes, "Hang on, it's on the tip of my tongue …" I point at him, "Caaa … Cass …"

"Cassie?"

"Yes! Cassie. That's her." I clap my hands. "Cassie Wright. Do you know her?"

"Err, no. Don't think so." He shuffles, awkwardly, then turns back to the TV.

"Cassiopeia Andromeda Wright. How could I have

forgotten that name?" I laugh. "Wonder what happened to her."

He shrugs and takes a sip of beer.

"Yeah, it's all coming back now. I know her boss, as well. Rachel Hazlewood. Maybe I'll give her a shout." I pull my phone from my pocket. "I think I'm friends with her on LinkedIn."

Brian looks nervously at me, then down at my phone.

"What's your name, mate?"

"Paul. Paul Underdown." I stick out a hand in his direction.

"Pleased to meet you, Paul. I'm Martin."

Brian or Martin, as he's calling himself, grabs my hand and shakes. I take the opportunity to churn out some heavy wavelengths, but there's a strange tingle in my hand, like a wash of energy flooding through as he squeezes hard. I stop my flow and allow whatever is happening to continue.

"You're looking for a job, you say?" He releases my hand.

"Yeah," I sit forward in anticipation.

"I might know of something in the green energy area. I'm staying just down the road, if you want to come back, I'll see if I can dig up the name and number. I think I've got it on my laptop."

I feel a powerful compulsion to go with him. In fact, it seems like an absolutely brilliant idea, and I feel a grin spring onto my face. "That would be amazing. Cheers, Martin."

"Yeah, no worries." He gulps back the rest of his

beer. "Whenever you are ready." Brian slaps me on the shoulder and the tingling feeling returns.

I chug down my beer and stand up. "Now is as good a time as any."

Brian uses the torch on his phone to light the road back to the farmhouse. I follow, resisting the urge to break the fucker's arm off and shove it up his arse. No, I need him to get me inside, so I play it cool. A gentle flow of energy seems to glide away from Brian back towards me. I can't see it, but I can feel the wavelengths and visualise the frequency. I tune in and resonate with the energy.

I can't be sure, but I would guess that he also has the frequency harmonising skill. How is that possible? Evelyn told me that no one else in the world has used her system. Maybe they haven't, and the Department has their own system that they have been working on all the time since the 80s, when they took away Evelyn's project. Damn. Brian could have a much better version than I do. He could be capable of anything.

Evelyn was right, these guys are dangerous. They don't know I have run Flash Gordon, though, and I still have the element of surprise.

We get to the driveway of the farmhouse and Brian turns to check I'm keeping up. We go to the front door and a light above turns on as we approach. I look around, but I can't see any cameras. Brian unlocks the door and ushers me into a large hallway, then quietly closes the door behind us. He shows me into a living room off the hallway. Sumptuous, with antique-looking furniture and a fire that is now mostly deep red embers, gently dancing in the small, but ornate grate.

"Have a seat here, and I'll fetch my laptop. Back in a moment."

"Right, thanks."

He closes the door, and I hear footsteps go up the stairs in the hallway.

I look around the room some more. There's a record player connected to a couple of ancient speakers, a drinks cabinet, bookshelves stuffed to the brim with worn tomes, pot plants galore, and a deep thick rug on the floor that ends with six inches of polished wood at the edges. Very fancy. I take a seat on one of the ornate couches, faded gold colour seamed with green tassels, and more cushions than seem necessary.

I ponder on bursting out of the room now and storming up the stairs, taking them by surprise and finding Cassie quickly. But who's to say they don't have a gun, and Brian is already swinging it in my direction? He doesn't know who I am, but he knows I know Cassie, and that has definitely set off an alarm in his head. The story of bringing me back to give me a contact name is pure bullshit. So, I'm here for something nefarious, coerced with his frequency harmonising charms. What if the others have the skills too? I'm going to be outnumbered at least three to one, possibly more, and they could all have a better version of Flash Gordon style software installed.

This could end badly. I need to act fast.

I check my phone, and there is barely a one-bar

signal. I send a quick message to Evelyn with my map location.

> I'm in the house. Brian is here. I haven't seen Cassie yet, but I'm sure she's here. Can't talk now. Stay tuned.

The message delivers, and I'm thankful for modern cell modem technology.

The door opens and Brian returns.

"Sorry, couldn't find the laptop, and when I did, it was dead. Just charging it up for a bit. Shouldn't be long."

"Ah, no worries."

"Can I get you a drink, Paul?"

What are the chances that he drops a roofie into it? I shouldn't risk it, but it would break this charade if I declined. "Cheers, you got any beer?" Beer has to come from a sealed can or bottle, so should be safe. I don't want to touch a spirit, anyway. Too soon.

"Yeah, should have something in the fridge. One sec."

Brian returns with two bottles of Budweiser. Not exactly what I'd call beer, but beggars can't be choosers. He offers me one, and then picks up a bottle opener from the drinks cabinet, handing it to me. I open the bottle with a satisfying fizz. It seems as safe as any bottle of Bud.

"Cheers."

Brian opens his bottle, then knocks his against mine.

"Slainte, as they say here."

"Ha, yeah." I take a sip. "So, what brings you out here, Martin? I can't help but notice the accent." I grin. He sounds like he's from anywhere vaguely southwest of London, but you never know, depending on what school he went to.

"Doing some work with the folks here." He waves a hand noncommittally.

"Here, in this house?"

"Err, yeah." He admits.

"Right, many here?"

"A couple." Brian, or Martin, because I don't know which of those is his real name. Maybe neither, sits down in an armchair by the fire. The red glow shifts and hisses. "So, tell me about yourself, Paul." He changes the subject.

I sigh. "Not much to tell, really. Grew up on the Isle of Man, parents were both potters, went to college to become a botanist, but somehow ended up in green energy." The lies churn out of me as if on a motor. I've never even been to the Isle of Man. "I've had three wives, but I'm in-between marriages right now." I chuckle. "My dream is to settle down somewhere on a big wind farm, harvesting all those breezes." I find myself yawning, uncontrollably. "Pardon me."

Brian smiles. "No, please. Go on."

I open my mouth to talk, but a fog of hazy fatigue droops down with my eyelids. I'm suddenly exhausted and barely able to focus. Bleary-eyed, I look up at Brian who continues to grin. "You fucker. You drugged me?" I spit out the words with the dregs of energy I can summon.

"No. No need for drugs, here." He laughs, and the sound carries through the thick blanket of soporific waves that resonate around me, into my brain, into my subconscious, and deep, deep into my dreams. I try to pull free, but the black hole of narcolepsy is too strong, and I'm sucked down into the dark depths of sleep.

CHAPTER
THIRTY-FOUR

5:17:34 am

A DIGITAL CLOCK displays the time in bright red digits in front of me. Darkness all around. The seconds tick on.

I'm in a bed. Soft and comfortable. A warmth of body heat comes from behind me. Female frequencies. Something I recognise.

"Cassie!" I bolt up and turn to face the other side of the bed, but the darkness is solid, and I can't penetrate it. There's movement and a fumbling sound, and then a tiny light flicks on above the headboard.

It's her.

"Cassie!"

She blinks and rubs her eyes, then stares up at me.

"Shhh." She puts a finger to her lips. "You'll wake those bloody idiots up."

"You're okay?"

"Yeah, fine." She shuffles up in the bed and yawns. "What time is it?"

"About twenty past five."

"Bloody hell. Bit early."

"Let's get out of here before they wake. Quick." I throw off the covers and jump up, noting that I'm still dressed. Only my shoes have been removed, which are neatly tucked under the bed below me. I slip them on.

"Door's locked." She waves a hand, then grabs for a bottle of water on her bedside table. "You're Toby, aren't you? We met in a pub, once."

"Err, yeah. That's right."

"What the bloody hell are you doing here?"

"That is a good question and a very long story. Can I get back to you on that? For now, we need to figure out how to escape." I reach into my pocket for my phone, but it isn't there. Nor is my wallet. Shit.

"Don't you think I've tried? The door is thick as a whale sandwich, and the windows are barred. I'm stuck in here, and so it seems are you, now."

"How did I get into your bed?"

"Oh, Brian … He came in late last night and dumped you here on top. Unconscious. Didn't say much, just that I had a visitor. I didn't know if I should … you know, undress you, so. Err." She blushes and motions towards my clothed body. "Sorry. You were out for the count, so I thought I'd let you sleep it off."

"No, that's fine. Thank you. He put me to sleep, somehow."

"Yeah, he can do that." Cassie scoffs. "At first, I thought it was his dull conversation, but then it kept happening. Dunno how he does it. He must have some little gadget, I reckon. God knows what secret weird James Bond stuff they have, here."

"I have an idea of how he does it, but what do you mean James Bond stuff?"

Cassie blows out her cheeks. "Where do I start?"

"Tell me everything you know."

———

"They call themselves the Department for the Prevention of World Changing Technology, or just the Department for short. They say they don't exist, officially. A top-secret government department, and that's why we are here, in the middle of bloody nowhere, rural Ireland." Cassie tells me her story in hushed tones, cross-legged on the bed in front of me. She's in a nightgown, but she pulled on a pair of leggings. "They can't be in any way connected with the UK. This was the easiest and cheapest choice, apparently, and remote enough that they would be hidden and invisible. Been here years, I think." Cassie shrugs.

"But why did they kidnap you and bring you here?"

"Because of my work." She rolls her eyes.

"At EverGreen Power?"

"Well, yes, and no. No, mostly."

"Sorry?"

"Well, it was meant to be a secret, but I suppose everyone bloody knows, now. So I may as well tell you."

"Tell me what?"

"I had this idea a couple of years ago about waveforms in water. And how if you get just the right frequency, you can resonate and amplify the energy. You know, like if you run your finger around the rim of a glass, you can make it ring much louder than it normally would."

"Yeah. I know something about that."

She nods. "So, I wondered if you could use that energy to heat things. Specifically, water."

"Oh. Interesting."

"Yeah. I made a model. Not a real one, but inside my computer at home. A model of a tank of water, and a mesh of thin wires that goes throughout. Then, I ran a high voltage, but low power signal through it, and, well, long, long story short, I finally found a combination of metal alloys and frequency that will fracture the water, causing it to heat incredibly quickly, but using barely any power. Harmless. The only by-product is steam. The metal doesn't break down." She pauses for effect. "It generates more power than you put in. Much more. Imagine boiling a full kettle four times using only a tiny watch battery."

"Wow. Really?"

"I mean, it isn't tested in the real world, but I've checked every aspect of the simulation that I can think of, and it seems solid. All my tests worked. All my calculations and variations, the physics engine down to the molecule, all theoretically sound. The next step was to try to get an actual model built. I was going to show it to my manager, Rachel. We deal with some companies that could potentially build a prototype."

I nod. "I know Rachel."

"Oh?"

"Err, long story, again. Sorry, go on."

"Well, then Brian … that isn't his real name, by the way, told me we were going to Spain for a break, and

next thing I know we are here in fucking Connemara."
She throws up her hands.

"Okay, but, still — why did they bring you here?"

"To wipe my memory." She sniffs, matter-of-factly.

"What?"

"Yup. If it works, and they think it will, my technology would most definitely change the world, and
they can't have that, they reckon. Their remit is to
prevent world-changing technology for some bullshit
misguided reason. Ian reckons he has predicted that if
my technology became real, the culture, businesses and
governments of the world would all fall into chaos.
Revolution, rebellion, disasters and war. All that fun
stuff. Stochastic cultural breakdown prediction he
called it." She looks me in the eye. "I reckon he's a
proper loony. Says that humans aren't ready for this
level of technology yet. They want to prevent this revolution and destroy all evidence of my invention, and
that includes inside my brain. They have this gadget
downstairs. A helmet thing. You put it on, and they
fiddle around with dials and switches, and then there's
a buzz of electricity. It's meant to wipe your memory.
Not everything, but just the bits they care about.
Targeted memory dissipation or something. They ask
questions and show pictures about the memories they
want to wipe, to bring them to the surface, but nothing
happens when they do it on me." She giggles. "May as
well be at the hairdresser. It's driving Ian and Cynthia
bananas. I think she's on the verge of killing him." She
pauses. "Or maybe me. Bloody hell."

"The helmet doesn't work on you?"

"Doesn't seem to. No. They must have tried it a

dozen times now, and nada. They reckon they've done it loads of times before on other people, and it worked fine, so they can't understand what is going on. To be honest, I don't think they know what they are doing. There are only three of them, as far as I can tell. Not much of a department, if you ask me. I don't think they have any money, either. Things seem to be tight. They eat soup or beans on toast for dinner a lot of the time. Spend everything on gadgets."

"Wow," I repeat. "How did Brian and the Department find you in the first place?"

Her face falls. "I let down my guard and led them straight to me. I used to post on this physics forum, and I needed to ask some questions. I thought I was anonymous, but apparently not. They told me they monitor all the crazy, outlandish perpetual motion type claims all over the internet, and of course, most of it is bollocks, but my questions and posts threw up a red flag, so they dug deeper, traced me and then I think they hacked into my computer. Brian, the sneaky little twat, was planted to become my boyfriend and bring me here." She shudders at the thought. "I don't even fancy him, so God knows how it happened."

Now is not the time to remind her I knew he was never serious.

"Do they know you are related to Evelyn?"

"Gran? No, I don't think so. Why would they?"

"Hmm. Never mind." They must do. Maybe they think she's harmless at one hundred and in a care home. Big mistake. "Go on."

"Well, it was all meant to be finished ages ago, and Brian was going to take me to Spain as planned, then all this," she waves her arms around the room, "would be forgotten. Wiped from my brain along with the water heater plans and ideas, but it ain't working, and they are panicking now." She laughs. "I'm meant to be back at work soon, and I've sent some messages to my gran. The police will find me. Just have to sit it out. They've wiped my computer, of course, but that's okay. Made me log in and delete all my forum posts and stuff, too."

"About that," I start, but there's a creak from the corridor beyond the door.

Cassie presses her finger to her lips and stares at me with wide eyes. I shut up and listen.

The door tentatively opens and Brian, or Martin, or whoever pokes his head in, flicks on the main light and points a gun at me, then Cassie, and back at me. A Glock, I think.

He moves aside, and a woman comes in after him.

"Well, good morning, Mr Steele. I'm so glad you two have had a chance to become reacquainted."

I know her. It's Cynthia Payne. Much older than the memories I have, but there's no doubt. She's the woman who tormented Evelyn in the 80s. I have the same lack of trust in her that Evelyn had all those years ago. The current situation only backs up those fears.

"Look, I don't know what is going on, but there's been a big misunderstanding here. Just let us go and we'll forget it ever happened. Okay?" I flick my gaze between Cynthia, Brian and Cassie.

"You can drop the charade, Toby, we know who you really are."

"Do you, now?"

"We know more than you can possibly understand. However, I can't imagine how you came to be here."

"Fishing holiday." I shrug.

Cynthia almost rolls her eyes but scowls instead, then shrugs and shakes her head. "No matter. We will let you go, just as soon as you've been processed. Last thing we need here are more moochers," She turns to Brian. "Go wake Ian up. Lazy bastard can do some proper work, now."

Brian shrugs, hands Cynthia the gun, and darts out of the room.

I could probably rush her and grab the gun, but I don't know what abilities she has. She could be equally capable of the sleeping skill that Brian has, and I could be knocked out and on the floor in a second. I play it cool.

There's an exchange of loud, but muffled words out in the corridor and some footsteps back and forth, and then a man in his mid-sixties appears in the room, clad in an ancient brown dressing gown that is much too short for modesty. Doctor Ian Davidson, again far older than I remember. The memories are in my head, but they aren't mine. A strange feeling, a bit like déjà vu.

"Ah, who do we have here? A new one?"

"We'll bring you up to speed, Ian. Go get the machines ready for deletion."

"Oh, what fun!" He turns to leave, then comes back. "Time for a coffee, first?"

"Yes, good idea. Put a brew on." Cynthia turns to me. "We'll be back in a moment." She backs out of the room, still pointing the gun at me, and closes the door.

The sound of at least three bolts being pulled over rattles through the thick wood.

"What are they going to do?" I turn to Cassie who is still sitting on the bed.

"Probably try to wipe your memory with that stupid helmet thing downstairs. Maybe it will work on you. Dunno."

"Shit. That can't happen. We need to get out of here."

"I agree, but who knows how?"

"I have a plan, sort of. But for now, I need to ask an urgent question."

"Yeah?"

"Where is the toilet?"

She smirks and points to a door behind me. "The flush is weird, just jiggle it."

"Thanks."

———

The door opens, and we go through the same rigamarole. Brian flashes his gun around, and Cynthia comes in to do the talking.

"If you'll follow me, Toby, then we can get this all sorted out and you can still be home in time for breakfast."

They took my wallet, so they must have looked up my details. My driving license was in it, so they could have access to all kinds of information. Do they know

I've run the Flash Gordon software? Probably not. Only me and Evelyn know that. I still have the edge.

I follow, but I turn to Cassie and mouth the words 'Get ready' before I leave the room. She nods. Brian, behind me, pulls the door closed and slides over the bolts. I watch in my periphery. They don't use a key. Only the bolts. Good.

I'm led downstairs and through to the back of the house, then into a large room. I notice my coat, wallet, and phone are sitting on a small antique table in the hallway. How convenient.

"Holy crap!"

"Impressive, isn't it?" Doctor Ian Davidson, now clad in more suitable attire, sits on the edge of a desk in a room filled with junk. Old technology on every shelf and table, piled on the floor, pushed into corners. Dials, switches, tape machines and more brushed aluminium than a 90s Dixons. Standing out from the midst of the chaos is a bright red monolith of a thing.

"Is that a Cray-1?" I point, in awe at the old beast of a machine, crammed into the corner.

"It is! A classic, and worth an absolute fortune. Still in mint condition."

"Wow."

I'm nudged towards a chair in the middle of the room, and I plop down into it. There's a helmet on a table next to me, connected to dozens of cables in a rats' nest mess that leads to various other devices around the room. This is Evelyn's lab. I recognise all of her equipment, even her old Cray computer. They lifted the whole thing and brought it here? I know all of these things, inside and out. I notice a desktop computer stuffed under a table and a couple of laptops perched on top. I guess that would be Cassie's PC from home and her and Brian's work laptops. The only modern things in the room.

"Are you ready, Ian?" Cynthia folds her arms and goes over to stand next to him. Brian remains at one side, swinging his gun like a total dork.

"Yup. Calibrated for male, sweep and wipe. Should be no problem."

"Good." She comes over to me and picks up the helmet. "Now, you won't feel a thing. Here we go."

Brian stands in front of me, hinting with his weapon that I should comply. I calculate the odds of being able to brute force this, and they are low. I sit still.

Cynthia lowers the ridiculous helmet onto my head. A metal bowl, with a mesh of wire inside that blossoms into faded red rubber circles around the rim, and over the crown. Each one with a domed-off electrode protruding in the middle. It weighs heavy, and I feel like a complete idiot sitting here.

"Excellent. If we all cooperate, we'll be out of here in no time." Cynthia grins.

Ian flicks on some switches and fiddles with dials. Cynthia moves back away from me. Brian edges over to the window on the other side, still aiming his gun.

"Here we go. Initiating dissipation protocol." Ian flips a large, exaggerated knife switch on the desk and a hum of electronics breathes into life.

The helmet buzzes, a current flows around it. A frequency I'm not familiar with. It bites, acidic, angry and forceful. I flinch and shake. Brian urges me to stay sitting with a wave of his gun.

I grit my teeth and take in a long breath. The waves become stronger as Ian nudges a dial on his desk. They drill into me like needles. I taste metal and smell burning. Confusion and the roar of an angry crowd churn in my mind. Thoughts explode, images appear and then vanish like bubbles popping, I feel sick, and bile rises in my throat. I cough and try to back away from it.

Nope. Absolutely fuck this for a laugh.

I focus and take another deep breath. Concentrate, filter out all else and taste the frequency of the energy. Elusive, but I find it after a confusing moment. A complicated pattern, but a pattern nonetheless. It takes all my brain power to keep up with it. Like playing a video game on hard mode. I surf the waves of the signal, blasting out an inverse oscillation to cancel it out. I strain at the energy it takes from me, but it works, fading out to nothing. The sensations and nausea subside. I am in control.

The helmet buzzes louder, and the hum from the electronics in the room increases. Fans spin up and Ian looks nervously at the Cray in the corner.

I boost my output, taking a deep breath and closing my eyes. The equipment is my friend; I know these circuits. I traverse them in my mind, finding the power supply, reverse the polarity and increase the energy. Fans spin louder, and the buzzing is intense now, like a hive of angry bottle bank wasps.

"What's going on?" Cynthia asks, nervously.

"Nothing, just …" Ian is cut off by a muffled bang from the corner of the room inside the Cray. I smell acrid smoke, but I don't stop. The buzzing increases more. I amplify the frequency, resonate the energy and blast out another spike, using the equipment itself to boost my signal through the wall, out to the two wheelie bins that, by my estimation, are just outside the window.

I open my eyes, and the room is filling with smoke. Panic on their faces and Brian looks extremely agitated. He can't decide if he should leave the room, or stay with his gun pointed at the helpless man, sitting still and quiet on a chair.

Under my breath, I countdown. "Five, four, three, two, one. Blast off."

There's an almighty boom from outside the window, as the lithium in the battery power banks sparks and catches fire in my butane bombs. The fire heats the canister, which in turn expands, the pressure inside too much and the thin metal gives way to compressed, highly flammable gas, exploding in the confined wheelie-bin space. The lid bursts its duct tape seal and flies off at the window with force, smashing the thin old glass and knocking Brian down in a rain of broken shards and flaming plastic. The other bin follows quickly with another intense, louder boom that leaves a ringing in my ears, and with it, the five-litre can of petrol melts and whooshes up into a sudden raging inferno. Some of the flaming liquid flies in through the broken window, barely missing Brian on the floor, catching the antique rug in patterns of smouldering flames. Acrid, stinking smoke rises up. The room is now ablaze. Smoke and chaos rain down in equal parts as Cynthia scrambles to leave the room, and Ian bends down to help Brian. I rip the helmet off my head, get down low to avoid the smoke that now also billows in through the window from the burning bins, grab the gun from where it fell and exit, stage left.

I run up the stairs and unlock the door to Cassie's room.

"Quick. Get out!"

She's already standing near the door, dressed and waiting with a bag over her shoulder.

"What happened?" A look of panic on her face.

"No time to explain. This place is going to burn!"

We fly down the stairs and I grab my coat, wallet and phone as we rush through the hallway, and then out of the front door that is already open.

Cynthia, Ian and Brian all stand outside in the half-light of morning, staring, bewildered in shock and horror at their house that is now pouring out thick black smoke.

"There's a small fire extinguisher behind your garage," I yell to Brian who takes a moment to respond. A smear of blood runs down his face. He takes off in a run around to the back of the house. Not that it will do much, now. I may have gone a bit overboard with the petrol. Oh, well.

"What have you done!" Cynthia screams at me. "We don't have the budget to replace any of this! What have you done?"

"Oops, sorry." I grimace sarcastically towards the gawping Ian and Cynthia, then grab Cassie's hand and set off in a jog down the driveway, and back along the road.

I look back, waving the gun in their direction, but they don't even attempt to chase us. Cynthia has fallen in a heap on the ground, and looks like she's about to burst into tears, and Ian seems to be away in a world of his own, staring at the house. I don't think this has registered as real to him yet. This could be game over for the Department.

"My computer was in there!" Cassie mourns as we run down the road.

"I'll buy you a new one."

"Where are we going?"

"I have a car hidden down here."

We reach the gateway and slow our pace. No one is following still, so I pause to put my coat on. First, I check the gun that's still in my hand. Safety off, loaded. They weren't playing around. I flip the safety on the gun and stash it in my coat.

"You okay?"

Cassie takes a few deep breaths. "Yeah, fine. Thank you."

"No worries." I grab the key from its hiding place on the front wheel, unlock the car and we both get in. "Sorry about your water heater simulation, thing. Is it lost now, can you make it again?" I start the engine and drive around the side of the house.

"No need." She smiles. "It was gran's hundredth birthday recently, just before I met you in that pub … I gave her a necklace with a silver locket on it. A photo of me inside it."

I've seen the necklace she means. Evelyn was always wearing it.

"Gran doesn't know, but behind that photo is a tiny micro SD card with a total backup of my software."

I turn to Cassie. "Really?"

"Yup, so no. Nothing lost."

"Nice one." I hand her my phone. "As soon as there's a signal, call your gran. She's worried."

Cassie takes the phone with a nod.

We drive back along the road and past the farm-house, which is now pouring thick black smoke up into the air. Outside, Ian seems to be trying to get a phone signal, while Cynthia stands watching, crying and waving her fist at us as we go by. I beep my horn, wave back and speed away.

Cassie chuckles. "Thanks for rescuing me, Toby!"

"All part of the service." I smile.

"But, how on earth did you come to be here?"

I slow down as we get to the turning to Clifden, then look over at Cassie with a grin. "Oh. Winnie the Pooh sent me."

EPILOGUE

SATURDAY, 12 JUNE, 2010.
BANGKOK, THAILAND.

MY DEAREST EVELYN,

I don't know if this letter will ever find you alive, but I can hope. I have been sworn to secrecy, all these long years, but now there is little that can be done to me as punishment for breaking the silence.

Evelyn, I don't have much time left, so they say. I won't bore you with the details, but suffice it to say I won't see Christmas.

I'll be brief.

The Department.

I'm sure you have wondered as much as I have who and what they are.

Well, I have spent my life since PFG was disbanded either hiding from them, or investigating them. What I can tell you is they are not officially recognised. According to the powers that be, they don't exist.

This means two things.

One. They don't operate within laws and policies.

Two. They don't receive a budget like other government departments.

They are funded entirely by private donations.

Oil, waste, pharmaceuticals, brewers, finance, insurance, mining, and any industry that needs a convenient way to dispose of surplus money without drawing attention.

They are in the business of destroying progress. Of wiping out anything that they deem as too good for humanity. They censor the future. Cull anything innovative and world-changing.

To be frank, they are a bunch of evil plotting bastards! Pardon my French.

They took PFG after you were kicked out. The whole shebang. Uprooted, and transported to a secret location in Ireland. Reassembled and continued development, but without your keen eye and honest heart. I know they outsourced some code development, and the rest, Doctor Ian Davidson has tinkered with for decades.

They went down roads you would never have travelled, and they use the device to delete memories, somehow.

You were right, as always, not to trust them.

. . .

All I can hope is that you and your loved ones never need to hear about them again. In recent times, they seem to be dwindling in popularity. The world of today doesn't much care for the idea of dulling down progress, so they are finding it harder to source investment, but there will always be those who will pay anything to preserve their own misguided ways.

Be careful, Evelyn. You and I will always be on their radar.

In all my years of service, I can happily say that working with you was the highlight of my career, if not my life. I never married, as you know, and I came to think of you as a partner, of sorts.

May you live a long and happy life, and this Flash Gordon and Department nonsense be far behind you and your family.

I hear your granddaughter is a remarkable young lady, and I expect her to change the world as you did. Yes, even out here in my dark days of retirement, I still know far more than I care to about the world.

Faithfully yours,
    Spencer.

DO ME A FAVOUR?

I genuinely hope you enjoyed this story and I'd love to hear about it. So would other readers. I would be eternally grateful if you would leave a review on Amazon for me.

I don't have a big-name publisher or agent, or any marketing help. I rely on the kind words of readers to spread the word and help others find my books.

In a world of constant rating requests from everything you buy, I know it's a pain, but it does make a huge difference and it encourages me to keep writing.

Thanks!
Adam.

www.AdamEcclesBooks.com

ALSO BY ADAM ECCLES

In order of publication:

Time, For a Change

The Twin Flame Game

Who Needs Love, Anyway?

Need a Little Time

The Soul Bank

System Restored

———

facebook.com / AdamEcclesWrites
twitter.com / AdamEcclesBooks

AUDIOBOOKS

Need a Little Time, unabridged audiobook.
Narrated by Mark Rice-Oxley

———

System Restored, unabridged audiobook.
Narrated by Mark Rice-Oxley

ACKNOWLEDGMENTS

———

TOP-SECRET
CONFIDENTIAL MEMORANDUM

This list of names are people who have been exposed to Project Flash Gordon.

They are extremely dangerous and should be avoided at all cost.

Sarah Hopkins, Sian Richards, Paul Cusack, Jonny Thomson, Tracy Fisher, Keith A Pearson, Jennifer Dege, Kirsty Scutter.

———

Thanks :)
Adam.